He brought her hand to his chest where his heart was beating harder than he liked.

"Feel that? That's me worried you're going to flake, and I'm going to mess up because you haven't told me enough about what we're doing here for me to handle it alone."

She stilled, waited, did nothing but breathe.

Harry pressed. "It's your ball game, sweetheart. I'm just a rabid fan."

She'd stopped shaking. That much he was glad to see. What he wasn't sure about was how to react when she flexed her fingers against his shirt, testing the muscle beneath.

And he was really lost when she stepped closer and leaned her forehead against him. Especially since he could smell the wild rain scent of her hair.

He stood there unmoving, his heart pounding even harder now when the whole reason for bringing her here was about staying calm. Calm was the last thing he was feeling.

DEEP BREATH

ALISON KENT

BRAVA

KENSINGTON PUBLISHING CORP.

http://www.kensingtonbooks.com

BRAVA BOOKS are published by

Kensington Publishing Corp.
119 West 40th Street
New York, NY 10018

ISBN-13: 978-0-7582-1117-0
ISBN-10: 0-7582-1117-1

First trade paperback printing: April 2006
First mass market printing: November 2009

10 9 8 7 6 5 4 3 2 1

Printed in the United States of America

To Lieutenant Junior Grade Bryan Estell, USCG
for being a true hero

Acknowledgments

and a host of thank-yous to . . .

Emma Gads, for handling everything so beautifully

Stephanie Tyler, for the emergency brainstorming

Larissa Ione, for being a survivor

Kara Lennox, for the Dallas help

HelenKay Dimon, for the legal help

Jan and Annette, for waiting patiently for lunch

Kate Duffy, for waiting patiently

Walt, for the therapy sessions, the cooking and cleaning

Holly, for the cleaning and shopping

Casey, for the shopping and cooking

Megan, for the dinosaur food and waiting patiently for lunch

A Gala Reception and Auction in Honor of
General Arthur Duggin

Symposium 4:00 P.M.
Auction Preview Reception 7:30 P.M.
Friday April 7, 2006
Benefiting The Duggin Scholarship Foundation
$100 per person—$175 per couple

Speaker: Paul Valoren
Professor Emeritus Political Science
Stanford University

Auction 2:00 P.M.—Sunday April 9, 2006
Open to the public—Free of charge
Grace Emerald Auction Gallery, Dallas, Texas

Thursday

This must be Thursday. I never could get the hang of Thursdays.

—Douglas Adams, British writer
(1952–2001)

March 15, 1989–10:15 A.M.

TOTALSKY CONVICTION CASTS SHADOW ON MILITARY CONTRACT

Associated Press
BREAKING NEWS

Washington, D.C.—Dr. Stanley Dean McLain, vice president of purchasing for the TotalSky Corporation, was today convicted of treason for his part in the failure and subsequent loss of two communications satellites contracted and built by TotalSky for the U.S. military. Sentencing details to follow soon.

She had expected better security.

Seriously.

For someone in his position, a man whose life had been devoted to rights and freedom and keeping honor clean, whose final years had been dedicated to homeland defense, General Arthur Duggin hadn't been quite as careful with things down home on the ranch.

She'd come in with the final tour group of the day. The final tour group of forever, actually. The General, his health failing, had spent his last years at his Dallas home, opening his 160-acre ranch near Waco to the public. Now with the passing of the military legend, history—and tourism—had reached an era's end.

The cataloging team from Sotheby's working with the Grace Emerald Gallery in Dallas was scheduled to finish tomorrow with the General's city estate. The packing crew in place at the ranch was ready to move into action tonight.

First thing in the morning, the antiquities set for auction would be shipped from here to the city. The sale of all residential furnishings would begin this weekend. The first of next week, both homes went up for sale.

She didn't understand the rush.

She did understand the time frame—and the decided lack of wiggle room it gave her.

Already the workers had started classifying the personal mementos the general had amassed throughout his career, as well as sorting documents from his private library. Those dealing with his life as a public figure would be divided and donated to the university libraries spelled out in his will.

Items of a more personal nature—those of interest to soldiers who had served beside him, to cadets who had studied beneath him, to friends, to collectors, to military hobbyists who had their hearts set on priceless keepsakes—were slated to be auctioned Sunday afternoon. The proceeds would benefit the general's educational charity.

And then there was the dossier she was here for—the one she wouldn't be leaving without.

Even knowing as little as she did of the file's contents, she was certain the general would have bequeathed it to no one. Would, in fact, have preferred to have the file's explosive details buried beneath his own grave.

More than likely, the dossier had been rounded up with his personal papers intended for auction—though there was the off chance that it hadn't been found.

She was hoping the latter scenario turned out to be true since she knew exactly where it was.

Any minute now, the tour group would be exiting the 8,500-square-foot ranch house through the main entrance and boarding the tour bus that would return them to the visitors' center at the property's entrance.

The doors would be locked at six P.M., and a security sweep made for lingering tourists. At six-thirty, the day staff would begin to leave. At seven, the exterior patrol would commence. At eight, the perimeter alarms and motion sensors would activate.

Her battle with the wiggle room had only just begun. The entry recess inside the second floor visitors' rest room hid a dumbwaiter, one used by the staff to transport linens and cleaning supplies. That much she'd deduced by the overwhelming smells of bleach and pine cleaner, and the stack of towels on top of which she now crouched.

She'd discovered the dumbwaiter on her visit last week. Never having used these particular facilities in the past, she couldn't believe her luck. Or the fact that she managed to fit inside. This time, however, before climbing into the small wooden box, she'd jammed a pocket knife into the motor to make sure she didn't end up where she didn't want to be.

She knew the cleaning crew worked mornings before visiting hours rather than coming in nights. Unless there had been a sudden change in that five-year routine, she didn't fear discovery as long as she stayed where she was until the guard doing the walk-through cleared the room.

She hit the button on her watch to light the face: 6:05. She held her breath, listened. Another minute and the door opened and closed. She heard the squeaking swing of all five stall doors, the flush of a toilet, running water, a metallic smack before an air dryer kicked on for thirty seconds. Then the door again, opening, closing. Silence followed.

This was it. She had to move and she had to move now. She had less than twenty-five minutes to get her hands on what she'd come for and exit with the rest of the staff into the employee parking lot behind the house. Once there, she'd choose her quarry and beg for a ride out.

She had her story set, that of a temp hired for the busy spring break day and abandoned at the last minute by a friend who had sworn to be there at six-thirty to get her. She knew how to flirt, how to wheedle, how to whine, and wasn't above having to beg. All she needed was a lift.

Once in Waco, she could make her own way to the transit center and the locker where she'd stored her things. From there, a few short hours would see her back safely in Houston at her brother's place.

She would wait until after the auction, let the media blitz surrounding the general's passing die down. Then she would pull out the dossier, her ace in the hole, and for the final time plead her father's case.

Beneath her Baylor University pullover, she wore the same western cut, red bandanna print shirt as did the staff. Her blue jeans and boots matched as well. The uniform store that outfitted the help supplied temps with ready-to-wear, including patches monogrammed on site. She'd learned that when doing her prep work and had found identical items at Wal-Mart, deciding to call herself Pam.

Pushing open the dumbwaiter panel, she climbed out, shucking her pullover and her spiky blond wig. She shoved both into the trash receptacle, buried them beneath the used towels, and gave herself permission to forgo washing her hands, fearing the guard's return at the sound of running water.

Fluffing the layers of her coffee-brown hair, she avoided her own mirrored gaze. She was a university coed out to make a few bucks, not a treasure hunter intent on clearing her father's name. She lived in a dorm, not in her brother's guest room. She was twenty-two, not thirty-four. She was Pam. She had every right to be here.

And with that, she took a deep breath and eased open the rest room door.

The General's study and bedroom were both in the wing at the end of the long hall she stepped into.

When she'd come here to see him three years ago, she'd sat in one of the huge leather chairs in front of his desk.

He'd sat behind it, a stately presence, though even then he'd appeared wan and frail. He'd appeared even more so when she'd brought up the reason for her visit. He'd been devastated to hear of her father's passing, but told her she needed to accept that Stan's deathbed ramblings simply were not true.

No matter her father's insistence, the general did not know the location of the dossier chronicling the TotalSky scandal and missing from government archives now for almost twenty years. What he did know, however, was that the content of the file would in no way change the public's perception of the man her father had been.

She hadn't believed Arthur Duggin then; of course he wasn't going to admit knowing where it was. And dirty his own reputation? Neither did she believe him now. The dossier *would* tell the tale, would help her clear her father's name. And, thanks to her father, she knew exactly where to find it.

Hearing no chatter and sensing no movement, she headed for the study. The door stood open. The desk sat to the left and overlooked the massive room. A fireplace of hand-hewn stones along with a cluster of cowhide club chairs took up the space on the right.

The wall connecting the two ends was nothing but a sprawl of windows looking out over grazing lands that she imagined took a fortune to irrigate. But that wasn't the wall holding her interest. So, with her heart thudding in her chest like a big bass drum, she turned toward the wall of bookshelves that towered behind the desk . . . and jolted to a stop.

Byron Corgan, the general's assistant, stood with one of the auction house employees between the bookshelves and desk. One held a pencil and clipboard, one a stylus and PDA. They both looked up at her entrance, which turned bumbling once she got a look at the spread of papers over the desktop and the drawers standing empty and open.

"Oh, I'm sorry. I have the wrong room." She waved her hands breezily, trying to hide her choking panic and her face from Byron. He'd only seen her once three years before, but still. This was not good. *So* not good. She took a quick turning step in reverse . . .

. . . and plowed right into a broad uniformed chest. Uh-oh. She cringed, totally screwed, and looked up into stern brown eyes that she doubted knew the meaning of mercy. Crap. Just . . . crap.

"This section of the house is off limits to everyone but authorized personnel." The security officer's voice was deep, his tone unyielding, his body doubly so.

"I'm sorry." She gave an apologetic shrug, her mind racing, plotting, searching for an escape hatch, a way out. "I didn't know."

"Let me see your agency card." His eyes narrowed, his lips, too.

Agency card? What was he talking about? Had she actually missed something that vital? She patted her pockets, her palms sweating. "I don't have it with me."

"If you've got the wrong room, then you're obviously part of the spring break crew." He held out a meaty hand. "The employment agency would've given you an ID card and told you to carry it at all times."

"They did." Damn, damn, damn. Forget the flirting, wheedling, and whining. It was begging time. "I guess I just . . . left it somewhere . . ."

He nodded, but it wasn't an agreement. And it

certainly wasn't forgiveness. It appeared to be a judgment call, one that had him reaching for the radio at his belt. "Tim, meet me at the employee entrance. I'm bringing down an unauthorized temp hire. We have a trespasser on our hands."

Friday

Only Robinson Crusoe had everything done by Friday.

—Anonymous

January 2, 1988

General Arthur Duggin faced the windows of his second-floor study, which looked out over the pastures where his herd of Black Angus grazed. He held his hands clasped behind his back, his chin up, his head high, wondering if he would ever stand here again, if he would ever again enjoy the peaceful sight, the comforts of home, the fruits of his lifetime of labors.

In two hours, he was bound for Washington, D.C., for months of senate hearings and the endless questions he'd be compelled to answer. He was, after all, a key witness in the government's investigation, one seeking to expose corruption in the contract for communication satellites his committee had awarded to the firm TotalSky.

He thought of Paul, of Stanley, of Cameron. This was certainly not an ending they had conceived happening throughout the long year of work that had brought the seed of their plan to fruition. They had dotted every *i*, crossed every *t*, covered each and every base they had run. Or so they had erroneously assumed.

He had yet to understand which of the decisions they'd made had been the one to bring it all crashing down—one satellite at a time. The first had landed in the North Sea between Stavanger and Aberdeen eighteen months ago, plunging into thunderous waters that would have rendered the pieces impossible to identify. Or to recover.

At that, he had breathed a sigh of relief. They had not been so fortunate the second time. That one, only a scant six months later, had landed on the side of a mountain deep in the Tanzanian jungles. Parts of the onboard computer, including the motherboard, had been found. The mezzanine board, thankfully, had not.

Two satellites remained in orbit. Convincing the powers in charge to leave them there, to monitor them closely, to ensure their functionality while benefiting—as intended—from the information both procured was not going to be easy, but he was the one elected by the TotalSky alliance to make it happen. And so he would.

The four men had known at the first failure that a choice had to be made, that last year's discovery would result in this year's hearings, that one of them, as agreed from the beginning, would be the first and—because of his connections to TotalSky—the most obvious to take the fall.

The other three would see to the future of those their comrade left behind. Monetarily, emotionally. Whatever doing so required. That time had now arrived. General Arthur Duggin took a final look at all he owned, returned to his desk, and prepared to do what he had to do.

Current day—11:00 A.M.

Morganna.

A beautiful name. A beautiful car.

And a beautiful, never-ending stretch of concrete reaching into the distance and inviting SG-5 operative Harry van Zandt to give the fully restored 1958 Buick convertible her head.

Oakleys in place, a wrist draped over the steering wheel, he lifted his face to the bright blue sky and rested his arm along the back of the aqua, tucked-and-rolled leather seat.

It was April in north central Texas. Weather he could get used to. Weather he could love. Especially after the last ten months spent in New Mexico, where he'd experienced both the fire and ice of hell.

He hadn't minded so much in the end; before leaving, he'd flushed a big chunk of Spectra IT down the tubes, finishing up a mission that had originally been assigned to another of the Smithson Group's newest recruits.

Due to a rocky ride at the wrong end of a rope held by one of two Spectra thugs, Mick Savin had wound up out of commission, and Harry had landed the job of infiltrating Spectra's western U.S. command center.

With a little help from an inside and unexpected source—namely one Ezra Moore, Spectra assassin and all-around bad guy—Harry had managed to derail the international crime syndicate's money train.

Before New Mexico, he'd worked another Spectra scenario in Old Mexico, holding down the proverbial fort for Eli McKenzie, one of the original members of SG-5. He'd spent a grueling four months in a crude, generator-powered barracks, living with men in the business of supplying Spectra's international prostitution ring with kidnapped and underage girls.

Interestingly enough, Ezra Moore—right hand to Spectra boss Warren Aceveda—had been instrumental in the Smithson Group successfully bringing down the very house in which he lived.

Finally, Harry had a mission of his own. Naturally, it involved Ezra Moore. And the deal the two had made in New Mexico—Ezra's release of a Spectra hostage in exchange for Harry's locating a confidential and long-time-missing government dossier—played right into Harry's plans.

Hank Smithson, Harry's boss and the principal behind the Smithson Group, wanted to know exactly who Ezra Moore was. Wanted to know how he managed to be in so many right places at so many right times. Wanted to know why he'd stepped up on recent missions for Julian Samms and Kelly John Beach—two other SG-5 operatives—as well as for Harry, Eli, and Mick.

It was Harry's job to find out. But then finding things had always been Harry's job, and was exactly the reason Hank had recruited him into the SG-5 ranks. He was the go-to guy, the Rabbit—his nickname—that his fellow agents pulled out of the proverbial hat when they needed something, needed it now, and needed it without strings.

He'd procured motherboards while in the middle of the Sea of Cortez. He'd procured antibiotics while in the middle of the Gobi Desert. He'd procured electrical wiring, waterproof socks, and tickets to sold-out theater performances while in the Bering Strait, Siberia, and Sydney.

For this role, the first thing he'd laid his hands on was Morganna. And what a babe she was, he mused, stroking the rich leather seat as he drove. No one made cars like this anymore. She could suck a gas pump dry and empty a man's wallet without ever coming up for air. Hard to resist a beauty with that combo of skills—especially when she made the man feel so damn good while it happened.

Harry'd been a sucker for a slick set of wheels his entire life. Make it a convertible, he was over the moon. A muscle car, and he was in hog heaven. His mother had driven a classic and fully decked out 1971 Riviera GS, his father a 1969 Camaro. He'd never cared who took him to school. He only cared about not riding the bus.

For his sixteenth birthday, he'd wanted a '69 Pontiac GTO. His parents had given him a '71 Cuda ragtop instead. Black and bumblebee yellow. He'd been voted junior class president right then and there.

He who dies with the most toys wins. Wasn't that what the bumper sticker said? It was always about the coolest car, the fattest wallet, the hottest honey, the biggest dick. Funny how so little had changed.

The second thing he'd done was to hunt down the one single person most likely to lead him to what he wanted—the dossier he'd promised to find for Ezra Moore. The dossier that would never see Ezra's hands without first seeing the fine-tooth electronic comb belonging to the analysis team waiting even now at the Smithson Group's Manhattan ops center.

Inquiries, both discreet and not so—the first made as an SG-5 operative, the second in his role as a collector of modern military memorabilia—resulted in one name popping up repeatedly. A Texas treasure hunter named Georgia McLain. He'd found her in jail in Waco, and he liked her already.

What wasn't to like? The woman wouldn't take no for an answer, went after what she wanted with a vengeance, found no lengths too far. That dedication played into Harry's hands. Especially since sweet Georgia McLain appeared to be after the same thing he was.

The background check he'd run yielded a mother who had died of pneumonia when Georgia was five, and a father who had died in the federal prison where he'd been incarcerated seventeen years before for his role in the TotalSky scandal—a detail Harry knew not to tuck too far away.

She had one living relative—a brother, Finn—and Harry had no trouble tracking down his photo, driving record, vehicle identification number, and license tag as well as the make and model of his truck. Then he'd spent the night in McLennan County and waited for little brother to show.

The thing he found most interesting about his treasure hunter went back to the cool car, fat cash observation of earlier. For someone who hunted treasures for a living, the woman had zero in the way of assets, liquid or otherwise. He'd found no property in her name, no DBA, no Bahamian, Cayman, or Swiss accounts.

It would appear she pocketed the proceeds from one find and lived off those funds while hunting down the next. It would appear that way except for the fact that there were no records of her locating any items of significant worth in the last three years. There had, in fact, been little activity notched on her notoriety belt since her focus had narrowed.

Not such a big market out there for specializing in military papers. Her interest, he·reasoned, had become personal at the same time she'd dropped off the map—right after her father's death. To Harry, that obsession was the best kind of news.

And when combined with the death of General Arthur Duggin, the upcoming auction of the man's library items, and her arrest for trespassing on the General's property, well, this beautiful, never-ending stretch of concrete between Waco and Dallas seemed to be exactly the right track.

He glanced beneath the dash at the GPS navigator that doubled as a tracking device. The signal sent out by the transmitter he'd slipped inside the wheel well of Finn McLain's pickup showed brother and sister a half mile behind. Harry had cut across a couple of county roads to get in front of them, but now it was time to slow down and let them take the lead.

He planned to stay on their tail all the way to Dallas. He wasn't worried about being seen. He wasn't worried about Morganna drawing attention. She had, after all, once belonged to one of the highest ranking military officials to serve during the Korean War. And that gave a whole lot of credence to his cover story.

When he ran into sweet Georgia McLain tonight at the auction preview, she'd have no cause to think he was there for any reason other than getting his hands on the General's 1948 Jaguar XK120 Roadster.

Harry was the only one who would know the truth.

"One question, Georgia. That's all I have. One question."

Georgia McLain slumped down as far as the seat belt would let her and stared out the passenger window of her brother's truck at the flat nothingness whizzing by.

Finn had not been the least bit surprised to get

her phone call last night. He was used to bailing her out of this scrape and that. Neither had he been the least bit happy. But he would get over it as he always did.

He had paid her nominal trespassing fine—thank goodness nothing more serious had been filed against her—and driven her from the McLennan County Jail to Waco's transit center to pick up her duffel and backpack, stored in a locker there.

He'd done everything she'd expected, making her feel even worse for the trouble she'd caused. And so she finally grumbled, "What?", wondering why she bothered when she knew exactly what he was going to say—and when he knew exactly how she would answer.

When are you going to give up this ridiculous quest? When are you going to let the past go and deal with the present? When are you going to grow up?

She knew those would be the questions he asked her because they were the ones she constantly asked of herself. And the answers always came in one form or another of "you know when."

Finn reached across the truck's cab and poked her in the shoulder, jouncing her out of her pity party. "When are you going to take the break you've been promising me for weeks and pack up the stuff you have at my house? I'm moving in less than a month. In case you've forgotten?"

Hmm. Not what she'd expected. And she hadn't forgotten. Uh, not really. She'd just been putting it off because she'd been busy. Wasn't she always busy? And because she had no idea where she was going to keep her stuff now that Finn was giving up his investigator's business in Houston and moving to the Florida Keys.

She sat up a little straighter, rubbed at the spot on her arm. "I have a couple of things I need to do first once we get to Dallas. I should be finished by Monday, and I'll head down then, okay?"

Duggin's auction would be history by then, and the rest of his assets ready to be sold. She'd damn well better have the dossier in her hands. If she didn't, well . . .

"What if you go ahead and rent storage space for me? In case I get hung up?"

"You're not going to get hung up." Finn glanced in his rearview before looking over. "We're both going to be back in Houston on Monday. I'll help you pack up your things. And then instead of a storage space, we'll rent you an apartment. How's that?"

An apartment. Utility bills. Neighbors. She wasn't sure she'd ever be ready for that responsibility again. She'd have to get a car . . . "We'll see. Let me get through the weekend first."

"Sure. But I'm sticking around until then."

"Finn, no—"

"Look, Georgia. You don't have wheels—"

"I have feet. I know how to rent. I can even call a cab." Her brother, her keeper, was the last person she needed hanging around. She scrunched down again, propped her boots on the dash. "That's all I need."

"Maybe so." He paused, the ground whirring by beneath the wheels of the truck, the road's center stripe a blurry and hypnotizing *thwap, thwap, thwap.* "But none of those will do you any good in a getaway."

He made it sound like she was Bonnie, sans Clyde. "I'm not going to need to be making a getaway."

Finn snorted. "How many times have I heard that?"

He was right, of course, but such was the nature of

even small-scale treasure hunting and wanting the same thing dozens of others would dismember to get their hands on.

Finn had come to her rescue near Fredericksburg when she'd walked out of an auction with a photograph of General George Armstrong Custer and his wife, Libbie, to find that a competitor had backed into her rental and left her on foot.

He'd intervened at a flea market in the valley when she'd found an 1852 Treasury Certificate issued to an officer in the Navy of the Republic of Texas and a collector had broken her pinky trying to snatch it out of her hand.

He'd swooped in when a dealer in Baton Rouge had given her a black eye and bloody nose while shoving her away from an 1835 Letter of Passage signed by Stephen F. Austin, commander in chief of the Texas volunteer army.

So, yeah. Sooner or later a getaway car would come in handy. Especially with her reputation for having a nose for sniffing out things no one else could, and everyone wanted, preceding her everywhere she went.

The only reason she'd been so successful was because she didn't have an apartment, a car, and a cat. And because she refused to believe having any of those was as important as clearing her father's name.

Finn didn't disagree with the latter. He just wasn't keen on her approach. Or on the fact that what had once been a quest was now a fixation. And that she refused to move on from her vagabond ways until she'd accomplished the task.

She really was too old not to be more settled. Then again, settling, when she'd done it, had gotten her nothing but a broken heart and a lot of useless community property.

Her ex of eight years now had wanted to start a

family. Problem was, he hadn't thought dawn-to-dusk road trips and constant exposure to mold, mildew, dust, and spider webs was any kind of life for a kid.

She couldn't have disagreed more, but hey, he'd insisted he was the boss. It had been her life for a very long time, and she'd loved it, going from garage sale to estate sale, from auction barn to antique shop to flea market.

And doing it all with Caroline Sorter. Caroline, who'd been her and Finn's nanny since she was five and their mother had died of pneumonia. Caroline, who'd been appointed by the court as their guardian when their father had gone to prison only weeks before Georgia had turned eighteen.

Wondering if she would've had it in her to be half as good a mother as Nanny Caro, Georgia glanced over at Finn, whose eyes were back on the road. "Why do you put up with me?"

His crow's feet crinkled, and his grin scooped a deep dimple into his cheek. "Because that's what baby brothers do," he said as they passed a wooden billboard, faded, beat all to hell, yet still professing: *Nobody Knows A Grill Like Phil—Waco Phil's—5 Miles.*

Her stomach growled, and she huffed. "You need a haircut."

"I also need a hamburger," he said, checking his mirrors and his blind spot before passing the slow-moving vehicle in front of them. He let out a long low whistle. "Now that's what I call a car."

Georgia looked down from her window at the boat-sized convertible, noticing little about the car because her attention was all for the driver sitting back and soaking up the sun. His hair was dark and cut short in a near military buzz. He had just enough of a shadow on his face to bring to mind a bad boy or two that she'd known.

She liked the way this one sprawled all over the big bench seat like he owned the world and the car was his throne. His legs were long, his arms, too. His hands big with long fingers, and beautifully shaped. She couldn't tell a thing about his eyes behind his shades, but his mouth was wide, his lips caught in the hint of a smile.

And then he was gone, Finn returning to the right lane, rendering the car behind them nothing more than a blue-green speck in the mirror on her side.

She dropped her head back and closed her eyes. "Now that's what I call a reason for taking a ride."

The black luxury car was silent as it hugged the long straight road. Move fast, keep low, stay quiet. His favorite way to travel. He hated public transportation. Too busy. Too much pushing, shoving. Too many people.

Charlie Castro didn't like people. Not those he worked for. Not those he worked with. Human beings. Lying, scheming users. Always with the excuses. The better good. The needs of the many. The end justifying the means.

Bullshit.

Charlie prided himself on being straight up. Behind the excuses lay the truth. Power, sex, money. The triumvirate ran the world, and history was the proof.

He did what he did for the almighty buck. And he did it because lying, scheming, and using were what he did well.

Power was overrated. It came with too much attention. Sex had never been a priority. His abbreviated time in utero had shorted out that gene.

But money. Money provided every pleasure wanted, every pain desired. Charlie didn't buy much. Good clothes. A choice car. First edition hardcovers. Fine wine.

Offering the services he did let him see what other men hunted, how much they would spend to obtain it. How much they would spend to keep it from another's hands.

He'd dealt in antiquities for the last eight years. A no- man's-land of finders keepers. Robin Hood with a twist. Taking from the rich, giving to the richer. Underground. Off the record. The items he located would never see the light of day. Ownership equaled power. Money was no object.

He sat straighter in the Mercedes' reclining leather seat as, ahead on the right, a diner came into view. He didn't care about food. He noticed the nondescript metal building for one reason.

The pickup Georgia McLain had climbed into in Waco sat parked beside a second car in front.

He motioned for his driver to pull in and circle to the rear. Two more trucks. Empty fields behind. Charlie weighed his odds. A spring break weekend. A sparsely traveled road. A little-visited eating establishment.

Two trucks likely equaled two employees. Georgia was traveling with a man. The second car was an unknown factor. He, his two men, and their arsenal were not.

The property his current client wanted was hot. The client himself at risk for exposure. Charlie made his choice. He would get what he wanted.

Georgia would do all the work.

11:45 A.M.

Tracy Dunn double-checked that she'd locked the bathroom door before leaning over the sink to splash her face with cold water. It was too early in the day for her to be sweating; between the heat from the grill and that from the sun, not to mention carting hot coffee and steaming plates from one end of the diner to the other, she ended her days smelling—and looking—like she'd been rode hard and put up wet.

But here it was not quite even noon, and she was already sticky and hot. If she wasn't twenty-nine, she would swear she was going through menopause.

She grabbed a handful of paper towels and blotted the water from her cheeks and her neck, staring at her reflection and thinking for the millionth time that she hated the tan uniform even more than she hated the pink.

Not that the white was any better. What with her skin so splotchy and her hair falling out in clumps and being unable to eat without wanting to throw up and crying herself to sleep every night, she pretty much looked like leftover crap all the time lately.

Who knew stress could turn a body into such a pathetic, sloppy, ugly mess?

She kept waiting for Phil to hand her a pink slip with her paycheck, except being here as long as she had, she knew how much trouble he had getting dependable help to stick around for what he was able to pay.

She finished drying her face and neck, then blew her nose, tossed the towels into the trash, and opened the mirrored cabinet above the sink. Since she and Patty—Phil's two female employees—were the only ones to use the ladies' facilities regularly, they both kept a few personal items—deodorant and hairspray and tampons and the like—stored here.

She pulled the scrunchie from her ponytail and grabbed the hairbrush from her shelf, closing the cabinet door so she could use the mirror. Pulling the brush through her hair, she wished she'd said no when Patty called last night to switch today's shift with tomorrow's.

Tomorrow wouldn't really be any better, but today really sucked. And then seeing the flash of her gold wedding band reflected as she pulled back her hair made everything suck a million times worse.

She was going to cry. She just knew it. Damn stupid Freddy Dunn. This was all her stupid-excuse-for-a-husband's fault, though she kept waiting for the paperwork to show up that would make him her stupid-excuse-for-an-ex-husband. Half the time she wanted him back. Half, she never wanted to see him again. She couldn't remember ever being so confused.

They'd both been their parents' only children, and he'd been a part of her life forever, running with her through summer sprinklers when they'd been four, teaching her at six to climb over the Cyclone fence from the postage stamp of her front yard to his. He'd kissed her for the first time at ten, added the French twist of his tongue at fourteen.

At sixteen, she'd given him her virginity. At seventeen, she, a Dunbar, had graduated two minutes before him, a Dunn. At eighteen, they'd decided one last name would suit the both of them. For the last eleven years, she'd been Tracy Dunn, Mrs. Freddy Dunn, and living in his family's house since.

After deeding them the property, his parents had moved to Louisiana, his mother wanting to be close to his grandmother, who was ill. The following year, Tracy's own mother had passed, leaving her father living next door alone. Ten years she'd been all that her father had. And now Freddy wanted to sell both places, send her father to a home, and move . . .

At the sound of the kitchen bell signaling a customer, she shoved her hairbrush back into the cabinet, blew her nose, and quickly wiped her eyes. Phil would be banging on the door if she didn't hustle her backside out to see to the order.

So she pasted on the best smile that she could and reached over to flush her thoughts of Freddy, along with the tissue, down the commode.

She waved cheerily at Phil and his arched eyebrow as she wound her way from the bathroom through the kitchen and down the alley, where she grabbed two laminated menu sheets and two glasses of ice water before heading toward the couple who'd just settled into the far corner booth.

"Morning, folks. I'm Tracy," she said, having glanced at the clock over the door on her way by. Eleven-forty-five. "Are you here for breakfast, lunch, or supper? Eggs are good all day long, and if you want tonight's pork chop special now, I'll sweet-talk Phil into whipping it up for you."

The man, really cute, hair falling over his collar and forehead and into his bright blue eyes, didn't even bother with the menu. "Hi, Tracy," he said, and grinned. "I'll have a bacon cheeseburger basket, extra fries, and the biggest Coke you can bring me."

She didn't need to jot down the order to remember it. She just smiled right back and took the unused menu from his hand. "Sounds like someone skipped breakfast this morning."

He chuckled. "Someone got called away from last night's dinner and is short on both food and sleep."

The woman with him snorted and rolled her eyes. "I'll have the same."

"Good deal," Tracy said, tapping the two menus against the edge of the table, and wondering how this couple fit. "I'll bring y'all's Cokes right now. You go on and take a nap until I get back."

The man slouched down in the booth, the vinyl squeaking beneath him, and laughed as she walked away. She found herself sucking in her stomach and using the menus to fan her face. *Whoo-boy.* Men weren't supposed to be that beautiful.

If she wasn't married . . .

Yikes. Talk about cold water slapping a girl in the face. Tracy moved back into the alley, shoved the menus into the plastic tub beneath the counter, wrote up the ticket, clipped it on the carousel hanging from the order window, and spun it around for Phil. Then she scooped ice into two giant soda glasses and set the first beneath the fountain to fill.

The syrup and the carbonated water blurred into one big fizzy stream. She blinked away this newest batch of tears, used her wrist to push back her bangs, and focused on what she was doing. If she screwed up something as simple as two large Cokes, she deserved to get fired.

She couldn't afford to get fired. Not with Freddy gone, and now having to make up the difference all on her own between what Medicare paid on her father's bills and what the nursing service charged for his in-home care. She needed a new job, a better paying job, but waiting tables was the only thing she knew, the only thing she'd done for eleven years.

What she was going to have to do was get a second job. Maybe get on an evening shift at the Wal-Mart Super Center in Waco, and have one of her father's old friends come sit with him while she was gone. She could get a DVD player and a bunch of old Jimmy Stewart and Robert Mitchum movies.

That might work, she thought, grabbing up the two Cokes and carrying them to the couple in the booth, smiling widely and feeling a little less down in the dumps. She didn't need Freddy. She could figure this out on her own.

"Here y'all go." She placed two Coca-Cola coasters on the speckled Formica, set the drinks on top, nodded toward the glass dispenser at the end of the table as she tucked her serving tray under one arm. "Straws are in the jar there. Burgers'll be up in a few, if y'all can hang on that long?"

"We're doing great, Tracy, thanks," the man said, his smile so bright she wanted to give him a hug. The woman didn't say anything, just reached over for a straw. She wasn't exactly scowling, and Tracy wouldn't call her rude, but neither would she call her happy.

She would've tried to make small talk if she'd thought it would be welcomed. But the couple was too hard to read, and she was fresh out of any extra friendly today. And then a second later, the door opened again, bringing a new customer, more work, another distraction to keep her moping at bay.

This was good. A busy Friday. She turned, hearing the woman behind her mutter, "Holy crap." She didn't look back to see what the brunette was talking about because she knew. The man climbing onto a stool at the counter looked like he'd stepped out of a Hollywood limo.

He was wearing simple clothes. Deck shoes and blue jeans and a yellow T-shirt with the long sleeves pushed up to his elbows and the buttons at the neck undone. And even if she was still married, she wasn't dead or blind.

His dark hair was cut short and he needed to shave. And when he took off his sunglasses and tossed them to the counter, "holy crap" were pretty much the only words that came to mind.

"Hey, there," she said, stepping into the alley, reaching for a menu, and scooping ice into a glass for water. "Gorgeous day out, isn't it?"

He took the glass and drank down half. "Just about perfect," he said as she refilled him. "Thanks."

"Can I get you an iced tea or a soda? Coffee?" Grinning like some movie star groupie, she hooked her thumb back toward the coffeemaker. "Pot's fresh."

"How 'bout orange juice?" He nodded toward the menu she still held. "I was thinking of a couple of eggs, over easy, toast, and bacon?"

"You got it." She dropped the menu back into the bucket with the rest of the laminated sheets and turned to jot down the order for Phil. Reaching up, she clipped the ticket to the carousel, gave it a spin, and froze.

Time froze, too, the aluminum wheel spinning and spinning, the green and white ticket flapping like a flag in the breeze. Phil stood with his hands raised shoulder level, facing a man who wore sunglasses and a light summer suit, was clean-cut with dark hair, and held a pistol-grip shotgun like the one Freddy showed her at the pawn shop when he bought his thirty-thirty for hunting season last year.

Tracy squeaked. The man turned, the barrel of his gun swinging toward her. She screamed. The customer at the counter scrambled up and over, sending salt and pepper shakers and ketchup bottles flying, and tackled her to the ground.

He lay half beneath her, his arm around her middle, his heart beating as hard as hers, her chest heaving harder. Water from his glass dribbled off the edge of the counter onto the floor, the sound making her need to pee even worse than her fear. She swore her chest was about to explode.

What the hell was happening?

The front door opened. She heard footsteps, followed by a loud, booming, "Sit. Don't move."

She wanted to get up, to see what was going on. The man holding her wouldn't let her go. He whispered a soft, "Shh," waiting, his body tense, alert, still, then leaned forward to grab a steak knife from the utensil bucket beneath the counter and slipped it into his sleeve.

The diner's interior dimmed as the window blinds were closed. The front locks *thunked* into place, that noise followed by the screech of the door sign sliding from Open to Closed. "Everyone quiet. You don't talk, you don't get hurt."

Eyes squeezed shut, Tracy prayed, wanting to see her father, wanting even more to see Freddy and tell him so many things. She got to "Our Father who art in Heaven" before she and her rescuer were hauled to their feet.

Her eyes flew open. The man who'd been holding the gun on Phil now held it on all three of them. At least until he figured she wasn't much of a threat, and ordered Phil and the customer to cross the room and join the couple guarded by a second man with a darker suit and lighter hair.

The third man who'd come in stood silently at the door, doing nothing but watching everything going on. The first man, the one nearest Tracy, reached beneath the counter for the tub of menus and shoved it into her hands. "Get over there. I want cell phones, car keys, wallets, pocket knives, nail clippers. Everything they've got on them. You, too. Pockets, purse. All of it in here."

She nodded, then stood there shaking, trying to make her feet move, afraid she was going to barf all over the menus Phil had paid a pretty penny to have laminated.

Behind her, the man slammed shut the warped back door and locked it. The order window's rolling cover came down next with a metallic bang. And when the side door leading to the hallway between the bathrooms and the kitchen thudded closed, she jumped.

"Hurry it up," he said, nudging her forward. She caught a sharp breath and shuddered, feeling like a traitor, unable to meet any of the other hostages' eyes. Because that's what they all were, wasn't it? Hostages? Like on *Law & Order* or *CSI* or something?

Her shoes felt like lead weights as she crossed the room, holding the tub while the second man, the one in the darker suit, first searched Phil, robbing him of his keys and wallet and the dog whistle his grandson, Sam, had made in Scouts. She watched all of his things land on top of the menus and wanted to cry.

Phil squeezed into one of the booths as the crook patted down the man from the counter. She lifted her lashes and met his gaze, drawing a bit of strength from the way his brows came together over his dark green eyes and the way he gave a shake of his head as if telling her not to worry.

His key ring and cell phone and wallet ended up in the tub with Phil's stuff. When the steak knife was discovered, the man searching him shoved him into the table, cursing rudely, and she bit at the lip that threatened to tremble.

The woman came next. She had nothing in her

jeans pockets but a business card holder with her driver's license and her cash money. She grumbled under her breath while being searched, glaring at the man who still stood near the door.

He had to be the boss, what with the way he lifted a finger and signaled for his men to move onto the last man, the customer who'd been sitting with the woman and ordered the cheeseburger basket and Coke.

He tried to chat up the thug searching his pockets, asking how the guy's day was going, wondering if a bag of chips wouldn't be too much trouble since he was starving.

She wanted to laugh—she wanted to get him the chips—and ended up fighting both tears and a smile. How could he make her laugh when she was so scared her stomach felt like she'd swallowed half of the rocks from her flower garden?

Once his pockets were empty and his belongings piled in with the rest, he was ordered into the booth with Phil and the other customer, and she was ordered to carry the tub to the table at the diner's far end, then to sit on a stool at the counter out of the way.

She didn't mind so much, and hoped they all forgot about her. Maybe when they weren't looking, when they were busy taking all the money from the register—wasn't that why they were here? what else could they want?—she could slip off unnoticed and call the cops.

But no one went for the register at all. The two bullies stood guarding their prisoners like they were waiting for a bomb to drop or something.

It was then that the quiet man moved, picking the two-person booth nearest the door. He was of average height and rather thin, sleazy looking in one way, and nice looking, like a fashion model, in another. As she looked on, he motioned one of the big thugs to bring over the woman from the booth.

The woman looked even more miserable and mad than earlier, but one thing she didn't look was scared. She slid into the other side of the single booth, slouched down, and glared. She didn't say a word.

Finally the man shook his head, laughed, the sound soft and spooky, and said, "Hello, Georgia."

"Charlie." Crap. Just . . . crap. First, the arrest. Second, no dossier. And now Charlie Castro. Could her day, no, her week, no, her *life,* slide any further downhill? "What do you want?"

"Is that any way to greet an old friend?" he asked, the bored look on his face telling the truth of their nonexistent relationship.

Still, she took pleasure in reminding him, "You're not a friend. You're barely an acquaintance."

But he was a threat. And that reality was one not scraped away as easily as slime from the bottom of a shoe.

The comparison was apt. If she got wind of Charlie Castro chasing down the same lead she was, she backed off. The stench of his ruthlessness clung like sewer waste.

Tangling with him was a no-win situation. And she'd grown attached to having all her fingers and ear parts and kneecaps in working order.

"And here I thought being in the same business made us colleagues," he said, his mouth smiling, his eyes not.

"Think again." She crossed her arms over her middle.

Time was ticking. This weekend was her best and possibly last chance to get her hands on the TotalSky dossier. She was not about to share with Charlie Castro that she had it on her radar. The fact that she was on his was bad enough.

"Whatever you want, I don't have it. You've searched me. You've searched"—she started to say *my brother*, held back the ammunition just in time, and said instead—"Finn. Have one of your thugs search our truck. My backpack and duffel are in the cab. If you think I've found anything of value, your sources are dead wrong."

He stared at her for several long moments, one dark brow lifted as he studied her, his expression flat. She knew her eyes gave away nothing; she'd been in this business long enough not to lose her poker face under pressure. But beneath the table, her left knee bounced up and down with a nervous tic that was giving her hell.

Finally, Charlie moved, leaning to the side yet never looking away as he reached into the pocket of his suit coat and pulled out a card-sized envelope with an embossed vellum invitation inside. He took his time, holding her gaze while removing the auction announcement and sliding it across the table.

Georgia wanted to choke.

The paper told her exactly what information he had, information he'd somehow used to connect her to Duggin. But it didn't mean he was aware that she knew the location of the dossier. It couldn't mean that. Not when she was days away from closing the book on this nightmare.

While Georgia tried to quell her rising panic, Charlie called over his shoulder to the waitress, "A cup of coffee please, black." The waitress, Tracy, nearly fell off her stool to comply. Georgia cringed.

The waitress, the cook, the cool-car hottie who'd made that heroic dive across the counter—none of them deserved this. Even Finn, who had done nothing more than end up in the wrong place at the wrong time, now had the barrel of a shotgun aimed at his head.

For not the first time in the past three years, Georgia questioned the cost of her search—to her physical health, her mental health, to Finn. But to have three strangers staring into the face of danger—a face named Charlie Castro—was more than she knew how to deal with.

Tracy arrived then with the coffee, having poured it under the watchful eye of one of the goons. At Charlie's clipped "thank you," she hurried back to the stool where she'd been sitting.

With Georgia facing away from the others, the waitress was the only person she could see. She gave Tracy the warmest smile she could muster, and the other woman fluttered her fingers hesitantly in response.

Charlie sipped at his coffee, returned the white stoneware mug to the table, then reached for the invitation and pushed it closer to her side. "You may not have found it yet. But you will have by the end of the weekend."

"Is that so?" And even as the words left her mouth, nerves coiled in her belly like a rubber band ball. Anyone interested enough could have made the connection between her, her father, and TotalSky.

But Duggin had been out of the picture since senate hearings had cleared his name almost twenty years before—hearings that had been closed, the records sealed in the name of national security.

There was no way Charlie could have linked her to the General without a lot of digging. Or an inside source. And for the first time, she wondered if she'd run into a situation with which even Finn couldn't help.

"Yes. It's so."

"I have no idea what you're talking about," she hedged.

"Then let me spell it out." Charlie pushed his coffee mug to the side. "A missing dossier detailing the TotalSky scandal. My sources tell me it will be available for bid at this auction."

The very thing she'd been trying to get her hands on for three years, begging the general, scouting around to see if it might possibly have found a new home. And he knew almost as much as she did.

The criminal element had all the luck. "Not all rumors in this business turn out to be true, Charlie. You know that as well as I do."

"You're going to help me prove this one true or false."

The rubber bands in her stomach began twanging. "And how am I going to do that?"

"I have a client interested in laying claim to the file."

She gave an indifferent shrug. "The auction is open to the public. Have at it."

"Crowds aren't my thing."

"Surely it's not a matter of money." She lifted a brow. "I hear you run in circles Donald Trump can't afford."

"Not all rumors in this business turn out to be true," he said, his head cocked to one side. "You know that as well as I do."

Grr, she hated hearing her words coming out of his mouth. "Sorry, Charlie. I really don't know how I can help."

"There are parties referenced in the dossier who wish to remain anonymous."

She wondered who he was working for since obviously it was neither her father nor General Duggin.

She knew there had been other men involved in the scandal, but their names had never been released.

Not that she cared what Charlie or anyone wanted since she planned to make the documents public. "Again, I don't see how I can help you. I barely have enough money to pay for the hamburger I never got to eat. I can't afford to bid on the General's grocery list."

"Then you need to find the item before it goes up on the block."

"And do what?"

"Steal it, of course."

"I don't think so. That's your area of expertise. Not mine." An obvious truth based in part on her recent arrest.

"I'm counting on your having learned from your mistakes."

One night in a county jail was hardly enough time to reflect on anything. "It doesn't matter what I know or might have learned. The preview is tonight, the auction on Sunday. There's no time to do what you're suggesting even if I was criminally capable. Which my record proves I'm not."

"Working under the gun will give you the motivation you need."

She really did not like the way he dropped the word *gun* into the conversation. And so she sat where she was, one leg bouncing, her short fingernails digging into her arms as she tried to hold herself together. She was not going to work for this man, do his dirty deeds, play his game.

When she didn't respond, he signaled for one of his men. The dark-haired thug came over, bent for Charlie's whispered order, retrieved the wallets Tracy had collected earlier.

Georgia's driver's license and forty-five bucks

seemed of little interest. He passed the card holder across the table; she raised one hip and slid the ID into her back pocket while he studied the others.

"The dossier is in the general's possessions. And, like my client, you know it's there." He tossed the cook's wallet back into the tub, picked up the one belonging to the convertible driver, and Finn's.

"I don't care how you get it." His gaze came up then, snagging hers coldly and with cruel intent. "But you're going to bring it to me. By Monday, one P.M. That gives you seventy-two hours. Use it wisely."

Was he insane? "And what? You're just going to wait for me here?"

"I won't be waiting alone."

The air conditioner kicked on, a chilling buzz in the silent room, and Georgia began to shiver. "I can't do what you're asking in seventy-two hours. Not by myself."

He held Finn's wallet in one hand, the stranger's in his other. "The name McLain gives you a stake in this one's well-being."

She didn't say anything. She barely managed to swallow.

"Mr. van Zandt. Please come here," Charlie called out, and behind her she heard vinyl squeak and what sounded like shoes and men scuffling. A quick glance at the waitress's wide-eyed expression confirmed for Georgia that Mr. van Zandt was less than willing.

Finally, and under escort, he arrived at the table and stood without speaking. Honestly? After that dive he'd taken across the counter, she'd expected no less. A man of action, this one, rather than a man to mince words.

She sensed a restrained energy and waves of pulsing anger, and cast a quick glance to the side, taking in no more than the fit of his blue jeans and the size of his hand, curled into a fist, before dropping her gaze to the auction invitation that seemed to be mocking her failure.

"Mr. van Zandt. This isn't your battle. You could abandon Ms. McLain and go on your way. For, I believe, her brother's sake, I'm asking you to accompany her to Dallas while she retrieves an item of interest to me."

Her knee stopped bouncing. Her anger rose. "This is between you and me, Charlie. Leave Finn out of it. Leave everyone out of it."

"Make up your mind, Georgia," Charlie said with no small hint of sarcasm. "You just told me you couldn't do it alone. I'm giving you the help you said you need."

"If you want to give me help, then give me Finn."

"Remember what I said about the right motivation? I keep your brother. You bring me the dossier. As long as you're back here by Monday, no one will get hurt. Otherwise, your brother will."

1:00 P.M.

"Pull over. Let me drive. I know where we're going."

"You? Drive this car?" Harry snorted. "Maybe in another lifetime."

"Then speed it up. If we don't get to Dallas and fast, we won't have any lifetimes left to worry about."

"Dallas I can do," he said, and pressed the accelerator to the floor. The huge car surged ahead.

He still couldn't get over the scene in the diner after Castro had delivered his not-so-veiled threat to Finn McLain. Georgia had come up out of her seat like a pouncing tiger, growling and scratching and clawing and mad.

Harry's first reaction had been to help her, to take out the bad guys like he'd been trained to do. Playing the part of the innocent bystander had required a lot of restraint and a lot of patience, and had left him feeling foul.

Once Castro's dark-haired goon had pulled her out of the boss's face, he'd escorted both Harry and the hellcat outside. Under the thug's watch and orders, she'd grabbed a duffel bag and backpack from her brother's pickup, and tossed both into the open backseat of Harry's car.

He'd been under the same watch, the same orders, but since he'd wiped out his water glass during his lunge across the counter, he'd taken two minutes to dig through his own things to find a dry shirt. That had apparently been too long for Miss Hiss and Spit to wait.

Sunglasses in place, she had stood there, her weight cocked, tapping the fingers of one hand against the opposite arm where she'd crossed them over her middle. He wasn't sure if she was trying to hold herself together or if she was really as aggravated as her stance made her seem.

That was when his foul mood worsened. He'd wanted to tell her not to worry, that he wouldn't let anything happen to her brother. But he couldn't tell her that without revealing things about who he was that she didn't need to know.

What was important right now was getting her to Dallas—and getting her to talk. That was the only way either of them would survive the weekend. It was also the only way to guarantee his mission's success.

He cast her a sideways glance. "You want to tell me what all of that was about back there?"

"No." The exact response he'd expected.

"You have a history with that man, Castro?" Charlie Castro. A name Harry would be transmitting to the SG-5 ops center at the first opportunity that came his way.

"Not a personal history, no." She relaxed a bit, her shoulders dropping as tension drained. "I've run into him in the past a time or two."

Not personal. That made it business. "You both hunt down antiques?"

"Something like that."

Harry ground his jaw. This lack of real information was getting him nowhere. He pressed, needing details. "I saw the auction invitation on the table. Whatever this man wants from you is something going up for bid?"

"It might be."

"But you don't know."

"I haven't seen the auction brochure yet. But, yeah. It could be there." She didn't say anything else for several seconds, leaving Harry to wonder exactly what she was keeping to herself. If what she did know was worth prying for. Whether another few hours would matter. If he could afford to wait for her to tell him on her terms.

Options weighed, he didn't insist, and she finally shifted sideways in her seat, pulled up one knee, and propped her elbow on the seat back. Her hair blew into her face when she turned to face him, and she gathered up the wavy brown strands in one hand. "Listen. I'm sorry Charlie involved you in this. Once we get to Dallas, I can rent a car and you can get back to your life. Just please don't go to the cops. Not yet. Not until this is over. I don't want anything to happen to Finn."

Harry nodded, pretended to consider her offer when what he was most interested in was the self-confidence implied in her willingness to write off his help. "So the guy you were with *is* your brother."

"Yeah," she said, her voice breaking softly. "My baby brother. I don't know what I'd do if anything happened to him."

An ace to store up his sleeve. "Then we'll have to make sure nothing does."

"Listen—"she started again, paused, shook her head. "I'm sorry. I don't even know your name."

"Harry."

"Harry, thanks. I'm Georgia, which obviously you know." She waved a hand. "That Mr. van Zandt thing sounded too much like you're somebody's grandfather."

"Nah." He liked her attitude. "I just drive somebody's grandfather's car."

"Yeah, Finn noticed it earlier when we passed you." She turned her attention back to the road ahead. "I cannot believe this is happening. I told him we should eat before we left Waco so we wouldn't have to stop once we were on the road."

"If this Castro was following you, he would've caught up with you sooner or later. Right?" Something else to look into. Where had Castro come from? How had he found Georgia? Who was he working for? "At least this way there wasn't a crowd around to suffer a lot of collateral damage."

She glanced over. He caught her frown from the corner of his eye. "Collateral damage. That's something I'd expect to hear from a news junkie or military type."

Point to the lady. "How 'bout both?"

"In this situation?" She blew out a heavy breath. "The latter would do me a lot more good than the first."

"Then you might not want to cut me loose when we get to Dallas."

"Why not?" she asked, looking back.

He leaned across the seat to open the glove box, brushing her knee when he straightened, his own auction invitation in hand. "I hesitated saying anything in case we had some friendly competition happening here, but we're going the same way."

"You're kidding me, right?" She grabbed the card from his hand. "You're not kidding me."

"Not kidding at all. There's a '48 Jaguar Roadster I've got my eye on."

"I know that car. I know the money that car's going to bring." She snorted. "Charlie should've sent *you* after the file he wants. I sure don't have the money it'll take to walk out of the auction with it."

Meaning she had never intended to bid on the

file in the first place. "You have an alternative solution in mind?"

A humorless snort. "Nothing I want to share with a military type."

"Ex-military."

"Semantics."

He let that go, thought about her father's history in the service before going to work for TotalSky, wondered if she was doing the same. "So, these documents. They're important to you personally?"

She slouched down in the seat, thought about propping her feet on the dash. He could tell that because he could tell when she changed her mind. She made a fidgety movement before planting her boots flat on the floorboard.

Head back, she cast a quick glance to the side. And just when he'd decided she wasn't going to answer, she said, "More important than you can possibly know."

2:20 P.M.

They stopped for gas on the outskirts of Dallas. Georgia hadn't eaten a thing all day and was starving. After using the station's facilities, she trolled the minimart's aisles and picked up a Coke and a bag of peanuts while Harry pumped gas into the tank of that incredible car.

Harry. What a normal name for someone she had a feeling didn't have a normal bone in his body. The bones that were there weren't too shabby, giving him a nice, buff-and-broad, Michelangelo's David sort of look.

But he was way too calm, way too accepting. He was dealing with a hostage situation as if it were nothing but another day at the office. Whoever he was, Harry van Zandt was no ordinary Joe Blow, ex-military, concerned citizen checking out an auction because he had a jones for an old car.

No way.

She'd seen that dive he'd made across the diner's counter to get Tracy out of harm's way. Most guys she'd known would've been too busy scrambling to save their own hides to worry about a small-town waitress. And then to slip a steak knife up his sleeve?

Speaking of sleeves, when he'd whipped off his wet T-shirt there at the car to exchange it for the gray athletic number he was wearing now, she'd spent a good thirty seconds oblivious to anything else but

his pecs and his abs before snapping out of her lust-
ful stupor.

She forced herself to snap out of it again now.
Grabbing a second Coke and another bag of peanuts,
she paid the cashier, pulled her sunglasses from the
top of her head, and headed for the car.

He was smart, sharp, and on her side. It couldn't
hurt to keep him around. At least for tonight. Hope-
fully, she wouldn't need him come tomorrow.

If the dossier actually wound up at the preview, he
might be willing to turn a blind eye to whatever means
she used to get her hands on it. Maybe she could
even get him to provide a distraction. What he didn't
know he couldn't get arrested for, right?

But this military background of his . . . She shook
her head, tucked his bottle under her elbow, and
screwed the top off hers. She knew next to nothing
about him. And she definitely needed a few details
before presenting him with an illegal proposition.

"I've been thinking," she said, walking up and waiting for him to settle the nozzle in the pump's holster
and tighten the Buick's gas cap before handing him his
peanuts and Coke. At his surprised, "Thanks," she
nodded and went on.

"Do you have dress clothes for tonight?" She
glanced at her watch. "There's a symposium first. We
can skip that. The preview reception starts at seven-
thirty, but being fashionably late works for me. Less
attention. We can slip in while things are in full swing."

He uncapped the Coke bottle. "Slip in for a hundred and seventy-five dollars, you mean. Since I'm assuming we'll be going as a couple."

"Right. A couple." She pushed away all thoughts
of marble David statues and guzzled down a quarter of
her drink. It fizzed. It burned. It jerked her mind out

of the lust gutter. "I can pony up for the donation, but I'm also going to need to buy clothes. I don't have anything with me but T-shirts, boots, and jeans."

"I have a suit, my bag's in the trunk." He tore the cellophane top from the peanuts, upended the bag into his mouth, and chewed. "It'll need to be pressed. And I'm going to need a shower."

A shower. Makeup, hair, shaving her legs for a dress. All she'd thought about was clothes and shoes. She groaned, glanced again at her watch. "There's no way we'll be ready in time."

Not to mention she still hadn't come up with a workable plan to walk out of the gallery with the dossier—and without being seen. Or a way to explain to Harry what she had really come to Dallas to do.

The more she thought about it, the more she couldn't help but wonder if she'd be better off on her own, no matter his familiarity with collateral damage.

Harry twisted the plastic top back onto his bottle and reached for the receipt the pump finally spat out. He headed around to his side of the car. "Sure we will. We need a room for the night, so we'll do that now. I'll send my suit to be pressed, we'll get cleaned up, then go shopping for you."

Sending his suit to be pressed meant something other than Motel 6, and she was on a limited budget. Making the donation to attend tonight's preview and buying shoes and a dress would pretty much wipe out the emergency fund stashed in the bottom of her backpack.

"Don't worry," he said as if reading her mind, sliding the key into the ignition and turning it to start the car. "The room's on me. I was headed here anyway, remember? I have a reservation."

"Oh. Okay," she said, getting in and shutting her door. Sharing a room with a marble statue wouldn't be that big of a deal since she had no plans to sleep until she was out of this mess. If she didn't come away from tonight's preview with the dossier, she'd need time to figure out her next step.

As Harry pulled the car into traffic, she popped back a mouthful of peanuts and glanced at her watch, wondering if she was going to be sick before or after she swallowed. Her hours were growing short, her cash limited, her acquisition of the dossier hardly guaranteed.

Altogether, her circumstances inspired absolutely no confidence that she'd get Finn out of Charlie Castro's clutches before it was too late for whatever brutal thing he had planned.

Once housekeeping arrived to pick up his suit, Harry left Georgia to stew and headed for the shower. She hadn't said much of anything since they'd checked in. She hadn't said much of anything since he'd gassed up the car, for that matter.

He didn't think it was the idea of sharing the one room that had her so quiet. More than likely the gravity of the situation was beginning to sink in. For most, it took going through the denial, anger, and bargaining stages before that happened.

She'd only had a few hours to deal, but maybe she'd hit the depression that came before acceptance. He didn't like seeing her suffer when with a word or two he could have eased her mind.

Problem was, he mused as he stripped down to bare skin, doing so would raise more questions than the revelation would answer. If he even hinted at what he did, she would no doubt demand he call in the cavalry right then and there, take-charge thing that she was.

He couldn't do that without blowing the mission, and her connections were still his best chance for success. He needed to convince her that he was with her all the way, in for a penny, in for a pound, that he was her best hope for freeing her brother.

But he had to convince her of that as Harry van Zandt, a collector of military memorabilia and classic cars, not as the SG-5 operative who knew a few things about pulling tricks out of hats.

Before he did anything, including shower, he needed to put the diner under surveillance, and do so without involving state or local authorities. Towel around his waist, he lifted the false bottom from his hard-sided shaving kit and retrieved the text messaging unit stored inside.

He lowered the toilet lid and sat, extending the device's antennae. Elbows braced on his knees, he used his thumbs to type in the password that would connect him to the comm desk at the Smithson Group's ops center in Manhattan. Ten seconds kicked by before a response flashed on the screen.

> Tripp Shaughnessey at your service.

The man did not have a serious bone in his body, Harry thought, shaking his head.

> Rabbit checking in.

> What can we do you for?

> Two things. Charlie Castro.

> Any relation to Cuba?

> You tell me. Start with antiquities theft.

> Number two?

Harry typed in the GPS coordinates to Waco Phil's.

> Monitor activity inside and out. No contact.

> No burgers?

Harry chuckled.

> No contact. Including food.

> Will send Simon. That it?

Simon Baptiste was one of the two newest members recruited into SG-5.

> For now. Oh. How's the chair?

> Slow as hell. Take care, dude.

> Will do.

Tripp Shaughnessey's never-ending quest to roll

his chair the width of Smithson's cavernous ops center was legendary, and the ribbing he'd earned as a result nonstop.

Harry returned the messaging unit to its storage space, quickly shaved, pushed away thoughts of Tripp and the rest of the SG-5 crew, jumped into the shower, and got back to thinking about Georgia McLain.

She knew he was ex-military. She'd admitted his being so couldn't hurt but help, or something similar. She couldn't argue that he had a viable reason to attend the preview and auction. So far, so good.

If she found what she was looking for tonight, he'd have to convince her they would be better served waiting until tomorrow to return. Harry needed to make sure Simon had time to get in place—not only for surveillance and eventually storming the diner, but for the handing off of the goods.

Especially since Harry was convinced that Georgia wasn't going to want to turn over the dossier to Castro any more than he wanted her to. And this was where things were going to get extra sticky.

Once Finn, Phil, and Tracy were safe, Harry would be taking possession of the dossier whether Georgia liked it or not. Meaning, he needed to figure out exactly what she wanted with it. He was certain it had something to do with her father. He just hadn't had time to figure out what.

He wasn't above a compromise or helping her. But he had a job to do. The dossier went back to Manhattan or he went back to the drawing board. That said, he would make sure Georgia and her brother were reunited by the end of the weekend.

He had just stepped from the shower and reached for a towel when a bright white light flashed and nearly blinded him. He reached over and shut off the silent alarm, the trigger to which he'd attached to the room's door when he'd closed it behind the maid. It wasn't that he didn't trust Georgia . . .

He flung the towel around his waist and whipped open the door, stepping barefoot, half-naked, and dripping into the small entry alcove. Georgia stood there with one hand on the door handle as if she were about to leave the room. Her eyes grew wide; her gaze traveled from his head to toe and back.

He didn't stop to think, but moved in, menacing, hovering, gruff. "Where are you going?"

She shook her head. Her throat convulsed as she swallowed. "Nowhere. It's housekeeping. With your suit." She took a step out into the hallway, her other foot braced against the base of the door, and returned with his clothes, which she shoved into his chest. "You owe me five bucks for the tip."

While Georgia had holed away in the suite's monstrous bathroom to shower, shave, shampoo, and pull on a clean pair of undies, her T-shirt and jeans, Harry had been busy. Busy doing more than getting dressed and ratcheting up the who-is-this-man-and-where-did-he-come-from stakes.

He wore serious grown-up clothes as beautifully as he wore casual, and as well as Michelangelo's David wore his marble skin.

She'd walked out of the steamy bathroom and only just stopped herself from demanding what the hell he was doing breaking into her room before she realized her mistake. He was that amazing. And her heart was still dealing with the unexpected lust.

The man was the most beautiful thing she'd seen in forever. Her first impression, made from Finn's truck when looking down from her window, had been right on the mark. But he was so much more than a girl's guide to getting off.

His smile—those lips and dimples, the dark shadow of his beard—was enough to melt even the most titanic ice queen. Not that she was one or anything . . .

Sitting as she was now in the hotel's salon, having her hair and makeup done, she kept sneaking looks over to where he sat waiting and reading a back issue of *Cosmo*. Every once in a while he'd frown, shake his head, turn the page. If she hadn't been ordered not to move by her stylist, she might never have stopped laughing.

When Harry told her he'd arranged not only this appointment but another with the hotel boutique's personal shopper for jewelry, shoes, and a dress, she'd asked him if he thought she was made of money.

He'd pulled out his wallet, handed her a five to pay back the tip, then reminded her she was the one donating to General Duggin's Scholarship Foundation tonight.

Making sure she arrived looking the part of wealthy collector rather than pack rat was the least he could contribute to the cause—a cause he'd then started to dig into, asking her questions about her family and the importance of the documents Charlie had sent her to find.

Since she'd been stuck on the pack rat comment, frowning as she ransacked her duffel for the sandals she knew that were there, thinking how she really *had* let herself go since being consumed by this quest, she'd almost answered, had barely caught herself in time.

The story of her father's wrongful incarceration and her determination to prove his innocence had been on the tip of her tongue before she had bit down. If Harry knew the truth of why she wanted the dossier, he would quickly figure out she had no intention of delivering it to Charlie Castro.

Then, no doubt, they'd get into an argument about the value of her brother's life versus that of her father's name, and he'd want to know why the hell they were going through all of this if not to save her brother.

She really didn't want to go there with Harry. She was having too much trouble going there with herself. Finn would understand; she knew he would. As long as he was alive to do so when this was over . . .

At that thought, she groaned, the sound eliciting the stylist's concern. "What's wrong, sweetie? Too much color? Not enough? The highlights are temporary, remember? Three washings max, you'll be back to being a brunette."

"Oh, no. I was thinking of something else," Georgia assured the other woman, meeting her reflected gaze. "I hadn't even looked . . ."

But now she did. And she swore the reflection in the mirror couldn't possibly be hers. "Wow," was the only thing she could think to say, and so she said it again. "Wow."

"Yeah. I thought so, too." The stylist beamed at her handiwork—and rightly so. Georgia had never in her life looked like this. The highlights in her hair gave off a coppery sheen. Her layers, too long and grown out—she was desperate for a new cut—had been trimmed, colored, and swept up into an intricate rooster tail of untamed strands.

And then her face . . . Was that really her face? The salon's makeup expert had used a similar color scheme, spreading sheer terra cotta on her cheeks, a blend of copper and bronze on her eyelids, finishing off with a gorgeous cinnamon-colored glaze on her lips.

And all of it matching the beautiful ginger-hued polish on the nails of all twenty fingers and toes. She could go for this girly girl stuff. Really.

Especially when she lifted her gaze to meet Harry's in the mirror. He stood behind the stylist, his shoulders wide in his designer suit coat, his hands jammed to his lean waist, his smile showing just a hint of teeth.

She had no idea when he'd moved from where he'd been sitting to her chair, but the look in his eyes, the fire in his eyes, and the low sweep of his lashes was enough to make her swoon.

It had been so long since a man had shown *that* kind of interest in her that she didn't know what to do, how to react, to respond. Except the truth was that it wasn't the men. It was her.

She had refused to let any man close enough to do more than notice her skill for ferreting out valuable antiques for years now, longer than she could remember.

But now, here came Harry into the middle of her personal catastrophe, a veritable stranger who had the body of a god and a killer smile and eyes that were telling her dangerously sexy things about wanting to get her naked. He was helping her in ways that went above and beyond.

And she still had the night to spend in his room. "Can we charge the makeup to the room? I'll pay you back."

"Sure." His eyes sparkled. His smile grew wicked. "And it's my treat."

The stylist swept the cape from around Georgia's shoulders and Harry offered his hand to help her from the chair. It was a Cinderella moment that she had no business enjoying, but she couldn't help it.

She hadn't done a single thing for herself in so long that it was impossible to brush aside this feeling of discovering someone she'd thought lost.

She was well aware of why she and Harry were together, the full extent of what was at stake. But it had been years, literally *years*, since she'd considered herself attractive—not to mention since she'd felt confident that someone of the opposite sex found her so.

Harry did. She didn't doubt it for a minute. Even if it did up the nerve-wracking factor of the long evening ahead in his company.

While Harry tipped the stylist and settled the bill, she took the bag of cosmetics from the cashier, absently noticing how the attention of every woman in the salon, whether overtly or subtly, was directed toward the check-out station and the fit of Harry's clothes.

She wanted to laugh; here she was, panicking over sleeping near him when he could crook a finger and have any of these women in his bed.

And then she didn't want to laugh at all.

She wanted to grab him by the arm and drag him out of there, leaving a battlefield of bloody cat scratches in her wake. Like he belonged to her or something, and how ridiculous was that? He was nothing but a man who happened to be in the wrong place at the wrong time, who was going out of his way to get her out of a jam.

Finn would have done the same for a woman in need. Her ex, hardly. They'd been married, and he wouldn't have done it for her. Unless there was something in it for him . . . Hmm. Too bad she hadn't snapped to that before.

Harry scrawled his signature across the bottom of the ticket, then handed the pen to the cashier. Georgia cocked her head and considered what he could possibly hope to gain from helping her out. He was going to a lot of expense . . . and sex was the first thing, the only thing, that came to mind.

He turned toward her, that amazing smile reaching all the way to his eyes, and she backed into the corridor that connected the hotel's lobby with the maze of others leading to meeting rooms, shops, sitting areas, gym lockers, and pricey amenities catering to the well-to-do guest. Like Harry.

"What?" he said, placing his palm in the small of her back and herding her toward the clothing boutique and her appointment there.

"Why are you doing this?" she asked, glancing up as they walked.

He frowned, kept looking forward, looking . . . edible. "Doing what?"

"Spending all this money to clean me up." She moved ahead, dislodging his hand and the possessive weight that she was liking way too much.

He caught up and settled it right back where it was, the spread of his fingers heavy and warm. "We've been over this already. You're forking over a hundred and seventy-five bucks to get us into this reception."

She snorted. "You just dropped more than that on my face and hair."

"So?" he asked, guiding her around the richly carpeted corridor's next corner.

"So, in this place, a dress and shoes are going to double your outlay, and we won't be so even anymore." When he didn't respond, she added, "We could make a stop at Foley's or J.C. Penney and save a bundle."

This time he shook his head. "We're out of time."

"I just hope you're not out of money."

"Why's that?"

"Because if things don't go well tonight, I'll need another dress for Sunday's auction."

He laughed, a chuckle that was low and deep and vibrated all the way to his palm where he touched her. "You're forgetting something."

She wasn't surprised. She could barely even think. She was surprised she hadn't tripped over one of her own two feet. "What?"

"I'm bidding on a 1948 Jaguar."

"Oh." That shut her up. What? A good ninety thousand or so? Expensive hobby.

"And I've been thinking that if I draw the attention as the one interested in the auction, you can do your thing without anyone getting in your way."

It sounded good anyway. At least until they reached the boutique and she saw the dresses and shoes the personal shopper had selected in advance *and* in her sizes—Georgia wasn't sure how she felt about Harry snooping through her things—based on the event details he'd given when he'd called.

She glanced from the dresses hanging on the rolling rack to Harry. "These dresses are not going to do a damn thing to help you draw attention away from me."

"Maybe not. But you'll make for good arm candy."

Earlier this afternoon, when Georgia had walked out of the dressing room and made her way to where Harry had been sitting, showing off the first dress the boutique's personal shopper had selected for her to try on, he'd come damn close to swallowing his tongue.

The two hours he'd spent in the salon flipping through the magazine had been bad enough. He was as clueless now as he had been then to the content of the pages he'd turned. All he knew was that he'd done a piss-poor job of focusing on the night ahead and working out a game plan.

Instead, he'd been consumed with the transformation of Georgia McLain.

He hadn't paid her a whole lot of attention in the diner, but then all of them had been pretty busy back there. Based on the pictures he'd seen of her during his mission prep work, he'd known she was a looker. What he hadn't known was that she was a *looker*.

She'd walked from the dressing room into the sitting area where he'd been waiting, and all he'd done was stare. He hadn't known what to say; the woman in front of him was not the woman he'd expected to see. She had legs, bare legs, legs made even longer by the height of her heels and the thigh-high hem of the dress she'd chosen.

She'd turned in a circle, arms out to her sides, a smirk on her gorgeously made-up face. She'd enjoyed seeing him pinned to the cushy chair as if he'd been run through with a spike—an apropos comparison because he had not been able to move.

The neckline of the little black dress was scooped low, the back scooped even lower, leaving no doubt that she was wearing very little beneath. What sleeves there were fell off her shoulders, tiny caps of fabric barely hanging on and leaving her arms bare.

Sitting beside him now in the back of the cab for the ride to the gallery, she shifted forward and hiked up the lace wrap the boutique's shopper had insisted on adding to the package of dress, shoes, and diamond drop pendant.

Hank Smithson was going to throw a cow when Harry turned in the receipts in his expense report, but if Hank could see Georgia . . .

"You never did tell me why we're taking a taxi," she said, cutting into his reverie.

He'd planned to, but somewhere between leaving the boutique and having the doorman call the cab, he'd lost his tongue—not to mention his entire command of the English language.

Glancing over at her now, seeing the way the streetlamps caught the colors in her hair as the car passed beneath, he wasn't sure he'd found enough of either to reply.

He cleared his throat anyway. "The Buick isn't exactly a car to lose on a crowded street. Just in case we need to hit the road in a hurry."

She bobbed her head a couple of times. "Funny. Finn said something this morning about me needing a getaway car."

"Yeah?" He heard the catch in her voice when she'd mentioned her brother's name.

She looked his way briefly before dropping her gaze to her lap and twisting her fingers in the fringe of the wrap. "All I could think was that I was a Bonnie without a Clyde."

He wondered if she was referring to her love life or her life of crime. He knew she'd once been married, that she wasn't in a relationship now. He also knew calling her a criminal based on her history was a stretch. After tonight, well, things in this spy business changed in a hurry.

Leaning toward her, he rested an arm along the seat back. "You can call me Clyde. If it makes you feel better."

"That's okay," she said with a laugh. "I kinda like calling you Harry."

"Want to know what my nickname is?" he asked, toying with the hem of her tiny nothing of a sleeve.

She hesitated, shivered, answered shyly, "I don't know. Do I?"

"It's Rabbit."

Lips pressed together, she shook her head. "I'm not even going to ask."

This time he was the one who laughed. "It's about tricks. Pulling things out of a hat. Trust me. It has nothing to do with, uh, taking my time," he said, feeling the beginnings of an uncomfortable heat sliding down the length of his spine. "That I know how to do."

"That's good to know." A blush crept up the back of her neck. "Not that I was asking or anything."

"Just so we're clear," he said, laughing again because otherwise he was going to do something really dumb. Like drag her across the seat and into his lap.

"Don't worry," she said, her voice having dropped to a near whisper. "As thorough as you've been getting things ready for tonight, it wouldn't occur to me to think anything else."

The car hit a bump in the road, jarring her shoul-

der into his hand. Her whisper had led him to believe she was testing the sexual waters between them.
The icy skin of her shoulder changed his mind.

He opened his fingers over the slope of her neck.
Damn. "You're freezing. Here. Take my coat."

She stopped him before he'd done more than start
to shrug one shoulder. "No, really. I'm fine. I'm not
cold."

"Right," he said, sounding more harsh than he'd
intended. "Tell that to your skin."

"It's nerves," she said, her teeth chattering. "I don't
do well with anticipation. Or dreading everything
that might go wrong. I'll be fine once we're there."

He wanted to pull her close, rub his hands up and
down her arms to warm her. Instead, he sat where he
was and watched her huddle in on herself, wondering if she was going to be able to pull it together and
hold it together once she had.

They had a hell of a long night to look forward to,
and he didn't know enough of the details of the
dossier they were both after to play her part in addi-
tion to his.

But then the cab began to slow, pulling in between the line of parked limos and the personal cars
waiting to be valeted, and what he did or didn't know
no longer mattered. He had a job to do, and it was
time.

A gallery doorman slipped through to open Harry's
door. He climbed out, reached back to give Georgia
his hand. And when she stepped out, her back straight,
her head high, he knew from her show of strength
that the only thing he had to worry about tonight
was keeping his hands to himself.

Still, with the evening's air being nippy and Georgia
hardly dressed, he draped his arm around her shoulders as they made their way beneath the gallery's

portico and down the pebbled walkway to the double glass doors.

At the entrance, the hostess pointed them to a short line at a table in the dimly lit and richly carpeted lobby where a cashier waited to take their donation and provide them with a receipt and the reception brochure.

At the mention of the brochure, Georgia's case of the shakes returned. He wasn't even touching her, was simply standing at her shoulder. The hem of his suit coat brushed the hanging ends of her wrap, but that was the extent of their contact. And still he felt her tremble. Whether a chill or nerves, her reaction set him on edge; a surge of heat rose along with his blood pressure.

This wasn't going to work. They needed to settle this now. Once inside the exhibit room, it was game on. No going back. He wasn't going to let her walk through those doors until he knew she was ready.

Casting a glance the length of the darkened lobby, he took hold of her upper arm, leaned close to her ear, and whispered, "C'mon."

She came willingly, seemingly relieved as he propelled her toward the private phone bays separated from one another and tucked behind thick decorative columns. She slipped inside the first empty alcove.

He followed, taking up the rest of the room and blocking the lobby's light. Chin down, she leaned against the high-backed chair pushed up beneath the bay's built-in table and shook her head.

"I'm sorry." She brought up both hands to cover her face, shuddered. "I thought this was going to be easy. A walk in the park. That we'd go in, the dossier would be right there for our taking, we'd grab it and leave. End of story."

Her honesty—and her naiveté—sent an unexpected

rush of softness flowing into his heart. He didn't doubt that she was tough. That she was strong. That she was not a cream puff who burst into tears at the slightest provocation.

But he was used to working with operatives who looked at a mission objectively, dispassionately. Not with a woman this personally involved in the outcome.

Georgia McLain was dealing with stakes even higher than he'd realized.

He weighed the odds of running this on his own, factored in the hellcat he'd seen in the diner this morning, came away confident that she had it in her to do this, to do anything. All she needed was a reminder.

"Look, Georgia—"

She cut him off with a wave of her hand. "I'm fine. I'll be fine."

He grabbed her fluttering fingers. "No, you're not. And I can't let you go in there until you are."

Her chin came up. "You can't let me? What the hell kind of chauvinistic crap is that?"

The kind that got her attention. He moved closer. Brought her hand to his chest where his heart was beating harder than he liked. "Feel that? That's me worried you're going to flake, and I'm going to fuck up because you haven't told me enough about what we're doing here for me to handle it alone."

She stilled, waited, did nothing but breathe.

Harry pressed. "It's your ball game, sweetheart. I'm just a rabid fan."

She'd stopped shaking. That much he was glad to see. What he wasn't sure about was how to react when she flexed her fingers against his shirt, testing the muscle beneath.

And he was really lost when she stepped closer

and leaned her forehead against him. Especially since he could smell the wild rain scent of her hair.

He stood there unmoving, his heart pounding even harder now when the whole reason for bringing her here was about staying calm. Calm was the last thing he was feeling. And the way she pressed against him, nuzzled him, bringing up both of her hands to do whatever it was she was doing . . . He shuddered, reached up to grip her shoulders and set her away.

Instead, he took a deep, deep breath. "Georgia?"

"Shh," she whispered, laying two fingers against his lips. "I know. I'm sorry. I know."

He had no idea what she was saying. All he knew was that her fingers were soft, that she smelled like heaven, and that the tingling heat at the base of his spine was about to make itself known in a very large way.

His hands on her shoulders tightened, sliding down her bare arms to her elbows at the same time she slipped her hands from his chest up to his neck. He closed his eyes and groaned.

This wasn't happening. Any other time, any other place, sure. Not here. Not now. But it was too late. She'd cupped the base of his skull with one hand and was pulling him down. The air she blew out brushed his cheek, and she touched her mouth to the edge of his in the barest hint of a kiss.

She moved closer, catching the corner of his top lip between hers, whispering, "I'm sorry," as she nibbled and tugged, as her tongue followed to wet him, to tease him, to make him horny as hell.

A growl rolled up from his throat. His hands found her waist. He backed her up into the table and opened his mouth fully over hers. He held her there, held her still, but she wouldn't have it.

She wanted the movement, the motion. Her hands found their way beneath his suit coat to his chest, his ribs, around to his back. She massaged tiny circles between his shoulder blades, all the while kissing him, her tongue tangling with his.

Her response wasn't about him. It wasn't even about sex or attraction. It was about fear and panic, about worry and stress. About her brother's life. About reaching the end of a search, about possibly reaching the end of her rope.

Knowing all of that didn't mean he stopped her. He did the opposite, in fact. He gave her every bit of the movement and motion she was looking to find.

He planted his palm in the small of her back and pressed her into his body, grinding down with his mouth while she pushed against him with hers. He played with her tongue, with her lips. He caught her with his teeth just hard enough to cause her to growl and bite back, to gouge her short nails into the muscles on either side of his spine.

He laughed, and she swallowed the sound, snarling when he palmed the round of her ass and squeezed. He wanted to take her, to lift her up and drive his cock home, to spread open her pussy, to rub all her hot spots, to make her come.

It wasn't going to happen. He knew that. But knowing it didn't keep him from bunching the fabric of her dress in one hand until he found skin. A lot of skin. Her bottom was completely bare.

He stopped. She stopped, pulling back to look him in the eyes. As dark as it was, he couldn't see much, but he definitely saw them glitter. "What? You thought I was wearing something under this dress, the way it fits? There's only one sure way to avoid panty lines."

"That so?" he asked, thinking how much he'd like to take her shopping again. Thinking how much he liked her bare backside. He slid his hand lower and palmed the swell of her cheek. "And here I was thinking you made it a habit to go commando."

"Well, there is that," she said, breathless, lifting her leg and hooking her knee around his thigh before she got back to killing him with her kiss.

Her nimble tongue mated with his, swirled through his mouth. He could hardly keep up because his attention had gone south the moment she'd raised her leg. She was wet and she was warm and she was naked and open.

All he had to do was slide his hand lower, his fingers deeper, to find the source of her heat. And so he did, slicking her moisture over her skin, teasing the downy lips protecting her slit until she whimpered.

"Please," she murmured against him. "Please. I'm sorry. Please."

He'd never had a woman beg him so sweetly, and he couldn't help but wonder what she kept apologizing for. He'd figure it out later, if later he still cared. Right now, he had his hands full, and too much else on his mind.

He let her go, reached for the chair and pulled it from under the table. Slipping his hand beneath her knee, he moved her foot to the seat of the chair. The position left her vulnerable. His position kept her hidden.

He tickled the skin of her thigh until she shivered, then slid his hand higher. She pulled her mouth from his, buried her face between his lapels where she'd crushed them in her fists. The sounds she made were low and throaty vibrations, all about what she was feeling, none of it faked.

He stroked his way up her leg, breathing deeply of her scents, which were clean and sweet, earthy, like fields of flowers, like the sea. He found her center, brushed aside her soft thatch of hair, thumbed the hard knot of her clit.

She gasped, tensed, shuddered, pulled his jacket closed and tightened her grip. The intimate space grew smaller. He turned her, holding her weight as she leaned back. Her hip hit the wall for support.

And then his head bowed, the darkness around them encompassing, he slid his middle finger inside of her and teased in and out of her folds with his thumb.

He felt her muscles contract as she began to move, rolling her spine like a snake and thrusting slowly to meet his rhythm as he fucked her with his hand. She was wet and wild; he wanted to taste her, to pull his finger free and lick away her sticky sweets.

But she was close, clenching him, milking his fingers when he added another, grinding against his wrist. When she came, she burst in a silent wave, one powerful and sweeping. He felt the pulse of her contractions like a riptide pulling him down, and he straddled her leg and rubbed the engorged head of his cock against her.

"I'm sorry," she muttered again moments later. "I'm so sorry. That was so unfair."

He pulled his hand from between her legs and helped her smooth down her skirt before, gingerly, he took a step back and sat down. "Why are you always apologizing?"

She struggled with the hem of her dress. "Because I'm horribly selfish. I'm always thinking about me and what I want."

"There's nothing wrong with looking out for number one," he said, slouching back to adjust the swollen goods.

"To the extent I do it? Even I think I'm a pig."

He would have laughed if he wasn't trying to catch his breath. "I think the ladies' room is across the lobby. I'll wait here if you want to freshen up."

"Oh, Harry. I'm so sorry."

"Are you still cold?"

She shook her head.

"Nervous?"

The same again.

"Then my job here is done."

She brought up her hands to her cheeks. "You'll let me make it up to you?"

He groaned at the thought, grew harder rather than soft. "Let's not go there right now."

She gave a mewling sort of guilty-sounding whine, leaned down, took his face in her hands, and kissed him. Then she scurried away. And it wasn't until after she was gone and his hard-on was halfway to hard-off, that he realized she'd left without an apology.

At least they were making progress on one front—though he would've been a lot more satisfied if they'd been making it on others. Specifically, finding what they'd come for and figuring out a way to get it, get out of here, and get back to the diner all in one piece.

The sex thing could wait. Hell, the sex thing didn't even have to happen. Georgia McLain, with her face, her hair, her outstanding body, and her hellcat ways were not a priority point of this mission. His cock might think differently, but he had yet to let the bastard run the show.

He enjoyed women. He loved women. He liked being with them in bed and out. Women were the finest thing to have ever been created—so fine that men could never have done the job of designing the same perfect fit.

That didn't mean Harry would risk life, limb, or the covert nature of what he did for the Smithson Group for a little bit of nookie on the side.

Of course, thinking about nookie was the moment he happened to look back up and see Georgia walking toward him, her wrap in place, her skirt straight, her hair a tousled mess of strands colored like a copper mine.

All the work he'd done convincing himself of his immunity to the way she walked and looked and wore her clothes went to hell in a fiery handbasket. He was monumentally doomed. He got to his feet, adjusted his shirt and his belt and buttoned his coat, trying to decide if he had it in him to walk.

He met her in the lobby hallway before she got the chance to corner him again in the dark. He was feeling about as weak as a man could get. He needed space.

She handed him the money she'd had zipped inside a pocket smartly designed at the edge of her wrap. "Here. I'm feeling all girly, so you can be macho and pay."

"Now there's the smart mouth Georgia McLain I've come to know and love."

She hooked her arm through his. "If you knew me, you would never have taken me shopping for a dress I can't even afford to have dry cleaned. And if you loved me, well"—she stood on tiptoes to whisper since they'd moved back into line—"you did okay on that score."

"Please. Don't use the word score. Not until I've recovered from the fact that I didn't." When she opened her mouth, he quickly silenced her with two fingers pressed to her lips. "Whatever you do, do *not* say you're sorry."

She nodded, stood beside him while he handled the business of the donation and the receipt, then nearly ripped the reception brochure in half pulling it out of his hand.

"You're supposed to blend in, remember?" he leaned down to remind her, catching a whiff of the soap she'd used to bathe. "That kid at Disney World act isn't what I call blending."

But she wasn't listening. She was scanning the tri-fold color brochure. The first section, the second, the third, the back side of each, before starting at the beginning again. And she did so without looking where she was going. He had to guide her by both shoulders through the door from the lobby into the exhibit hall.

The low-ceilinged room didn't have the museum-quality ambience Harry had expected. There were no glass-cased displays, ornately carved wood bases, engraved brass plaques. There were no special spotlights or velvet-draped stands. Instead, the setup reminded him of a hotel meeting hall. Dry and businesslike.

Tables covered with maroon cloths circled the room's perimeter and were made off-limits to the public by roped dividers. In the center of the room, carpeted in an industrial gray, the caterers had set up their tables. Food, drinks. Mucho drinks.

After the earlier symposium, he figured there would be a lot of takers. And, indeed, a large segment of the crowd of a hundred and fifty or so did seem more interested in the refreshments than in the memorabilia displayed.

Not Georgia.

She had her fingers wrapped like a claw around his elbow as she propelled him toward the section designated for the personal papers the general had deemed too insignificant to warrant inclusion in his university bequests.

Harry had expected—and wasn't disappointed to find—such things as letters from military dignitaries, correspondence from government officials, notes for the general's soon-to-be-published memoir. The dry cleaner receipts and grocery lists did raise his brow. But hey, if people could auction Britney Spears' chewing gum on eBay . . .

What he'd been surprised since the beginning of this mission to learn was that a dossier of this one's apparent importance would be included with the rest of the junk. Except he was beginning to doubt that it was. Not with the way Georgia had nearly ripped his arm and the brochure to shreds.

"Okay. Something is wrong," she finally said, having matched up every item on the table with those listed in the leaflet. She reached for a flute of champagne from a passing server, gulped half of it down. "There's a lockbox of miscellaneous documents related to Duggin's contract work that's supposed to be here. It's not. I can't find it."

"You sure?" A lockbox of miscellaneous documents? Was that where she expected to find the dossier?

She punched him in the shoulder, downed the rest of the champagne. "I've done everything but look under the table. It's not here."

"Maybe it's in one of the other sections." He glanced around. There were a lot of other tables set up around the room. They'd only looked at this one.

They could have looked at two hundred. It wouldn't have changed the fact that he'd put all his eggs into the basket of an unreliable source. He knew better. He should have spread his inquiries further into the field. In short, he'd fucked up. What Georgia was looking for—meaning what he was looking for—wasn't even here.

"C'mon," he said, wrapping an arm around her shoulders and guiding her away from the table she was reluctant to leave. The champagne wasn't much of a help. By the time they'd made their way around the entire room, she was holding her fourth flute. And she wasn't walking so well.

Neither one of them had eaten anything since she'd bought the Cokes and peanuts this afternoon, so he took the drink from her hand and herded her forcefully toward the food.

He loaded a plate with shrimp things and crab things and puffy ham and cheese things before following her back to the original table and forcing her to eat.

"What makes you think this dossier you're looking for is in this lockbox?"

"Where else would it be?" she hedged.

Avoidance wasn't going to cut it. He had to pin her down. "Unless you've actually seen it in there, then it could be in almost any city in any country in the world."

"Don't be silly," she said. "General Duggin lived here. In Texas."

"He traveled all over the world, didn't he?"

"He lived here," she said, her words measured, clear, and sharp.

Harry was seconds from writing off this exercise as a huge waste of time. And if not for the innocent people being held at the diner, he would.

But until they were out of harm's way and he picked up another lead to follow, he didn't have much in the way of options but sticking this one out.

That didn't make him any happier. "What you're saying, then, is that you really don't know."

She swallowed a cheesy quiche thing almost whole. "What I'm saying—"

"Georgia? Georgia McLain?"

Both Harry and Georgia turned at the interruption. The man who had butted into their business was older, probably the general's age, and dressed in a three-piece tweed complete with a watch fob and wire-rimmed glasses.

When Georgia didn't respond except to frown, Harry stepped in. "I'm sorry. I don't believe the lady knows you."

"She wouldn't, of course." The older man smiled, held his lapels, and laughed. "I only recognize her from a photo I once saw. It was a long time ago, so I wasn't sure. It's just your eyes. They still look the same."

At Harry's side, Georgia was shaking her head. "Where would you have seen a picture of me?"

"Your father showed it to me. He always carried pictures of both you and your brother."

"You knew my father?" she asked, sagging into Harry's side. "When? How?"

"Oh, I apologize. Let me introduce myself." He removed his glasses, pulled a handkerchief from his pocket. "My name is Paul Valoren."

"You were the symposium speaker," Harry said, taking in the other man's head of thick white hair and his even thicker waistline. What else had the invitation said? "You're a professor . . ."

"Political science, yes. At Stanford." Valoren returned his clean glasses to his face. "I take it you didn't attend my speech."

"We were late getting into Dallas," Harry said, a weak explanation but all that came to mind, and true enough. He was still waiting for Georgia to react. Valoren seemed to be doing the same.

She finally did, rubbing a hand over her forehead.

"I'm sorry. I don't recognize your name. Then again, I have had way too much champagne."

Valoren laughed, a strangely deep twitter. "Don't worry, Miss McLain. I knew Stanley a very long time ago. I doubt he would have had reason to mention me to the little girl you would've been."

"You served with him in the military? Or did you know him when he worked for TotalSky?"

"Actually, both," he said, scuffing the sole of one shoe over the carpet.

Harry wondered what the other man was thinking because the nervous gesture was a dead giveaway that his mind wasn't in the moment. "If we'd known that, we would've made an effort to get here in time to hear you speak."

"Oh, who wants to hear an old man blather on about politics in the military, uh, I didn't catch your name . . ."

"Harry." He extended his hand. Valoren's grip was firm, his palm damp. "Harry van Zandt. And from the look of things, you had a decent size crowd."

The older man smiled. "Ah, but how many came late as you did, for the food and the drink and the preview?"

"Professor Valoren—"

"Please call me Paul," he said to Georgia.

"Paul, do you know anything about the documents up for auction? Looking at the listing"—she glanced down at the mangled paper she held—"it seems there are some items missing from the display."

Valoren leaned to the side to study the brochure. "I don't really know anything, no. Were you interested in something in particular?"

"Yes," Georgia got out before Harry managed to grab her elbow and squeeze. She nudged him in the side. Hard. "It's nothing important."

"If you're asking, then of course it's important," the professor insisted.

Georgia gave a small shrug. "It's just that he kept up a correspondence with my father while he was away. I thought it would be nice to have those letters. No one's been able to find them for me, so I was hoping they'd turn up here. I'm being too sentimental, I suppose."

"One either is sentimental or isn't," Valoren said, reaching for her hand. "I don't believe it is possible to be too much so. Maybe one of the employees from the auction house can help you?"

"I'll check with them, thanks," Georgia said, adding a sigh and impressing Harry all to hell with her improv skills. "It's so nice to meet someone who knew my father."

Valoren looked from Georgia to Harry and back. "How long will you two be in Dallas? Perhaps we could do lunch tomorrow? Or Sunday before the auction? I'm actually scheduled to fly home Monday evening, so that day isn't out of the question."

Harry wanted to find out more about the man before making a commitment. He liked an even footing. Right now that was not what he had. "How can we get in touch with you?"

"Oh." The other man scrambled to find a card. "I'm staying at the Adam's Mark. You can reach me there, or leave a message with my service. The number is on the card."

"Thanks." Harry flicked the card once, then pocketed it. "It's been a pleasure to meet you, Professor. But I think I need to get Georgia back to our room. It's been a very long day."

"Of course, of course. And I see a colleague trying to get my attention." He looked beyond Harry's shoulder and raised a hand in acknowledgment. "Please do call. I'd love to tell you anything I can about the years I worked with Stanley. That is, if you want to know."

"I would love to know, oh yes, please." Georgia glanced up at Harry, her gaze imploring and just a little bit buzzed.

He wanted to tell her no, they didn't have time for side trips or distractions. That whether or not they found the dossier, there was the bigger consideration of her brother and the other innocent lives.

But he thought about her father knowing Duggin, about Valoren knowing her father, and realized his gut was telling him to listen.

"Sure," he finally said. "We'll talk tomorrow after you get some sleep."

Finn McLain couldn't remember a time in his life when he'd been as bored as he was now. He knew there was nothing he could do about the situation, not with Georgia out who knew where in the company of some macho hothead liable to get her killed.

Having his hands tied like this when he should be there for his sister really, really pissed him off.

He knew the guy had been acting on instinct, diving across the counter for the waitress the minute he'd seen the shotgun-toting thug taking aim in the kitchen at the cook. But Finn had always been of the mind to look at the big picture before leaping.

Then again, who but a six-eyed psychic could've seen this big picture coming?

Sure, Georgia got her fanny in a hell of a lot of silly—even unnecessary—scrapes, but he'd never seen her crawl across a table to claw out a man's eyes with two hired guns aimed her way. If that wasn't the closest his heart had ever come to seizing up . . .

Even now the remembering caused a massive blip in his pulse. And as much as he would've preferred to shitcan the memory as a whole, it did chase the boredom away. For about ten seconds. Then he got back to being a crabby, worried, bored-to-the-bone bastard.

There was no way he was going to be able to sit here like this until Monday noon. They were in a freakin' diner. He was going to get some damn food.

The place was dark. Castro had kept off the lights all day. Except for trips to the rest room, there hadn't been much movement. There'd been even less talking.

Finn had stayed in one booth, Phil in the next, while Tracy sat on a stool and napped, leaning into the elbow she'd propped on the bar and snoring softly.

Now, the big sodium arc lamp in the parking lot tossed light through the slats of the window blinds to sprawl like a zebra across the floor. It was enough for Finn to see where he was going, but not enough for the thugs to worry about anyone outside seeing in.

Sitting sideways in the cramped little cage of his booth, he reared back and heaved himself forward, hooking his knees over the seat and pushing to his feet before his captors figured out that he wasn't just squirreling around to get more comfortable.

The light-haired goon was the closest. "If you gotta piss again, do it in your pants. I'm not taking you for another potty break."

Finn ignored the thug and kept walking, ducking behind the counter and nudging Tracy. "Sorry to wake you, but do you have a box of cereal somewhere? I'll eat it dry. I don't need a bowl or a spoon."

"Hey." The thug prodded Finn's shoulder with the gun barrel. "Get over there and sit down."

"Or what?" Finn asked, turning around slowly. "You'll shoot me?"

"I'll make you wish I had."

"Fine. Do what you will. But let me eat first. Hell, you've got to be hungry." The thug made no comment, so Finn pressed on. "No need to fire up the grill or anything. It's just a freakin' box of cereal, man."

The thug glanced over to where Castro still sat in

the booth nearest the door. He hadn't moved since Georgia had left with the hothead. Even in the dark, Finn could make out the boss man's nod.

"Groovy. Thanks." He turned to Tracy. "Cheerios? Wheaties? Froot Loops? I'm not proud."

"Let them have milk."

Finn couldn't have been happier had Castro called out, "Let them eat cake." And considering that any moment the guillotine could fall . . .

"Just no lights in the kitchen." The thug added his two cents. "Including the fridge."

"No problem." Finn held up one hand in a three-fingered oath. "I'll unplug it, plug it back in."

"The bulb's burned out anyway," Tracy offered hesitantly.

"Even better," he said, rubbing his hands together as he salivated over fruit-flavored, sugar-crusted rings of corn or wheat or rice or who even the hell cared? He waited for Tracy to climb down from her stool, then gestured for her to take the lead. "After you, ma'am."

She gave a small laugh. "I'm not a ma'am. I'm only twenty-nine."

He followed her down the short hallway past the rest rooms into the kitchen. It was darker back here, with only a small shaft of light streaming through the half-moon gap where one of the holes in the ceiling cut for the exhaust vents gaped on one side. Tracy, bless her, knew the place like the back of her hand and pointed out the cereal boxes while gathering milk, bowls, and spoons.

Finn imagined for the first time in his life what it felt like to be a kid in a candy store. No little miniature boxes here at Waco Phil's. Uh-uh. These were big, man-sized, hunger-whacking boxes, bushels of whole

grain he could dig into and pretend were baked potatoes and steaks.

He grabbed three, headed back to where Tracy
was juggling a half gallon of milk with the dishes and
utensils. He took the carton, nodded at her and whispered, "Thanks," and followed her back to the counter.

She climbed onto the same stool where she'd been
sitting. He took the one on her left. Fuck the thugs if
they thought he was going to spend the next sixty
hours crammed in that skinny-ass booth. He needed
room to move, a change of scenery, new air to breathe.

He rubbed his hands together. "Lessee. Do I start
with flakes or rings or pellets."

She giggled softly. "I've never seen anyone so ex-
cited over a bowl of cereal."

"And how many starving men have you met in
your time?" He reached for the Raisin Bran, filled his
bowl, frowning as he realized he'd left little room for
milk.

"None, I guess." She poured her own bowl of
Cheerios. "But I think you've got a long way to go before you're truly starving."

"Tell that to my empty tank," he said, pouring
what milk he could before passing it to her, and turning when he sensed movement on his other side.
"Hey, Phil. Belly up to the bar. We're pouring everyone's favorites."

"Shut up over there," called Finn's personal guard
dog. "Or the only thing you'll be pouring is your
concrete boots."

He rolled his eyes at the thug's threat. "That one
needs to lighten up. He's taking his job way too seriously."

Tracy bobbled the milk carton. "How can you joke
about all of this? You act like you're not even scared."

"Good. That means I'm a damn fine actor," he mumbled, digging his spoon into his cereal and filling his mouth so he didn't have to say anything more right then.

"You mean you *are* scared?" she whispered, her face so close to her bowl when she leaned down that he almost didn't hear her.

He nodded. "Yeah. I'm scared. Boss man over there did leave the impression that he wouldn't mind killing me."

"Or killing all of us," Phil reminded him, pouring milk into a third bowl and dumping Corn Flakes on top. "Damn mobster jack-offs."

Finn found himself smiling at the older man's wrath. "You know, Phil, I think that's the first thing I've heard you say all day."

"Phil's not much of a talker," Tracy put in, reaching for a napkin to catch the milk dribbling from her chin.

"Nothing wrong with a thinking man." Finn scooped up another big bite.

Phil snorted. "You might not say that if you could read my mind."

"Oh, I'm pretty sure we're all thinking the same thing about now," Finn assured him.

Phil stabbed his spoon through the pile of flakes in his bowl, stirring them into the milk. "I was remembering a couple buddies I had in 'Nam. Both could teach this bunch a thing or two about manners."

Tracy leaned closer. "When Phil does talk, lots of the time he talks about Vietnam."

"Times like these, the past does spring to mind." Finn's own memories had been popping in his head like the Black Cats he and Georgia used to set off in neighborhood mailboxes as kids. Talk about getting in trouble. His sister had gotten a way early start.

"What have you been thinking about?" Tracy asked.

"My dad. The nanny who raised us when my mom died." He shrugged. He didn't want to think about what he was most thinking about. Georgia putting herself at risk to save him. "My sister."

"Oh, dear. I'm so sorry to bring all that up." She reached over, patted his arm.

"Don't mind Tracy." Phil added more milk to his bowl of mush. "She's our local Mother Teresa, caring for everyone's problems."

Finn sensed Tracy's embarrassment in the way she pulled back her hand and hid it in her lap, in the way she seemed to curl into a tight little shell. "So, Tracy. Who cares for your problems?"

She chopped her spoon up and down, crunching her cereal. "My daddy, when he could. My mom died when I was young, too. Then Freddy did for a while. Now it's just me."

Phil leaned toward Finn. "Her old man took down with the Alzheimer's. And her no-account husband up and left."

"Freddy is not no-account," Tracy shot back before bursting into sobs.

The light-haired thug stepped up to the counter and slid his gun along the surface toward her. Finn reached over, slapped his hand down on the barrel. "Hey, dude. Knock it off with the arsenal. The lady's going through a rough time."

"Yeah, ain't we all," he scoffed, turning to Tracy. "One more peep and you'll be waiting out the rest of the weekend in the cooler."

"We don't have a cooler," she said, staring down at her bowl and causing Finn to smile. "Just a fridge."

"In the toilet then, smart mouth." The thug dropped the gun's grip against the counter with a bang. "Now shut it."

Tracy shrugged and got back to eating. Phil did the same. Finn had to force himself not to yank the shotgun out of the thug's hand and turn the barrel around on the son of a bitch. He wouldn't hesitate to fire. And that was the problem with being a crabby, worried, bored-to-the-bone bastard.

He couldn't put Tracy and Phil in jeopardy because he wanted payback for what this bunch was putting his sister through. And doing something that stupid would only bring Georgia more grief.

So he tucked away his temper and dug into his cereal, deciding he wasn't so much of a kid after all, because this candy store business sucked.

Dazed, Georgia leaned into the curve of Harry's body for the ride back to the hotel. She didn't care whether or not the body contact was appropriate. And really, after that kiss? Was there anything that wouldn't be? Could she have possibly tried any harder to crawl into his skin?

She pushed the thought aside. She didn't have time to think about kissing Harry. They had to regroup. *She* had to regroup. *Could one person regroup?*

The dossier had to be at the general's estate. The ranch had been closed up, all items of value sent to Dallas for the auction . . . unless the dossier had been mislabeled and included in the documents awaiting shipment to the university libraries.

No. It was in the document lockbox listed in the brochure, the one that hadn't reached the gallery prior to the reception. It had to be. She didn't know how the slipup had occurred, but if the dossier *had* made it out of Waco but not to the auction, logic told her that's where it was.

If that wasn't the case, then after the auction she'd have to find out who had purchased the general's desk and where it had been shipped. Because if the file had been misrouted, lost in transit, or, God help her, for some reason destroyed, she didn't want to consider how screwed she was—and how screwed that left Finn.

But the biggest question niggling at her now was

who in the world was Paul Valoren and why had her father never mentioned him to her? Valoren had acted like he and her father were the best and closest of old friends.

She couldn't believe it. Didn't believe it. Refused to believe it. Her father would have mentioned the other man. He wouldn't have kept their relationship secret. He wouldn't have had any need if there was nothing suspect in their relationship, nothing fishy, nothing odd . . . She groaned.

"You okay?" Harry leaned close to ask.

"Right now? I'd have to say no. You can ask me again in the morning."

"Is this about finding the dossier? Or about meeting Valoren?"

She shook her head. She had no answer. She wasn't even sure she could separate the two. The night had been a blur of disappointment and confusion, with an unexpected wrench thrown into the middle of things.

And, horrible, horrible sister that she was, she'd hardly thought of Finn all evening, ugh. She'd been so self-involved, so outwardly focused. Except for the intimate tryst with Harry. And hadn't *that* just been the epitome of narcissism?

Yet here she was leaning into him again, looking for the sort of strength and support she never looked for outside of herself. She wanted to pull away, to prove that her spine was ramrod straight and titanium tough.

But he felt so good, his body curving to take the weight and shape of hers like a pillow, like he didn't mind being molded and punched and used . . .

She groaned, watching the play of light through the cab's windows. "I hit you, didn't I? Earlier."

He shrugged it off. "It was nothing."

"It was frustration. It was wrong."

"If you want to say you're sorry," he began, his voice deep and soothing, "I won't give you a hard time about it."

She didn't say anything. She sighed and settled more comfortably into his side. "Yes. To both of your questions. The dossier and Valoren."

He stiffened slightly. "Oh?"

"My father knew about the dossier," she said, lacing her fingers in her lap. "He knew where Duggin kept it. Ergo, my unsuccessful attempt at theft."

Harry took a minute to react. "You were looking for the lockbox at Duggin's ranch."

"No." What was the harm in telling him bits and pieces of the story? She obviously needed his help. "The dossier was hidden in the desk in the general's study. The bottom file drawer had a false back. My father told me the last time I talked to him, right before he died, that it was there."

"So you didn't know about it before then?"

She shook her head. "I had no clue. And I'm not one hundred percent certain what the documents will reveal. I just know that my father wanted the truth to be made known."

"The truth?"

She hated talking about this to people who knew the TotalSky satellite story, discussing the fact that her father was innocent, had been wrongly accused and convicted.

But she hated even more talking about it to a stranger. She didn't know how he would react, if he would believe her, or accuse her of grasping at straws.

She blurted it out. "My father is Stanley McLain."

"Okay."

"Stanley McLain? The TotalSky scandal?" she added, and came this close to holding her breath while she waited for Harry's response.

"Okay."

"That's all? Okay? No shocked gasp?" TotalSky was as much a part of the cultural lexicon as Watergate.

He chuckled softly. She felt the vibration slide down her spine. "I guessed at the connection when Valoren mentioned his name. I'd heard the rumors of Duggin's involvement, and that there wasn't enough evidence to make a case against him."

"Right. And it's awfully convenient that the dossier went missing at the same time."

"Hmm." He shifted beside her. "That was quite a while ago. You think Duggin has had it all this time?"

"I believe that's what my father was trying to tell me. But he waited too long. He pointed me in the right direction so I'd know where to start, but he wasn't lucid enough to tell me the whole story." She swallowed the lump of emotion swelling up in her throat. "And then he was gone."

"What about Valoren?"

"What about him?"

"He knew both Duggin and your father."

Yeah, this was what was really bugging her. "I don't know. I'm trying to decide if this is all just some big weird coincidence."

"Or if it's a conspiracy," Harry said, inclining his head toward her.

"I can't imagine that it would be. What would anyone have to gain?" she asked, gesturing with one hand, grabbing for her wrap when it slipped.

"The same thing you're after."

She blinked, breathed, frowned. "You mean Valoren might have lied when I asked him about the lockbox?"

"He could have been telling the truth." Harry

paused, gathered his thoughts. "Or he could be the one responsible for making it disappear."

The idea now that Valoren might be involved . . . Were there more "friends" in his past her father had failed to mention? Ugh, what a headache of a nightmare this was turning out to be.

The twists and turns were nauseating. "You know, all this speculation might be a total waste of time."

"How so?"

"If no one else knew about the false back on the desk drawer," she said, rubbing at her temples, "the dossier might still be there."

"Wait a minute." He scooted up to the edge of the seat, turned toward her. "Shouldn't you be trying to get your hands on the desk instead of the lockbox?"

"Before getting arrested, I saw the General's assistant and a member of the cataloging team putting paperwork into the lockbox. It was on top of the desk, and all the desk drawers were open. The box itself didn't mean anything until I saw it mentioned in the brochure."

And wouldn't all of this be so much easier had she not been caught to begin with? Had she been able to walk into the study, crack open the desk drawer, and find the dossier waiting.

Again, she pulled her wrap tight. "Right now, I've got to keep the lockbox from falling into anyone else's hands. I can go back for the desk after the auction."

The cab pulled up to the hotel entrance then. Harry paid the driver and, when the doorman opened the door, climbed out, reached back to assist her.

She let him take care of everything, let him lead the way to the elevator, punch the call button, usher her inside the car when it arrived.

He stood behind her, rubbing his hands up and down her bare arms. "You're an ice cube again."

"I know." And this time her gooseflesh wasn't about nerves. This time she *was* cold.

"If I wasn't so beat, I'd spend an hour in a hot bath." Oh, but his hands felt good, so big and so warm. So comforting. It was impossible not to squirm. She wanted so badly to lean against him. "I'll settle for a bunch of blankets so I don't have to worry about falling asleep and drowning."

"I can help with the warmth thing, you know," he said, pulling his wallet from his pocket and fishing for the room's key card as they walked down the hall.

She sighed, uncertain if she was ready to go where she thought he was suggesting they go. And yes, she told the devil on her shoulder. It was a little late in the game to be saddling up her moral high horse after what had gone on at the gallery. She knew that.

But forgiving herself for a heat of the moment indiscretion made at a time she'd been a bundle of nerves was a lot easier on her conscience than a premeditated slaking of lust—even if she *had* offered to make up to him the one-sided affair.

"I don't know if that's such a good idea," she finally said once they'd reached the room.

He opened the door, gestured for her to enter, waited for the latch to click before he spoke. "I've been thinking about sleeping with you since, well, you know."

"I know."

He reached up, brushed her bangs to the side. "You do make it hard on a man. But all I'm offering right now is heat. Body heat. Of the external variety."

She loved the idea. She didn't trust either of them. Not after, well, he knew, she mused and shivered. "I still don't know if that's such a good idea."

He moved in close behind her, placed his arms

along hers, matching up their elbows, wrists and hands. He was much bigger, of course, and they didn't match up at all. But she'd been so right about his comforting warmth.

"You trust me to help save your brother's life, but you don't trust me to keep my hands to myself?"

She didn't know what she felt for him or about him. If he was someone she wanted to let even deeper into her life was a question still hanging in the air.

What she did know was that she didn't trust herself. Not now. Not with so much going on with her emotions. "You're not keeping them to yourself now, are you?"

He laughed, left her standing there, and stepped around her, loosening his tie, pulling it from his shirt collar, tossing it and his suit coat to the nearest of the two double beds. "Simply making a point."

"Point taken."

"Tell you what," he said, reaching for the top button of his shirt and drawing her attention to the way his fingers worked so deftly, a reminder of how he'd worked her. "You go to bed over there. I'll go to bed over here. If you have trouble sleeping because you're cold, let me know. I'll come over. I'll stay between the sheet and the blanket. No tempting skin-to-skin contact."

She shivered again because, no matter the lies she told herself, that was the very thing she wanted. Harry close, warm, holding her. "That might work. If I stay beneath the sheet and you stay on top."

"And I keep my hands to myself."

"Exactly," she said, wondering if he believed those were her wishes or if he saw through the sham. And then as more and more of his chest came into view, she frowned. "Do you have pajamas?"

"I have jogging shorts. And a T-shirt." Wearing a monumental smile, he let the shirt plackets dangle and reached for his cuffs. "Will that work?"

Why did he have to be so beautiful? Why did she have to suddenly be so weak? "Sure."

"And you?"

She nodded. "I have pajamas."

"Okay then." He peeled off his shirt and sat on the end of the bed to get rid of his shoes and socks. "You take the bathroom first."

She swore the man didn't have a single roll of fat lapping over his belt when he sat. Unfair, unfair, unfair. "Let me get my things."

She crossed the room to where she'd thrown her duffel bag into one of the sitting area's overstuffed chairs. As she kicked off the expensive shoes, she wondered if she'd ever have occasion to wear them again.

Or if she'd *want* to wear them again when they would remind her forever not only of tonight's failed venture, but of this man who was making her want him.

Shoving away the thought, she found her camo tank top and matching shorty bottoms. She wasn't much for makeup and skin products, but she did dig out her face wash and hoped it would do the job on the salon's studio paint job.

Taking down her hair was going to be another hassle, one she wasn't used to messing with. She found her hairbrush, her toothbrush, and then nearly dropped everything when she began to tremble.

What in the world was she doing even thinking about sleep with Finn in so much danger? If anything happened to him because of her stupid obsession, with her need to prove their father's innocence . . .

Dear God, she would never forgive herself. Both

of her parents were gone. Finn was all she had, and she'd selfishly dragged him into the middle of what was beginning to feel like her own private breakdown.

"Georgia?"

She startled, turned, clutching her things to her chest. "Sorry. I was thinking about . . . stuff."

Harry handed her a hanger. "For the dress. It's recommended you don't toss it in a corner or store it in a duffel bag."

She grabbed the hanger and stuck out her tongue as she pushed past him on her way to the bathroom. Once there, she slipped off the dress and hooked the frame of the hotel room hanger on the back of the door.

Naked and mindful of where Harry's hand had been earlier, she pulled on the shorty pj set. What she needed was head-to-toe wool. Her nipples stood out like twin peaks, and her arms were pale, pebbled, the hair ruffled on end.

She turned on the faucet and let the warm water run over her wrists, finally sudsing up a dollop of face wash and scrubbing away the evening's paint. She brushed her teeth, dried her mouth and face, then tackled her hair.

She took too long doing all of it, but there was a part of her that just didn't know how smart it was to spend the night wearing shorty pajamas while in the same room with Harry van Zandt.

She'd let him bring her off in a public place, for crying out loud. And now she thought she was going to be able to lie quietly in a bed separated from his by nothing but a nightstand and a six-foot expanse of plush carpet?

Still, she couldn't stay in the bathroom any longer. He'd be in here any minute checking to see if she'd flushed herself down the tubes. So, wrapped in one of the room's thick terry robes, she cut off the light and prepared to meet her doom.

He was lying beneath the sheet on the bed he'd chosen, the lamp off on his side of the nightstand, his head pillowed on both of his wrists, his eyes closed. She was glad to see he was wearing a T-shirt because, really.

A woman could hardly be held responsible for her actions when faced with a bare chest like his. It was bad enough taking in the sculpted bulge of his triceps beneath his shirt's short sleeves.

On the far side of her bed, she shrugged out of the robe and climbed beneath the thermal blanket, the quilted spread, and the crisp clean sheet. She pulled the triple layer of covers to her chin, thinking she should've checked the room's thermostat when she walked by.

But instead of getting back up to do so, she turned onto her side—her back to Harry—tucked a pillow to her chest, and settled in to go to sleep.

11:40 P.M.

Harry wasn't sure if he'd actually slept or if he'd only dreamed that he had. He did know that he'd climbed into bed while Georgia was in the bathroom and that he'd done his best to fall asleep before she came out.

She was uncomfortable being here with him, and he didn't want to add to her stress. He was working for an out-of-sight, out-of-mind scenario, hoping she wouldn't freak on him and run out in the middle of the night.

She needed her sleep—not for reasons having to do with beauty rest or decompression from the tension of the day, but because he was going to be heading out in an hour or two and he had to have her down for the count.

Before he left to take care of business, however, he would rig a couple of transmitters—in her boots, her duffel bag, her backpack—so he could find her again should she vanish before he got back.

She'd been in bed now for twenty minutes, and she still tossed and turned. He hadn't said a word. He didn't know if she was still cold, simply restless, or as frustrated as he was. Because he was. Frustrated. Very.

And as much as he was focused, concentrating on what he had to do once he put things in play, laying out the logistics of his plan while he stared at the play of light on the ceiling where the moon shone over a gap in the top of the drapes, his body was wired and tight.

So when Georgia flopped over again and sighed, he wasn't surprised. What did surprise him was several moments later to hear her whisper, "Harry?"

He waited, his heart racing, uncertain whether she really wanted him to answer or whether she was doing no more than testing the waters.

Then again, he mused, would she ask if she wasn't interested?

And what exactly was it she was asking? Obviously he would never find out if he just laid here like a lifeless slab of clay . . .

"Harry?" She was louder this time.

And so he said, "I'm here."

"I think I'd like it better if you were over here."

He tossed back his sheet, started to swing his legs over the side of the bed and sit up. But then something made him stop and ask, "Are you still cold?"

"Uh, yes. And no. I'm not sure." Her voice sounded tiny and lost in the dark.

He thought about everything she'd gone through in the last thirty hours. An arrest. A night spent in jail. The siege at the diner. The threat to her brother's life.

Whether or not she was cold didn't matter. She was alone. And that was one thing he could make better. He slid out of his bed and crossed the short space to hers.

Her eyes were wide and white in the pale oval of her face. She scooted over, making room, and he did as he'd promised her he'd do.

He smoothed the top sheet over his side and slid beneath the blankets, wearing his T-shirt and jogging shorts that nearly hit his knees.

He lay on his side facing her, but he didn't move any closer and he didn't touch her at all. The first move, whatever it ended up being, wasn't his to make.

He bunched the pillow beneath his head with one arm and stared at her while she stared straight up, as tense as any slick-sleeve new recruit who'd just been dressed down by his drill sergeant.

When several minutes later she said, "I don't know if this is any better or not," he had to laugh.

"As long as you're warm and you can get some sleep, then it's better."

She shivered, the vibrating tremor reminding him of how nervous she'd been before the preview reception, reminding him of the scent of her skin, the taste of her mouth, the way she'd come in his hand.

He closed his eyes, pushed aside the thoughts, and tried to catch forty winks. He'd learned a long time ago to grab his sleep when and where he could, never knowing when he'd get a chance to grab more.

He relaxed. It was all good. Except the minute he felt himself dozing, drifting, he also felt Georgia move over to his side of the bed.

He stayed where he was; if he'd been underneath the sheet, he wasn't sure he would have managed. And even with the barrier between them and the promise he'd made, he was tempted to wrap her up in his arms.

It was especially hard to stick to his position when she shifted, scooting up so that her head was nearer the headboard than his. That put his face scant inches from the crook of her neck. She smelled so damn good.

"Harry?"

His eyes opened at her whisper. "Georgia?"

"I know we agreed on no skin-to-skin contact, but I'd like it if you held me. You know. With the sheet between? Just your arm around my waist or something?"

Or something?

He groaned. He had no problem draping his arm over her and settling it into that curve, but *something* sounded so much better. Because, sheet or not?

Her waist was halfway between the good stuff upstairs and the good stuff down. And her face was so close that he could smell her toothpaste, a hint of soap and shampoo.

But he wanted more than anything to ease her distress, and so he hooked his arm around her and pulled her close. And he went ahead and kissed the slope of her shoulder above the strap of her tank top, breathing her in and growing hard.

"Better?" he asked once he'd calmed himself enough to speak.

"It is. I'm sorry. I thought I'd be okay by myself." She tried to laugh, but the sound was a tortured sort of bark. "I mean, I *am* okay by myself. All the time. I don't know why today should be any different."

That one was easy. "Maybe because today *was* different. Because yesterday was different. How many nights in your life have you spent behind bars?"

"Just that one, thank goodness. If not for Finn . . . " She begin to shake. Not the tiny quivers of earlier, but full-bodied tremors.

He tightened his hold, soothed her with quiet shushing sounds, with the stroke of his hand up and down her rib cage, with his lips against the side of her neck. "He'll be fine. He's a big boy."

"He's always there for me. Always," she said with a hiccupping sob, one that turned into a desperate cackle. "I've been so obsessed with finding this dossier because it's what my father wanted that I've completely taken advantage of Finn. Not to mention taken him for granted. He never even complains. He just comes when I call."

"Then I doubt he feels taken advantage of. He'd let you know if he did."

She seemed to let that sink in, then asked, "Do you have brothers or sisters?"

"None." He'd been a spoiled rotten only son with the best parents a kid could wish for. "But I work with a group of guys who are the closest thing I've ever had. And I can guarantee not a one of them would hesitate to tell me if I was using and abusing."

"Yeah, but you didn't grow up with them," she said, chuckling softly, her angst melting. "You didn't fight with them over who washed the dishes and who dried, or who got to use the car on Friday nights."

She wasn't shaking now, and her skin beneath the sheet had grown warm. He really needed to move away. He didn't. "And I'll bet you got it most of the time."

"Well, I am the oldest. Besides, Finn always had a lot of friends with cars. Better cars than our father's Buick LeSabre."

Harry thought of his own love affair with wheels. "Gotta side with the brother on that score."

"Heh," she teased, snuggling deeper into the covers. "You said score."

He smiled to himself. She wasn't going to let him live that down, was she? "It's not quite so painful when I'm in your bed."

"I am warmer now, thanks," she said, wiggling closer.

Closer, but not close enough. She could wiggle against him all night and he wouldn't complain. "Not a problem."

"And I'm not so panicked. Or so scared," she admitted moments later with a long breathy sigh, as if she wasn't sure she wanted him to know what she was feeling.

Hmm. This could get deep if he let it. He didn't

know if he wanted to go there, to get that personally involved. In the end, how could he not? Being here for her was the whole point of this torturous exercise.

He might be a spy, but he wasn't a heel. "So, what scares you?"

She plucked at the edge of the sheet she held beneath her chin. "The biggest one? That I won't find what Charlie wants me to find in time to save Finn."

"Don't be scared," he said, knowing she had no reason to put stock in his words, having complete faith that what he told her was the truth. "Come Monday morning, this will be nothing more than a bad dream."

"You're awfully confident for someone pulled into the middle of a nightmare."

He gave a sideways shrug, the best he could do lying down. "I was a few years in the army. I've seen worse."

"Combat?" The one-worded question came wrapped in too many others for him to deal with right now.

He gave her the Cliffs Notes version. "Of a sort."

"Hmm. Covert stuff?" When he remained silent, she added, "I'm only guessing that since you're not talking."

He was not talking because his military days were in the past. He brought forward his skills and his experience to apply to the present as needed. That was it.

The rest of the time he was simply Rabbit. "And here I was thinking you were just another pretty face."

She stuck out her tongue. "I was kinda wondering why you've been so calm while I've been a basket case."

If she thought she was a basket case . . . "I'm always up for a good adventure."

She huffed. "Or a bad one?"

"No such thing."

"Only bad outcomes?"

"I told you. It's not going to happen."

"Promises, promises," she grumbled, turning onto her side and spooning back against him.

"Hey, I've kept them so far, haven't I?" He loved having her this near, loved the feel of wrapping himself around her, loved the way their bodies fit.

Loved the fact that he actually had it in him to do no more than hold her. "No skin-to-skin contact? No between-the-sheets action?"

She chuckled, grabbed his drifting hand. "Just above the sheet kissing and groping?"

"Only because you asked."

"Hmm. Did I?"

"Well, maybe not for the kissing."

"Definitely not for the kissing."

She made him smile. God, but she made him smile. "I gave it up."

"I know," she said softly, pausing, then adding, "You can start again if you want."

That stopped him cold, even while it raised his temperature to a record high. "This isn't about what I want, Georgia. If it were up to me, we'd both be naked by now."

"I know," she repeated, adding a heavy sigh. "That's why this is so hard. I want the same thing. I just don't know if wanting it is right."

"I can't answer that for you." He wasn't having a problem answering it for himself, but then he was the one with a stick shift between his legs.

"I wish you could. I'm having hell trying to answer it for myself."

That settled it. "The only thing I can say for sure is that we both need sleep. And right now? We probably need that more than anything."

Saturday

Life is a wretched gray Saturday, but it has to be lived through.

—Anthony Burgess, English novelist
(1917–1993)

March 15, 1989

Paul Valoren pulled his glasses from his face and tossed them to the center of his desk. They slid to a stop at the edge of the blotter.

He rubbed his eyes, his forehead, the bridge of his nose. He'd thought he would get word via a phone call. He'd never expected to see the news splashed across the *New York Times'* front page.

Leaning forward and reaching for the switch on his lamp, he kicked the garbage can tucked deep in the desk's kneehole. He'd shoved the receptacle out of sight after crumpling the newspaper down inside.

Out of sight. Out of mind.

It wasn't working.

Never had he believed that any of his friends would see prison. He wasn't sure he would have agreed to the terms of the deal if he had. He had been assured— they had *all* been assured—that the negligible chance for failure made the risk one worth taking.

He'd been in charge of the financial arrangements, the budget, the backing, the international transfer of funds. That made it easy for him to see the monetary scope, the broad personal appeal, the opportunity for amazing wealth they held in their hands.

He wasn't even sure he remembered who was the first to suggest the alterations to the satellite specs. It had been made in jest. It had been taken to heart. It had been implemented with the resolve to never look back.

Now the decision would ruin one of their lives forever. It could quite possibly ruin them all.

As had the others, he had profited. He had bought and sold stocks, bonds, real estate, and other assets, making his investments based not on speculation, but viable, confirmable data. Data illegally obtained.

He enjoyed the life he now led. He could afford to travel for pleasure as well as for work, and he did. He indulged in small luxuries, exquisite food, cultural stimulation.

He didn't want to lose what had become a life of comfort, a life where he was held in high regard, where his opinion was sought out, where his name was whispered in awe.

Neither did he wish to risk his position at the university, or the rapport he'd built with his students.

His involvement in the TotalSky project had been immaculate in detail. Not one recorded cent had been wrongfully allocated. His name, in fact, had been the first to be cleared. But he had turned his head during crucial negotiations . . .

He knew there was a true accounting of the events that one day would have to be destroyed. One kept to be used not so much as ammunition, but as insurance. He trusted his alliance partners, was consumed with guilt that one had to pay, knew of no way around that inevitable end.

He thought of the newspaper beneath his desk, thought of the lives affected by the guilty verdict and sentence. Thought of his own most of all. His pleasures, his way of life, his promising career.

And then he picked up his pen to sign the papers that would change the world as he knew it.

Harry made the return drive to the Waco area in record time. Stashing Morganna wasn't hard, but he sure as hell didn't like doing it—even if she wasn't his car.

The Buick belonged to the Smithson Group. That didn't make driving her over the cattle guard, through the gate he'd jimmied open, and into the pasture he'd chosen any less of a crime against Detroit and automakers everywhere.

He'd put up the top before leaving Dallas, and now flung a dark tarp over the body. He had a couple of hours, closer to three, before dawn. From the road, the car would be near to invisible until then. He just had to watch his time.

Hunkered behind her and wearing dark fatigue pants, he shucked out of his T-shirt and tugged on the black ski cap, long-sleeved pullover, gloves, and boots he'd brought with him, finishing off the camouflage with grease paint.

He glanced at his watch, pushed one of the four buttons on the side of the face. This one activated the wireless receiver inside his earpiece.

He hit the switch on the side of the headset to trigger the mike, spoke the code word to signal the SG-5 ops center, and waited for a response.

Tripp came on the line seconds later. "You're good to go. No movement on the perimeter. When you're close, I'll walk you through the motion sensors."

"Roger," Harry said, adding a silent thumbs-up. Tripp's satellite surveillance of Harry's movements wouldn't pick up such a small detail, but Harry felt better for the connection, and for knowing his partner had his back.

Contact made, he headed across the pasture toward the ranch house at a crouching run. He didn't have a lot of time, but he did need to get this done. No lead left unfollowed, no stone left unturned.

Good news was that so far he'd had no transmission from Dallas. That meant Georgia was still asleep, or at least still in the room. Not only had he slipped the transmitters into her boots and bags, he'd set a trip wire alarm on the base of the door. He'd know if she opened it and walked out.

He'd left her a note in the bathroom, told her he'd be back by breakfast time, and asked her to order him up a double stack of pancakes and enough bacon to feed a platoon.

He smiled as he pictured her reading his backhanded scrawl, rolling her eyes as if following orders was the last thing she planned to do.

The sharp green smell of the new growth he crushed beneath his feet burst around him as he ran. Adrenaline fueled his sprint. His heart pumped. His thighs burned.

Getting from the car to the house and back was the easy—if physically grueling—part. All he had to do was keep his head down and his feet moving.

Getting inside and upstairs was going to be the mental challenge—one he would feel a whole lot better about tackling if he'd slept more than six out of the last forty-eight hours.

He'd learned over the years to survive on quick snatches of sleep, sure. He still felt a whole lot better about his work when he got more and knew he was in top form.

That was what he wanted to do when he got back to the room. Dig into the pancakes, bacon, butter, and syrup, then go lights-out. For about twelve hours. Of course he'd have to tie Georgia to the headboard to make sure she didn't hit the highway while he caught up on his sleep.

Thinking of having her in handcuffs or silk scarves was not exactly a productive train to travel. Because then he started thinking about having her. And he was already running against the clock. He didn't have time to stop and kick his own ass for not taking her when they'd been together in bed.

Thing was, he wanted to make love to her and with her because they couldn't keep their hands to themselves—not because she was scared or cold or alone.

But making love would mean getting involved; he was an old-fashioned kind of guy when it came to intimacy. And he had no business taking personal side trips when he had a mission swallowing all the space on his plate.

He reached the fence line separating the nearest pasture from the house, and turned his full attention to the moment, triggering the switch on his headset to make contact with Tripp. "Rabbit at the gate."

"I've got you on the scope," Tripp told him. "The alarm's wired in to the north. Two posts up. Three meters."

Harry hunkered close to the ground, found the post, and went to work disabling the alarm without setting off the built-in warning indicators. That done, he held his breath and hopped the fence, waiting for Tripp's all-clear.

"No movement. Stay low until you hit the patio. I'll take you through the sensors."

These external hurdles down, all he had left to deal with were the guards stationed inside.

Intel had put two on each floor until recently. Due to the increased interest in Duggin's property since his death, the service had doubled the security staff.

With Tripp picking up the infrared images, Harry wasn't worried about his own detection. He was, however, beginning to worry about the time.

It took Tripp twelve minutes to guide him from the yard across the patio. The next ten took him to the glass doors where he bypassed the second alarm and slipped into the first floor's great room. Once there, he dropped to a squat behind a hulking billiard table.

He checked his watch again, timing the quadruple intersection of the first-floor patrols, then heading for the main staircase and creeping up.

At the top of the stairs, he took a left, listening to Tripp lay out the guard's positions. The General's study was at the end of the hallway straight ahead.

Harry drifted forward, an unseen shadow, the room's dark interior swallowing him whole. He found the desk, dropped behind it, pulled a penlight from his pocket, and located the drawer Georgia had described.

Finding the dossier here and now would be about the best thing they could hope for. He could turn over the file to Simon Baptiste as soon as the SG-5 operative arrived, and have the analysis run without Georgia ever learning of the Smithson Group's interest.

The only thing left to do at that point would be to rescue the bunch held hostage in the diner—a plan still in the early stages of development. Charlie Castro was going to be a very unhappy man.

Unfortunately, Harry realized, his own happily-ever-after was going to have to wait.

The false back to the drawer came away easily. But there was nothing behind it. He slid the pieces back in place and clicked off his light, rubbing the base of his neck as he hung his head, disappointed but already moving on.

And now he was really looking forward to—and needing—the sleep he was going to get when he got back to the room, because he might just have to do this again tonight.

Only this time he'd be doing it at Duggin's Dallas estate.

Head back, eyes closed, Charlie sat in his seat and listened. The waitress was curled into a far booth asleep. She'd spent most of the night sniveling. The cook had collapsed across his table at the diner's other end.

Georgia's brother had been sitting all night at the counter building log houses out of stir sticks. It had been quiet. Charlie liked that.

After Georgia and van Zandt left yesterday, Charlie's men moved the vehicles off the lot. McLain's truck to the Waco airport. The cook's to Baylor University. The waitress's to a shopping center parking lot. Lost in the crowd.

Charlie's Mercedes now sat in a wrecking yard down the road. It was closed for the weekend. The car would be safe there until Monday.

The phone line had been disconnected at the building. Not cut. There was nothing pointing to anything afoul. He would be safe here until Monday.

As long as Georgia returned on time with the TotalSky dossier, he would be safe long after that.

The man paying him for the retrieval would be the safest of all, his participation in the TotalSky scandal wiped from the pages of history. Unless Charlie made him squirm.

Charlie had been thinking about that for most of the night. His client had made it clear that Charlie was to stop at nothing, that he was to succeed.

The latter wasn't an ultimatum. Charlie never failed. But he had never gone as far as he'd been instructed to this time. He had never seen the need.

If a first attempt was unsuccessful, he made a second. If necessary, he made a third. As many as he needed. Doing so was a part of the game.

This client's urgency had him curious. Too curious. Too interested. He knew never to let a job be more than a job. This one was different.

A chance to observe the human condition.

To witness the frustrated fear in those from whom he took.

To see the inevitable boredom in those to whom he gave.

He had yet to be hired by anyone content with what he delivered. He thought this might be the time. He'd spent the night weighing options. Considering courses of action.

There was nothing he could do until Georgia and van Zandt's return. That was when he would decide whether to deliver the dossier without incident.

Or to look into its true value. Pit interested parties against one another for the sake of the show.

At the sound of a loud rumble outside, he opened his eyes, squinted between the slats of the blinds. A tractor-trailer rig shuddered its way to the soft shoulder on the far side of the road.

Charlie frowned. There would be a wrecker. There would be police. He sat up straighter. His men noticed the activity. He motioned them to keep the hostages down.

The truck driver jumped from the cab. Climbed up and released the hood. Pulled it forward. Dug around. Returned twice for tools. The minutes ticked by.

When the waitress stirred in her seat, he motioned

for one of his men to have her put on coffee. He slid from the booth, checked his weapon, took up position behind the counter near McLain to wait.

Thirty minutes later came a knock on the door. It rattled and echoed like a gunshot. Charlie moved to the last booth, knelt on the seat, leaned against the wall, peered through the window.

The truck driver. He wore dusty boots and dirty jeans, a plaid shirt untucked, sleeves torn out. Muscles bulged in his shoulders. Matched those of his biceps in bulk.

His hair was long and black, worn in a thick tail bound at his nape. The straw of his cowboy hat was crushed. His sunglasses held Charlie's attention.

He knew those sunglasses. They did not fit a big rig trucker dressed like a woodshed hick. The man drove a lot. The glasses would be an investment. That didn't ease the itch at the base of Charlie's throat.

The driver knocked again, leaned one hand against the side of the diner, waited, finally slapped the metal in frustration when he received no response.

Charlie watched him walk back to the rig, scuffing up clouds of dust on the way, and tried to figure what the man could want.

If not a cell phone, he should have a radio. Unless the electrical system was the source of the rig's breakdown. He could have wanted water, use of the rest room. Neither fit a man who made his living on the road.

He watched the driver set out safety triangles behind the truck. The man was going to be here a while. He punctuated that by parking himself on the step to the cab.

Charlie moved back to the counter, poured a cup of coffee. He ignored the waitress as she skittered out of the way.

"Didn't count on that, did you?" McLain took the coffee the woman returned to pour and hand him. "Puts a definite kink in keeping a low profile when you've got an audience at your front door."

"I'm sure you're more worried about that than I am." He wasn't going to be drawn into this conversation. "Discovery would be more painful for you than for me."

"Not really worried, no." McLain lifted his mug, held it with both hands, blew over the surface. "I'm getting more of a kick out of seeing you squirm."

He never squirmed. He never had cause. "Someone will stop soon enough to assist. The audience won't be around long. There is nothing here to see."

"If you say so," the other man said with a shrug, setting his mug in the center of his stir stick log house. The narrow red straws scattered across the counter. He leaned forward, blew them further away.

Charlie ignored McLain and his big bad wolf demonstration. But he could not ignore the sudden tic at the corner of his eye. He was not worried. He had no reason to be.

And he reminded himself of that as he returned to where he'd been sitting, paying no attention to the laughter coming from the man huffing and puffing and drinking coffee at the counter.

When Georgia pushed open the bathroom door, Harry had just zipped his text messaging unit into place in his shaving kit, having checked in with Tripp and learned that Simon Baptiste was in position at Waco Phil's.

"Well, thank God I'm not naked" was the only thing Harry could think of to say. The truth was that he was pretty damn close, considering all the goods were swinging free beneath his towel.

"Where the hell have you been?" she asked, probably unaware her demand didn't have a lot of impact, coming as it had from a woman wearing camo short shorts. Her legs were everywhere Harry looked.

"So, you didn't see my note?" He nodded toward the paper propped between two water glasses on the counter, directing his gaze there instead of from her shorts to her top, which didn't cover much more.

She'd been asleep when he'd returned. He'd walked into the room, glanced from the entryway around the corner toward the bed before heading to the bathroom.

Once there, he'd shucked off his clothes and hopped into the shower to get rid of any face paint he'd missed when he'd wiped down before driving back.

"No. I didn't see any damn note." She barged into the steamy room, snatched it up and scanned it. "Pancakes?"

"Yeah. I'm starved. You want to call room service?" he asked, scrubbing a hand towel over his face and head.

She slapped the paper down on the countertop. "I woke up at four and you weren't in bed. I figured you were in here so I went back to sleep. I woke up at six-thirty and realized the bathroom door was open and the light was off."

"That's when you sent out the search parties?" he asked, wondering if it had occurred to her that they were both nearly naked. It had certainly occurred to him.

"I was tired." She crossed her arms. "I went back to sleep."

"But you promised yourself you'd be mad at me when you got up."

She tightened her arms, pushing up her breasts even further. "Yes. I mean, no."

"I think you mean yes." He looked away, finished closing up his kit.

"Where were you?" She jabbed a finger at the note. "'I'll be back for breakfast.' What does that mean?"

"It means I'm hungry."

She said nothing, just stared, jaw tight, shoulders back, before spinning to leave the room.

He reached out and snagged her by the wrist. "Georgia."

"What?" she snarled, but she didn't pull away.

He didn't get her reaction. She couldn't really think he would abandon her—even though she'd given him permission more than one time. "Stick with me here for a minute. Think about the last eighteen hours. Have I given you any reason not to trust me?"

She didn't answer. But she did shake her head. And she turned her hand in his.

He laced their fingers, pulled her out of the doorway and into the room. "Then what's wrong?"

"I just didn't know where you were." She dropped her gaze to the floor. "And trust or not, I didn't know if you were coming back."

He wanted to know what was going on. And then he remembered last night. What they'd done. The change in the dynamic of what they shared.

He really was dense at times. "I won't leave you again without telling you. I promise."

She seemed to settle. "Are you going to tell me where you were?"

Did she need to know? Would it hurt or hinder the mission in any way? That had to be his first concern, his first consideration. "I went to Waco."

She gasped. "To check on Finn?"

That much he couldn't explain. That one of his partners was in place to do just that. That Finn was going to be fine. "No. I went to Duggin's ranch."

"What?" Her eyes grew wide. "Are you insane?"

He shrugged, released her hand, and tightened the knot of his towel. "I wanted to check the desk, see if the dossier was still there. Save us a lot of mileage on a possible wild-goose chase."

"And?" Her voice shook. "Was it there?"

He shook his head. "Sorry. No. It must be in the lockbox."

She turned and backed up to lean against the counter, her pulse popping in her throat, her adrenaline still high. "Unless Duggin destroyed it."

Harry's heart blipped. "Would he have done that?"

"I don't know why."

He could think of a couple of reasons. "To keep it from hitting the media that the dossier had been in his possession all this time. To keep from having to deal with the fallout if it ended up that he was involved, and it was discovered all these years later."

"He knew. Oh my god." She blew out a heavy breath. "He knew what I was going to do."

"What? Georgia? Talk to me," he said, stopping himself from asking what it was she was going to do.

She talked, but not about what he wanted to know. "The dossier has been missing for over twenty years, right? The general's assistant would know what it was. So would the cataloging team. If they had come across it while going through his things, the discovery would've hit the news."

He followed her line of reasoning, but . . . "Meaning they didn't find it."

"No. Meaning he destroyed it. If it wasn't in the desk, that's the only thing that makes sense."

He didn't agree. He couldn't agree. "Or they didn't find it. Sometimes a cigar *is* just a cigar."

She thought for a minute. "He could've moved it, I guess. Hidden it. Buried it inside a file going to one of the universities."

"Or inside a file going to the auction." Knock out the obvious explanation first. "We're going ahead with the original plan."

"We have one?" she asked with a snort.

"Tomorrow night." He raised a brow. "The auction. The lockbox. Or have you already forgotten?"

"No. I remember that part," she said with a wave of her hand. "Between now and then, though. Is there anything else we can be doing?"

"Pancakes first. Then sleep. For me."

"And what am I supposed to do while you're sleeping?"

"Well, you could buy another dress. One for tomorrow night."

She rolled her eyes, pushed away from the counter, moved into the doorway. "That will take all of thirty minutes. How long of a nap are you planning?"

Longer than that. "Once you're done with that, boot up my laptop. You can do some research."

"On what?"

He put all he had into his grin. "Everything you ever needed to know to be a member of an auction house cataloging team."

Who in the world was Harry van Zandt? That was the only thing Georgia wanted to know.

The fact that he had gone to Waco. The fact that he wanted her to research an auction house cataloging team. Where was he coming up with this stuff? It was like she was playing a part in a spy novel.

Yes, okay, he'd been Army and possibly covert at that. But Finn had a similar background. He'd gone into private investigation after his discharge. Yet she'd never known him to be so . . . She couldn't even think of a workable word.

Reckless came to mind but implied a lack of caution she hadn't seen in either Finn or Harry. Granted, his middle-of-the-night exploits were proactive and definitely welcome; she would never have thought to return to the ranch.

They just weren't anything she was able to reconcile to his involvement here. He'd been pulled in off the street against his will, making it hard to figure out why he was acting as if he'd been enlisted from the beginning, as if this—as if she—were the reason he was here.

At least he had saved her from having to do something about the desk. Upon news of Duggin's death, that had been her first thought. Getting to the study. Getting to the drawer. Getting to the dossier.

Getting her hands on the file before the desk was sold or put into storage. Breaking into the general's house as she'd done had been an admitted act of desperation—one undertaken because she'd been, uh, desperate.

Why Harry had put himself at risk to do the same she couldn't fathom. It was almost as if his interest was personal, as if there was another agenda here of which only he was aware—a thought that brought her back to square one.

Who in the world was Harry van Zandt?

And who in the world was she, doing everything he said?

Well, she wasn't doing everything. She hadn't shopped for a dress. She hadn't booted up his laptop. She'd never ordered the room service pancakes while he'd laid down like a sheikh and waited to have them delivered.

What she had done was charge an hour's worth of Internet time in the hotel's business center to his room.

That way he couldn't revisit her keystrokes—she wouldn't put it past him to have such a program installed—or check into her cookies or browser history to see where she'd been surfing on the World Wide Web.

Her first Google search term, in fact, had been Harry van Zandt. She'd found an interview with a man of that name who'd served during World War II, but nothing on the man she'd curled up against before falling asleep last night. The man even now sprawled out upstairs in the very same bed.

She'd ended up spending most of her allotted time reading about the TotalSky scandal. Having lived with the aftermath of the project for more than half of her life, she thought she knew all there was to know, and was surprised at the obscure details she'd uncovered.

Like the passing speculation that the People's Republic of China had a finger or two in the pie. The parts that had failed on the satellites had been Taiwanese, not Chinese, leaving Georgia scrambling to make the connection.

Then there was the fact that she found no mention of Paul Valoren beyond his years of association with Stanford. And that left her to wonder if her suspicions about him were a big waste of time.

For the last half hour, however, she'd been trying to make sense of the previous twenty-four by pounding out her frustrations on a treadmill in the hotel gym. All she'd managed to do was exhaust herself, so she shut off the machine and headed to the locker room.

While showering, she decided she might as well buy a dress for the auction before returning to the room. She hoped she would have no need to wear it. Harry asking her to research the cataloging team was a pretty clear indicator that he had something other than a steak knife up his sleeve.

Another of his covert, middle-of-the-night sneak attacks, no doubt. Except this time he had let her in on the initial planning stage. Meaning it would probably go down during daylight, whatever it was. She didn't think cataloging was an after-hours sort of operation.

And listen to her. Talking about operations and initial stages and plans going down. That might be the life Harry enjoyed leading, his idea of a thrilling vacation. It was not hers. She wanted . . .

She wasn't even sure anymore. She'd been on her own for so long, content, no worries, no stress, no responsibilities beyond taking care of herself. And then her father had dropped this bomb into her lap from his deathbed. And nothing else had existed since.

It wasn't a healthy way to live.

She knew that even without Finn reminding her constantly. Her brother was more pragmatic when it came to their father's case, telling her that neither of them could have forced him to fight the conviction. That what she needed to do—what they both needed to do—was respect his decision to accept his fate, whatever his reasons for doing so.

Part of her understood the logic of Finn's stance. But it wasn't her stance. And it wasn't her logic. If it was, then she probably wouldn't have found herself breaking and entering, and now keeping company with a man of a like mind.

She soaped up the rag and scrubbed the sweat from her body, letting the stinging spray pummel her skin as she rinsed. It wasn't that she particularly enjoyed the pain, but it did remind her that she was an entire body of limbs and muscles, that she was more than the parts that had been working overtime since Harry walked into her life.

It was wrong—she knew it, she felt it—that she was thinking about him in the way that she was. About his body, and the way he had touched her, and how being with him made her heart race and being away caused her to miss him.

How could she miss someone she didn't even know? How could she feel as if she'd known him forever? How could she be thinking about wanting to know him better after this? Blame it on the circumstances, that was all she could do.

He had ridden in like a knight in shining armor even though she would never describe herself as a damsel in distress. She was more like . . . a knight of a different color. One capable of rescuing herself, but not too proud to turn down the help—or to admit to the need.

Funny, but she'd never thought before that her quest would be easier with the burden shared. It always seemed like her responsibility. The only person who even knew to help was Finn, and he did enough by taking care of her.

But now here came Harry when she couldn't have been more ill-prepared. No, this adventure had not been his choice. Yet here he was, going above and beyond the call, taking chances, plotting, scheming, following through.

What was a girl to do when faced with a Prince Charming hero packaged like a marble statue, who kissed like he'd been saving up for her all of his life? Long term, she couldn't even begin to say. For now, she would simply do what he'd asked and see about buying a dress.

Having finished with her shower, she toweled off, pulled on her clothes, and blew her hair most of the way dry. She dropped the towels she'd used into one bin, the complimentary gym shorts and T-shirt in another, and made her way to the boutique.

It was almost noon, so she wasn't sure if the personal shopper who'd assisted her last evening would be working today. She hoped so; she hated shopping, and the woman had been incredibly helpful.

She also had a better eye for what worked with Georgia's height, shape, and coloring than she could ever have figured out on her own.

"Good morning. May I help you?"

Georgia returned the salesclerk's smile as the slender young woman met her just inside the door. "Hi. I was here yesterday—"

"Ms. McLain." A second female voice cut off the clerk's and caused Georgia to turn. "How wonderful to see you back so soon."

Kim. That was her name. Georgia shook the personal shopper's hand. "I'm fine, thanks. Not quite as spiffy-looking as last night." She glanced down at her jeans and T-shirt, which showed the wrinkles of being packed away. "I just finished working out."

Why she'd been struck with the urge to explain away her appearance, she had no clue. She'd never given a second thought to the way other women saw her, and hated feeling as if she'd just entered a twilight zone of female competition, as if needing to prove herself worthy of Harry's interest.

But Kim was nothing but pleasant and professional, setting Georgia at ease. "How did the Indirie work out for you?"

The Indirie? Oh, the dress. "It was perfect, thanks so much. Now I need another one. This one for tomorrow."

"What sort of occasion?" Kim asked, a studied look on her face as she began scanning the shop's wall displays and circular racks. "Will one of the others you tried on work, or should we start from scratch?"

Georgia sighed. She really, truly knew nothing about dressing up. And blue jeans were all she knew about dressing down. "Well, it's not a party. It's . . . a business situation, but nothing big and corporate. I don't need a power suit or anything."

At that, Kim's brow arched. "I have something that should work perfectly. Why don't you find a dressing room, and I'll bring you a few things? Though, this one I'm thinking about may be all you need."

And that was exactly why Georgia was placing the fate of her wardrobe in this woman's hands. She returned to the same dressing cubicle she'd used last night and stripped down to her panties and bra.

Kim breezed through the saloon-style doors and down the short hallway three minutes later. She hung two or three outfits on the display hooks outside of the dressing room gate before handing Georgia a suit that had her eyes widening.

"Oh, wow." She held the hanger, afraid to touch the fabric. It was a sort of jade green, but textured to look as if it reflected a rainbow of colors—colors that reminded her of carnival glass. "This is gorgeous."

Kim stood with her arms crossed, admiring her choice. "It's a nice retro look. The fabric is going to do great things with your skin."

Georgia laughed. "If I don't destroy it first."

"It's indestructible. Trust me." She stood in the hallway while Georgia dressed. "The skirt is longer than the one on the Indirie, but most of the attention will be drawn by the top. And you definitely have the body to show it off."

Georgia wasn't sure about the latter, but she could definitely see why the jacket would turn heads. It hit just beneath her waist, the front closing with four matching, fabric-covered buttons. She checked her reflection, loving the way the skirt fit. Loving even more the fit of the top.

The collar was wide, a portrait collar, Kim told her. The top points spread to her shoulders, while the lower section of the lapel dipped into her cleavage. Way down into her cleavage. And as broad as the collar was, it left the largest portion of her chest bare.

She liked it. A lot. Until last night, she hadn't worn a dress in forever. And the little black thing certainly reminded her of that, the way it clung to her curves.

But this suit was different. It was elegant and classy and the sexiest thing she'd ever seen. The color, the cut, the cloth. The way it showed off the body she usually forgot about, the body Harry seemed to appreciate.

She couldn't wait for him to see her wearing it, and gulped at the thought even more than she did at the price. "What about shoes? Can I wear the black ones with this?"

Kim held up a finger. "Wait right there."

Georgia was having too much fun looking at herself to even think about moving. And yes, she admitted, half the fun was having someone to dress for—even if it was only for the auction and only one night. She didn't care. She wanted this. And even more than wanting, she needed the buzz.

The shoes Kim brought back were a strappy slingback style colored a caramel gold. They couldn't have been a more perfect complement to the carnival glass effect, and the polish on her toes looked great.

"You can charge this to the room, too?" she asked, reveling in the girly girl feeling for just a moment more.

"Of course," Kim replied. "You look amazing. Your husband will definitely approve."

"Oh, Harry's not"—she stopped herself from saying 'my husband' and scrambled—"hard to please as a rule. But I think you're right. This should catch his eye."

She thought about that on the way back to the room, her arms full, her heart buzzing with excitement. About catching Harry's eye. She wondered if he was married, divorced, engaged, or involved. Silly her, making out with a man whose current romantic situation had never crossed her mind.

Again with the circumstances. She would never have pulled a first date into a dark closet were it not the fate of everything she'd worked for hanging in the balance.

That explained last night, but she wasn't doing so well explaining away this morning when she'd barged into the bathroom and nearly tripped over her tongue. He'd been wearing nothing—*nothing*—but a towel.

And even then it looked as if he hadn't fastened it well, that one wrong step and he'd lose it. Not only that, he'd been wet. And clean. She'd wanted to sniff him all over and lick him all up.

Neither did it explain her imagination running wild last night while they'd been in bed. She'd agreed to his no-contact rule because she'd wanted him near. But if he'd pressed, she would have given in. It had been a long time since she'd wanted a man the way she wanted Harry van Zandt.

And she didn't quite know what to do about that.

"Hi, honey. I'm home."

At Georgia's greeting, Harry looked up from shoveling a last monstrous bite of syrup-and-butter-soaked pancakes into his mouth.

He was sitting on the far bed propped against the headboard, the room service tray in his lap. The tracking receiver picking up the signal from the transmitter in Georgia's boots sat wedged between his thighs beneath it.

She'd been on the hotel's first floor for so long in what he calculated to be the business center, the gym, and the boutique, that when his food had arrived, he hadn't checked to see if she was on the move. He'd simply dug in.

Bad spy. Bad.

She slid open the closet door, hung up the bag from the boutique, and tossed a second containing a shoebox on the floor. Then she bounced into the room, stopping, her smile sliding away when she saw his plate empty of food.

She twisted her mouth to one side. "I never ordered your room service."

"So I woke up to notice," he said, watching her deflate and wondering why she did. If his comment had kicked the wind from her sails, or if her own forgetfulness was the cause. He couldn't say he didn't find the latter interesting . . .

"Sorry. I did go shopping, though." She rocked

back on her heels, tucked her fingers in her back pockets. "I got a suit for the auction. And shoes."

He nodded toward the laptop case he'd opened after waking. "Yeah, but you didn't boot me up."

This time she crossed her arms over her chest and glared down. "You have two hands. And judging by that plate, they both work just fine."

Grinning, he tossed his fork to the tray, grabbed up the napkin, and wiped his mouth. "So, are you going to show me what you bought?"

"You mean what *you* bought?" She shook her head. "You can see it tomorrow. I don't want you thinking this is any more than a loan."

He wondered what she would think if she knew it all went on an expense report in the end. "It's not about ownership either. I just like seeing you in a dress."

"Then you can see me in one tomorrow."

"And after that?"

She frowned, perched on the end of the other bed. "What do you mean?"

"Best I can tell, you live out of a duffel."

"And?"

"Hangers, remember?" he teased to distract her. "Where are you going to keep the new clothes?"

"Oh. That." She pushed up from where she'd been sitting, crossed to where he'd left his laptop case in one of the side chairs, and set it on the table between.

Harry scrambled to shove the tracking device into his pocket, using the tray as a shield as he got off the bed. He carried the dishes out to the hallway, walking back in time to see Georgia bend over and plug in the laptop and high access cable, her heart-shaped bottom playing wicked games with his body and mind.

He wanted to kick his own ass. He should not be

having this much trouble keeping his head on what he was here to do—and off the woman he wanted. He watched as she straightened and turned on the machine. The light from the screen flickered in her eyes.

He clamped his jaw tight. She was the means to an end, nothing more. The way she looked in the clothes paid for by the Smithson Group didn't matter. Where she stored them was no worry of his. His only concern right now was prepping for this evening.

Instead, he was standing and staring like a fool unable to put one foot in front of the other, enjoying her shopping excitement. Even enjoying her ire at having him point out that she'd bailed on booting him up. "Guess that means I'm not going to like the answer."

"Actually, I don't have an answer. Or my answer is that I don't know. Finn was just reminding me yesterday that I need to get my things out of his guest room."

"Why's that?"

She pulled the laptop around to face the wall rather than the window and sat in the closest chair. "He's moving in a month or so."

"What does he do?" he asked, even though he knew.

"He's a P.I., but he says he's burned out and is giving up his business in Houston. I honestly think he's planning to do nothing but be a beach bum for awhile."

"You live with him?" Again he asked knowing that she didn't live anywhere at all. He wanted to hear her talk about herself, to see what he might learn about who she was from her self-perception.

She shook her head, but didn't look up from the computer screen. "I keep a few things there and stay when I'm not on the road."

He leaned against the wall behind her. "Where do you stay when you are on the road?"

"Motels, campgrounds." She looked over her shoulder, frowned at his hovering. "I've been known to sleep in the back of a rental."

"You don't have a car?"

"I did until a few years ago." She turned back around, launched a browser window. "I had a rental while my insurance company fought with the one covering the guy who had hit me. It took weeks, and I got spoiled having everything but the fuel handled for me."

"Uh-huh."

She waved him off. "It's not practical, I know, but it works for me. It's not like I have a bunch of other expenses or responsibilities."

"Seems a strange way to live."

She snorted, pulled up Google. "And throwing all this hair and makeup and clothes and shoes money at a cause you know nothing about isn't?"

"Then tell me about it. Your cause." He knew a lot of the details. It was the emotional component hanging him up. This truth she was so desperate to reveal. What was it, what would she personally gain? Was there any of it he could use?

"I thought you wanted this cataloging team research done," she said, putting him off as he'd expected her to.

He returned to the bed, plopped down on the end, leaned back on his elbows. "Actually, I did it myself while waiting for breakfast."

"You mean lunch."

"Yours is over there, by the way." He jerked his chin toward the covered plate on the top of the dresser. "Just a club sandwich. I wasn't sure when you'd be back."

She glanced at the tray, smiled briefly, but ignored the food. "If you planned to do the research yourself, why ask me to?"

He shrugged. "So we could compare notes. Right now, I want to hear about your cause."

"Right now, we should compare notes. It's getting late."

"We've got time."

She sat back, her brows drawn as she looked over, her glare not so much about anger as curiosity—an observation she proved right when she asked, "Who the hell are you?"

He chuckled under his breath. It was a natural reaction to her frustrated demand, but one that was also part of his cover as a guy eating lunch in a diner who'd been hijacked into criminal service.

He thought that, then he realized that he really hadn't considered his two identities as separate for quite awhile. He was Harry and he was Rabbit, helping Georgia and working for the Smithson Group at the same time.

And so he said, "No one in particular. I just figured that since I'm up to my earlobes here, it would be nice to know what I'm doing this for."

She sobered, spoke softly. "You don't have to be doing this at all. I told you yesterday just to drop me off when we hit Dallas."

"You knew I couldn't do that."

"Sure you could," she insisted. "You don't know me or Finn. Even Charlie gave you the out. You don't have a real stake in any of this."

"I do have a stake. I have you." And even as he said it, he knew it to be true.

He didn't know why, he didn't know when, but in the last twenty-four hours she'd become someone he cared about more than was wise. Her gustiness, her fearlessness, her loyalty—each added another layer to a complexity he was certain would take decades to mine.

And the fact that he wouldn't be around that long and would never have the chance to know her well didn't stop him from wondering what it would be like if he did, if things were different.

"Harry, listen." She turned in her chair to face him. "I'm beyond appreciative of everything you've done, but I really ought to finish this up on my own. It's not fair to involve you further."

"Because I said I had a stake in the outcome?"

She fidgeted. "It's more about saying you have me. You don't want me. Trust me on that."

He wanted to ask so many things and none of them had anything to do with his mission or her quest. He settled on saying, "We'll have to agree to disagree on that."

She rolled her eyes, asked, "About tonight? The cataloging team research? Are you going to tell me what you've got up that magical sleeve of yours?"

He grinned. "Besides a steak knife?"

"Yeah. What were you going to do with that anyway?"

"Carve off a chunk of shoulder or loin if I got the chance."

"Eww," she said, and shuddered. "Yuck."

"Hey, if it would have gotten everyone out of there right then and kept us from having to go through all of this, I would've been the first to fire up the grill."

"You're gross." She paused. "Though I must be just as sick."

He pushed back up into a sitting position. "Why so?"

"I was just thinking if that had happened, I would have had to stay there and deal with the cops and the media." She picked at a scar on the desktop. "I might not have been able to get away in time for the auction."

The push and pull of her priorities flashed in her eyes. He watched with interest, uncertain if either finally won. "Would that have been such a bad thing?"

"What do you mean?"

"Well, obviously being here now is important because of your brother and the others," he said, ramping up to press harder for more of the emotional details. "But if Finn were safe and sound, how important would it be that you got your hands on the lockbox?"

She averted her gaze, huffed out her impatience. "If I didn't know better, I'd say you and my brother had been talking."

"He's not in favor of your quest?"

"He supports me. He just doesn't share my . . . obsession."

He could have pulled a mouthful of teeth with less effort than this. "Your obsession with . . ."

She fought responding. He watched the battle as she shook her head, heaved out a long heavy breath. And he wondered why she carried such a burden alone, why she kept it a secret if it was this heavy.

Finally she got up, moved from the chair and the table to the door that opened onto the balcony. She pulled it open, stepped outside. He followed, settling into one corner as she gripped the railing.

"My dad went to prison when I was still sixteen. Finn was a year younger. And it wasn't for some minor misdemeanor with local consequences."

"Yeah. I know." Now they were getting somewhere.

The look she gave him said he didn't know a thing. "He went to prison for a crime committed against the United States government, Harry. Total-

Sky wasn't small potatoes. We're talking large-scale reverberations. Hell, Finn and I kept waiting to get hate mail from the great beyond."

"Did you? Get hate mail?"

She shrugged it off. "I only saw some of it. Nanny Caro made sure Finn and I were kept out of the public eye. She did a great job protecting us from the backlash. We probably never knew half of what happened."

He knew the answer because of the prep work he'd done, but it seemed like a question the Harry van Zandt he was pretending to be would ask. "What about your mother?"

"I only remember her in snatches." She rocked back and forth, pulling and pushing on the railing. "Like mental photographs, I guess. She died when I was five. Caro came to take care of us then, and when my father went away, she was made our legal guardian."

"Wow. That had to be tough. Doing most of your growing up with both parents gone."

"It was. But it wasn't. It was just the life I had. Caro was a great mother. And she didn't do so bad as a father either." A smile took the edge off her angst. "You should've seen her throw a football."

"What did Finn think about that?" he asked as the sound of car horns drifted up from the street.

"He loved it. Think Jennifer Aniston with meat on her bones and muscles in all the right places."

Like you, he wanted to say, but didn't. "Bet your house was a popular place."

"Nope." Her hair flew into her face when she shook her head. "Caro wouldn't have it. No parties. Friends, sure, but she kept us on the straight and narrow."

"Sounds like your father picked the right woman to take care of his kids."

"Honestly? I think she loved him as much as she

loved us. After he was incarcerated, she worked through his attorney to sell our house, and the three of us moved across the country to be near him."

"Tough age to pull up roots."

"Seeing him regularly helped a lot. As did being in a new place where no one knew who we were. What I hated was that he couldn't see Finn's football games, or be there on Christmas mornings." Her voice softened, broke. "Those were the times I got angry that he hadn't fought harder to clear his name."

Good. This was getting close to what he wanted to know. He turned, leaned his forearms on the railing. "You weren't angry over what he'd done?"

She shook her head vehemently. "He did nothing. He wasn't guilty. Yes, he worked for TotalSky. And he was involved in working on the satellite contract they won from the government. But he would never have made a deal to buy the parts he was accused of buying illegally."

"And you think there's something in this missing dossier that will clear his name."

"He told me where to find it. He told me not to let it fall into the wrong hands. I have to believe he knew if it did, the truth would stay buried."

"Why didn't he fight the conviction?"

"The evidence was too compelling, even if it was circumstantial. And he refused to mount a real defense. He said if he took the fall, the story would go away, the country would forget."

"But if he knew where to find this dossier and knew it would clear his name . . ."

"I don't know. I just . . . don't know." She wrapped her arms around her middle and rocked back and forth. "I probably won't know until I get my hands on it and can see exactly what the files says. But, no.

I've never understood why he chose to be a martyr when he had so much waiting for him at home."

That loss aside, Harry could think of one good reason why. That the martyr was actually guilty. But he wasn't about to say that to Georgia now.

He headed for the closet. "Then I guess we should get ready and go."

"Go where?"

"To General Duggin's estate."

6:00 P.M.

Georgia thought Harry wanted the two of them to pose as members of the auction house cataloging team. Else, why the research he'd ordered her to do? The research he'd told her he'd done himself?

It seemed he'd changed his mind while she'd been gone from the room, shopping, working out, trying to dig up anything she could on who he was. Because now she was posing as his assistant.

And he was posing as the buyer for a historical conservation consortium interested in the home furnishings the General's estate was anxious to sell.

They'd left the hotel in the sedan Harry arranged to rent for the day. More of the planning he'd done when she'd been out of the room. She was beginning to wonder if he'd slept at all while she'd been gone.

Or if he was one of those ex-military types who was used to sleeping on his feet, used to existing on nothing but the air that he breathed.

Once on their way, they'd gone shopping. Again. This time, however, he'd driven them to a department store where the evening's outfits had not cost an arm or a leg.

She was going to wind up this weekend with a better wardrobe than she'd had in years—and none of it she'd paid for herself.

Harry had bought a navy sports coat, white dress shirt, and khaki pants. He looked very casually debonair.

She'd picked out a slim skirt in a charcoal pin stripe and a soft pink twin set with pearls. She looked very properly uptight. The low-heeled, gray suede pumps didn't help.

Neither had the way Harry wiggled his eyebrows and laughed.

She'd decided then and there, as they'd walked out of the store wearing their new clothes and carrying their old ones in bags, that he'd been having way too much fun at her expense since they'd met.

He'd reminded her that her end of the deal hadn't been exactly raw. She had new clothes, new hair, and a new face to show for it.

She'd countered that letting herself be bought equated to being his whore—and that she would feel a whole lot better about the situation if she got to be the consortium's buyer and he assisted her.

He'd shaken his head, told her he'd give up his pimping ways after the weekend, but until then she'd have to get used to calling him daddy.

All of that had happened on the drive from the store to the general's estate. Now that they were here, she couldn't even find a comeback. She was cold, and she was starting to shiver, and she so hated this about herself.

Especially since she hadn't discovered what felt like a massive character flaw until this weekend, when finding herself in the middle of this mess.

Harry nosed the car up against the gated entrance and stopped. He handed her the leather portfolio, the fountain pen, and the pair of clear-lensed reading glasses he'd bought just for her. Then he grabbed her icy fingers and squeezed. "Don't flake out on me now, sweetheart."

"I'm fine," she said, putting on the glasses before clutching the portfolio to her chest.

"Good." He squeezed again. "Because this car's not big enough for all the sex we'd have to have to calm you down. We'd need Morganna for that."

"Morganna?" she asked, because otherwise she was going to start thinking about how good his sex suggestion sounded. The warmth. The closeness.

"The Buick."

She pulled the glasses down her nose and stared at him over the rims. "You named your car Morganna?"

He shrugged, winked. "She put a spell on me, what can I tell you?"

"You can tell me what we're going to do if we walk out of here with the dossier in hand." She glanced through the railings of the monstrous gate. "All this planning and preparing and posing getting us closer is great. But it would be nice not to head into the endgame flying blind."

"I'll tell you. I will. As soon as I nail it down," he said, pushing the call button at the gate to the general's estate.

She deflated in her seat. "So you are flying blind."

"More like by the seat of my pants."

"Is there a difference?"

"Sure. Hold on," he said, telling the disembodied voice who'd answered his call that he had an appointment with the law clerk working for the General's attorney.

The gate began to roll open, and Harry looked over. "If I was blind, I wouldn't be able to see where I was sitting."

The seat of his pants. She got it. It was dumb, but it did make a twisted sort of sense. She stared out the side window as they made the short winding drive to the front of the Highland Park house.

The structure itself, a two-story colonial, wasn't overly large, especially not when compared to the monstrous ranch house in Waco. But the manicured lawn and gardens tucked inside the property's boundary ring of thick woods and the size of the lot earned it the designation of estate.

Harry parked the car in the circular drive. She slung her new satchel over her shoulder and opened her door before he'd even turned off the car.

He grabbed her by the wrist, keeping her from climbing out. "You get overanxious, you're going to blow this, you know."

"I'm fine. I'm sorry. I promise I'm fine."

"You sure? We can make the block." He wiggled both brows. "Park and swap spit for awhile."

The man deserved every bit of grief she gave him. "If anyone is going to blow this, I'd say it's the person using the head in his pants instead of the one on his shoulders."

His answering smile was so wide, his teeth so white, and his dimples so deep, she almost gave in and called him daddy. But he broke the spell when he said, "That's my girl."

She growled. She wasn't anyone's girl. She scrambled out of the car to let him know it, but stopped as the front door to the house opened and the law clerk stepped out onto the wide, white brick porch.

"Mr. van Zandt?" The man walked toward Harry without acknowledging her at all. Obviously she blended into the scenery even better than she'd hoped.

"I'm Bob Franken." The two men shook hands. "I have to say, even out of the blue, your call could not have been more timely. The general was adamant about disposing of all the property not bequeathed in his will before the reading. And I think your consortium will be more than interested in the pieces we have available."

Georgia, still invisible, frowned as she followed Harry and Bob into the foyer, swearing her next gig as an underling would be to a bigwig rather than a pimp who wanted her to call him daddy. But she quickly pushed that thought aside to make room for something Bob had said.

The general wanted all of his material possessions disposed of ASAP. She'd thought from the very beginning there was something strange about the rush to auction his memorabilia and distribute his library items. And added to that now was selling his things.

It was as if he were wiping away all evidence of his existence. He had no family, having never married and outliving his two older siblings. The instructions with regard to the auction proceeds reflected his life-long commitment to higher education.

She wondered if the money from the sale of his homes and furnishings would be similarly allocated. And then she wondered what in the world he had left to bequeath to anyone. Pondering the development, she followed the two men who had yet to stop talking as they left the foyer for the living room.

"As you can see," Bob was saying, "the General's formal pieces are primarily French antiques."

All Georgia heard was blah, blah, blah, and proceeded to write down the same.

While Harry and Bob stood near the fireplace, Bob pointing out the intricate scrollwork on the feet of the protective screen, she made her way around the room, jotting notes when Daddy Harry lifted a finger to indicate Bob had said something worth noting.

If the purpose of the visit had not been so vital,

the outcome so critical, she would have enjoyed working the room with Harry. She felt as if she were playing in an episode of *Alias*, complete with the conservative assistant costume and the hot operative for a costar.

The men moved from the formal living room to the formal dining room, again with more formal French antiques.

It was a gorgeous home, a showplace, but she hardly paid attention to the salon *canapé* or the matching *fauteuils* or even their Aubusson tapestry and pierced aprons. There was only one thing she was looking for, only one thing capable of holding her interest.

And just as she'd done in the living room, checking out the coffee and end tables, the shelves and glass-fronted cabinets flanking the fireplace, she snooped in the dining room's buffet, in the drawers of the *enfilade*, recording details of each piece as if she were truly interested in the hardware and the integrity of the interior woodwork.

Every once in a while she'd catch Harry's eye. And for the life of her she didn't know what to make of his expression. He was enjoying himself way too much, but this time it seemed less at her expense and more a case of laughing with her, of sharing a private joke, just the two of them.

She liked that, the intimacy of it, the fun of a secret that only the two of them had the code to unlock. It lifted her spirits. Harry lifted her spirits. And coming to that realization brought a hitch to her chest.

Why here? Why now? Why not a month down the road when this was behind her and she had the time to fully appreciate the possibility of having him as a permanent fixture in her life?

Because this is when you need him, you goon.

And that was the truth. If not for Harry, she would've barged into last night's preview reception without a clue or a plan. She would've come here today equally unprepared. And that was assuming she would have thought to come at all.

She certainly wouldn't have returned to the general's ranch house in the middle of the night, sneaking in, bypassing the alarms and the security guards to search behind his desk drawer's hidden panel.

Yeah, she needed Harry all right. Needed him to point out exactly how her full-steam-ahead approach was as welcome in this situation as a bull in a china shop. Obviously, her three-year obsessive search had left her with no social graces and very little common sense.

The entourage moved then from the dining room into the library where Bob immediately showed off the massive carved oak, uh, library. She followed the tea party of two closely, wondering how Harry managed to know so much about Louis the XV, XVI, and XVII when she wasn't even sure she was writing the Roman numerals correctly.

She of no social graces. He of many. Then there was his counter-diving ability, his knife-wielding skills, his bottomless bank account, his affinity for blending in, fitting in, playing a part. And she didn't even want to get started on the marble statue body, killer smile, and hands that had her panting like a dog for his touch.

She did not pant after men. It was not her personality, not her style. And the only reason she forgave herself the behavioral lapse was because she'd never met a man like Harry van Zandt. She had no experience dealing with his kind. No textbook to study. No files to pull. No history to use as a guide.

The man had actually asked if she wanted to make out in the car!

She knew that he had been teasing, but that hadn't stopped her from coming way too close to saying yes. Circumstances, again. And nerves. Excuses that were both growing stale and tired.

It would be so much easier to admit that her attraction for him was no longer just lust, that it had grown into something real, something more—

There it was! Oh God! The lockbox!

The one she'd seen in the study at the ranch, now buried amidst stacks of papers on a Louis XV partner's desk pushed up against one wall.

Blood surged hot and fast through her veins. Her fingers shook; she gripped her pen so tightly she thought her knuckles would crack.

Staring down at the portfolio's legal pad, she furiously scratched line after line after line on the paper to get Harry's attention. She needed to get his attention before her heart exploded in the center of her chest.

She glanced over the rims of her glasses. Harry caught her gaze, gave a sharp nod, and asked Bob to continue with the tour. Once the men were out of the room, Georgia went to work.

The plan, if they found the lockbox, was first to check that it was indeed locked. She tried the lid. It was. Step two was to see if she could find a key or pick the lock. If neither effort bore fruit, it would be up to Harry to find a way to try—meaning she would have to distract Bob.

They'd discussed the possibility of walking out with the box, then nixed the idea as reckless. It was in the auction brochure. If they didn't find the dossier today, they'd get their hands on it tomorrow night along with the rest of the documents labeled miscellaneous.

Today would be better. Today would be free. But Harry had insisted she not worry about the outlay of cash. She was trying not to. She was, however, worried about being caught as she lifted the backside of the box, slipped her hand beneath, felt along the bottom and then in the handle on top for a key.

She came up empty, and so scrambled around in front of the desk, pulling open and digging through drawers—all of which had been cleaned out—then dropped to her knees. She searched the bottom of the table, the legs, every stick of freakin' wood that Louis had glued together.

Nothing. And she was growing short on time.

She had also just run out of luck.

Because when she finally reached over the stacks of papers and turned the box around, she realized the bobby pins she'd pushed into the hair at her nape weren't going to do her a damn bit of good as a pick.

The lock didn't take a key. It took a combination.

And unless Harry was a closet safecracker, today was well and truly screwed, and tomorrow was going to cost them—uh, cost Harry—dearly.

She briefly visited the idea of loading the lockbox into her satchel, but knew if she got the metal box shoved all the way in, she'd never get the big bag closed. She'd certainly never make it to the car without being seen.

She could always revert to her pre-Harry plan, one that saw her at the auction house tomorrow afternoon, wearing a maid's uniform and conveniently dropping the lockbox into her barrel of collected trash.

Except that would leave her to deal with Charlie Castro on her own. And since she had no intention of turning over the dossier, well, she needed Harry's help.

Of course his help wasn't going to do her or Finn any good if the dossier wasn't inside the box. But borrowing that trouble now was unproductive. They were done here. She needed to let Harry know.

She reached over the piles of papers to rotate the box back into place. Her elbow knocked into a stack of files as she did. She managed to grab them before they fell, her gaze caught by a brown folder with what looked like the edge of a red classified stamp.

She stared down, unable to breathe, and slowly slid the file from between the others.

She opened the cover, saw the name TotalSky, and slammed it shut, quickly slipped it into her portfolio, and clutched the leather binder to her chest, her heart thundering, tears welling in her eyes.

Three years of wondering if it even existed. If her father had been delirious. If the general had been telling the truth. Three years of pleading and exhausting every avenue and praying the papers she now held had not been destroyed.

And to find it here so unexpectedly, sitting buried in a stack of other files . . . to realize if she had not knocked into the pile with her elbow . . . if the lockbox had required a key and not a combination and she'd spent precious time trying to get it open . . .

She caught back a huge gasping sob and stared out through the window at the plush grounds beyond, where roses and azaleas bloomed in riotous red and pink clouds.

She wanted out of here. She wanted a quiet place to sit and read and absorb. To make plans on how to distribute the information inside.

She wanted to share her discovery with Finn, to show him his faith in her instincts had not been misplaced. But even more so, she wanted to share her find with Harry.

He'd been her partner in crime and her extra backbone now for two days. He'd been the one who'd come up with a way to get her inside the general's house. Telling him would save him a lot of money to-morrow night.

But telling him would also mean losing what she'd just found. And until she was left with no other choice, that she couldn't do.

Even knowing what he did about her reasons for needing to get her hands on the file, she doubted he would ever understand her not turning over the original to Charlie Castro in order to free Finn.

A copy would do her no good. She needed the real deal, the stamps and the signatures to prove she hadn't manufactured the whole thing.

Finally, finally, she had in her hands the very thing she'd been searching for, the very thing she needed to prove her father had not been guilty of the crimes for which he'd been charged, for which he'd done time.

He'd told her as he was dying that the dossier would yield the truth. He'd also told her to make sure it did not go forgotten, that all guilty parties paid. She'd sworn to him that's what she would do.

Because of that promise, she had to figure another way to free Finn. And she had only thirty-six hours to do so.

At the sound of Harry's and Bob's voices behind her, she quickly dried her eyes and moved away from the desk to the huge walnut library.

With the open portfolio cover hiding her trea-sured find, she pretended to jot a few last notes be-fore tucking the binder into her satchel and making her meek and mousy way to join them in the door to the foyer.

But Harry didn't seem as eager to escape. "The

desk there. With all the papers. Is that staying with the house?"

"No. It's also available. The papers were brought up from the ranch this morning for the auction. Somehow they were overlooked during the original shipment out." Bob started to walk over. "Here, let me move everything to the floor so you can see the condition of the wood."

"Don't worry about it. I just wanted to make certain it was part of the inventory." He turned to the law clerk and held out his hand. "Bob, thank you for the tour. I'll relay the information to my clients this evening, and will be in touch tomorrow."

"Let me give you my personal cell number," Bob said, pulling a business card from the holder in his inside coat pocket and writing the number across the back.

He handed it to Harry, and Georgia realized she had not imagined his snub. The man only had eyes for the man. She snickered to herself, and Harry glanced over as he pocketed the card. "Miss McLain? Are you ready?"

"Yes, sir. I have everything I need."

"McLain?" Bob put in, halting their getaway. "The general spoke often of an old friend, Stanley McLain. I believe he had a daughter who would be about your age."

Georgia pushed her glasses further up her nose, hiding behind them and the makeup she wore. She also patted the back of her careless chignon, wishing she'd taken more care with her disguise.

She'd never met Bob, but still. If Paul Valoren had recognized her from a photo . . . "It's a fairly common name. I always think about the Bruce Willis character in the *Die Hard* movies."

Bob shook his head. "I'm sorry. I'm not familiar with those."

Now *that* she found hard to believe, what with the way Bruce had been all buff and sexy as he saved the day. Then again, that was probably her fantasy, not Bob's. And here she'd thought they had the same taste in men.

Harry interrupted her nonsensical musing and saved this particular day. "Bob, it's been a pleasure, and I will be in touch."

And then he placed his hand in the small of her back and herded her out to the car, not stopping to talk or letting up on the pressure until he pulled open her door, she settled inside, and he slammed it shut behind her.

She fastened her seat belt while waiting for him to walk around to the driver's side, and caught a glimpse of Bob on the front porch staring. With that picture in mind as they drove away—and with her dossier-rich satchel tucked between her feet—she couldn't help but feel giddy.

And so she laughed. "I think he likes you."

"That's not funny," Harry grumbled. "I'm kicking myself for using your name."

She waved off his concern. "It's not like my name is uncommon."

"He remembered it. He remembered you."

"He's never met me. He only knew the name. Don't worry about it."

"I was careless."

"Think how it would have looked if you'd made up a name on the spot and I hadn't responded."

"That's why I should have made one up before-hand. Like I said. Careless."

She could understand him beating himself up if he went around creating false identities every day. As far as she knew, he didn't. And as far as she was concerned, he was doing a damn fine job for someone so out of his league.

He was the proverbial calm, cool, and collected, while she was doing good to conjure up even one of the three. In fact, she was pretty damn close to the edge of losing what little composure she had.

They continued on in silence for several miles, Harry navigating his way through the posh residential area back to their downtown hotel.

Georgia didn't think she'd ever struggled so hard to keep a secret. Her left knee bounced up and down as she stared out the side window, her fingers twisting the strap of her satchel where she held it in her lap.

So she was actually glad for the distraction when Harry interrupted her musings and said, "When we get back to the hotel, I'm going to call in a friend to help."

She glanced over. His jaw was taut, his gaze focused, intense. "Help with what?"

He stared straight ahead out the window. "We obviously can't go into the auction now and bid on the lockbox without drawing Bob's attention."

Without you *drawing his attention,* she wanted to tease. But she could tell that he was not in the mood. "Would that really matter? If he saw us there?"

"It might not, but I'd rather avoid the spotlight. He could start questioning our interest in the furniture if what we really wanted was the box."

She wasn't following his logic. "It's not unbelievable that we would want both."

"I don't want to risk it," he said, checking his rearview, glancing back, changing lanes. "And I really don't think you do either. He might start wondering what's inside. Or question why we didn't ask about it when we were at the house."

She thought about what he was saying, how yet again he was looking out for her best interests when none of the stakes here were his. "You're probably right. And thank you. I don't think that would have ever occurred to me."

He smiled at that. "I told you that you weren't going to want to dump me in Dallas."

Right now she could see herself never dumping him at all. "You of the many tricks up your sleeve."

"And in the many hats."

The Rabbit. That reminded her. "Speaking of calling, who are you going to call and for what kind of help?"

"A friend, and I'll figure out what I need when he gets here."

Mr. One Step at a Time. "You know, you never have told me what it is that you do."

"I'm a project consultant. For an engineering firm based in Manhattan."

He rattled off the details quickly, without hesitation. Meaning he was either telling the complete truth or was a pro at popping the top on the canned response. "I would never take you for an engineer."

He chuckled, began to relax. "Why not?"

"I'm not even sure. I mean, yes, you are methodical. You think things through. You come up with workable solutions. You don't seem to be a spur of the moment kind of guy—" That was all she got out.

Harry picked that moment to make a right-handed bat turn. She grabbed for the armrest and still ended up halfway across the seat. The car bumped up into a parking lot and slammed to a stop before she managed to catch her breath.

Once she had, she narrowed her eyes and glared over. "What the hell was that?"

"A spur of the moment decision," he said, and waggled both brows.

She looked up through the windshield. A Tex-Mex restaurant. Men and their stomachs. "You know, Finn made a spur of the moment food-related decision yesterday, and look where it got us."

"It got you a big fat step closer to getting your hands on what you've been after for a very long time," he said, and she knew she had no room to argue.

He shoved open his door, climbed out, walked around the front of the sedan, and opened her door. "I'm starving and I'm tired of room service. We have a lot of hours to kill before the auction. I'd rather not spend all of them holed up in the room."

She made sure her satchel was securely closed before getting out. "We do have brunch at eleven tomorrow with Professor Valoren."

Harry frowned at her bag as he shut her door. "Why don't you leave that out here? You don't need it for anything."

Little did he know. "Actually, I have my hairbrush in here and I'm going to the ladies' room to take down this mess."

"I kinda like it up," he said, his hand in the small of her back as he guided her through the restaurant's entrance.

She breathed in the smells of jalapeño and cilantro and garlic and sighed. "Well, I kinda like that dark shadow on your face, but you keep shaving it off."

"I only do that so it won't scratch when you kiss me. But since that hasn't been happening . . ."

She stopped, reached out, grabbed him by his coat sleeve and spun him around. Once she had him facing her the way she wanted, she held onto his lapels, stood on her tiptoes, and planted her lips on his.

She kissed him hard. One big smack on the mouth. Then, as quickly as she'd grabbed him, she let him go, pulling him behind her all the way inside to the hostess station.

"I never thought in a million years I could get sick of eating cereal, but I am," Tracy said, lifting her bowl to drink the last of her milk.

She sat on the floor beside Finn, both of them leaning back on the wall with their feet against the base of the counter between the booths and the alley.

Well, her feet didn't quite reach. Finn's did, and he still had to bend his knees.

"What do you eat for breakfast?" he asked.

They'd talked all day, and off and on last night of equally silly things. "Usually oatmeal."

"Oatmeal is cereal."

"I know, but it's hot cereal. It doesn't count. So either that or scrambled eggs since I like to give my daddy a good start to the day."

"He lives with you?" Finn asked, pouring the rest of his milk from the bowl into his mouth.

She shook her head. "He lives next door. In the house where I grew up."

"Wow. So you're a real local girl, huh?"

"You could say that." She set both of their bowls and spoons on the floor and smoothed her apron over her lap. "The only time I've even been out of Texas was once as a kid when we went to Lake Catherine in Arkansas for vacation. I almost drowned."

Finn clicked his tongue. "That had to suck."

She laughed. "It's kinda pathetic when I think about

it now. The water wasn't even over my head. I just got scared and panicked."

"How old were you?"

"Five."

He huffed. "Five-year-olds are supposed to panic."

She laughed again. He made it so easy to do. To forget that if she leaned across him and looked around the counter, she'd see men with guns. "I guess you're right. Though I can't see Freddy ever panicking, even as a kid."

"Freddy. He's your husband, right?"

She nodded. She couldn't say anything else because she was afraid that feeling like she was going to choke meant she was going to cry.

"I figured he'd come here looking for you last night when you didn't come home."

She supposed it looked pretty sad to everyone that no one had come looking for either her or for Phil. Phil lived alone, had no family, and had been known to close up weekends to go fishing with no notice at all.

The diner wasn't his income as much as a way to keep busy. He had some sort of retirement pension from his years making cars in Detroit. She was the one who should have had people come looking. Freddy for sure.

"We're separated," she finally reminded him. "He wouldn't know I'm not home." It hurt to say it. Hurt even worse that Finn didn't say anything for awhile.

"What about your father? Wouldn't he have missed breakfast?"

"Any other day, he would have. But he went into the hospital on Thursday. I know they think I'm a horrible daughter, not visiting him for two days." She buried her face in her hands and sobbed. "And now they probably think I'm a deadbeat, too."

"Aww, Trace." Finn bumped her shoulder with his. "I'm sure they don't think anything like that. You're Mother Teresa, remember?"

She hated that stupid reputation. "Everything about my life has turned into a nightmare since Freddy left."

Finn waited a minute, then reached over, took hold of her hand, and squeezed. "I forgot about Freddy being gone. Phil mentioned it last night. I guess it didn't sink in. I'm sorry."

For what? For not listening or for her being alone? Maybe he was sorry that she was too much of a loser to take care of herself.

But his fingers felt strong and nice, and she really needed to feel like she wasn't alone, and so she let him hold her hand. "Well, it's my fault he's gone, so you don't have nothing to be sorry for."

"You can talk about it if you want. I'm a pretty good listener."

She couldn't be this pitiful. She had to suck it up. "Why would you want to hear about my problems when you've got a ton of your own? Aren't you worried about your sister having to go off like that with someone she doesn't even know?"

"Honestly? You pit those two against one another, I'll lay a hundred to one odds Georgia comes out on top."

"She sure looked like she was going to take off that Charlie's head."

"She's a scrapper. And a damn fine big sister."

"You're her baby brother?" When he nodded, she laughed.

"Oh, you think that's funny?"

"Only when comparing your sizes. You're about two feet taller than her and probably weigh twice as much."

"Hmm. You're probably right about the weight. But she's five eight. I'm six three. Not quite two feet."

Tracy sighed. "Freddy's only five nine. Standing up, I can lay my head on his shoulder."

"Sounds like you miss doing that."

"I shouldn't, but I do. I need to get used to being alone."

"No one needs to get used to that."

She didn't want to. She really didn't. "Do you have more family than your sister? Are you married?"

He shook his head. "Never took the plunge. It's just me and Georgia. Has been for a very long time."

"No cousins or aunts or uncles? No grandparents?"

"Nope. Not a one. Is that hard to believe?"

"It's hard to believe anyone doesn't have someone."

"You said Phil was on his own."

"Maybe it's because he's older. But that's stupid, huh? I mean, if my mom hadn't died, I know she'd still be here with my dad."

"Are you going to try and work things out with Freddy?" Finn asked. "Or is the split a done deal?"

"I don't know." Right now? This minute? She wanted him back more than she wanted to get out of here alive.

She didn't want to die without seeing him again, without telling him how much she still loved him. "We've got a lot of stuff we'd have to work out, and I'm not sure we could."

"Real stuff? Or are you both being hardheaded?"

She pulled her hand from his. "What kind of question is that?"

"An honest one." Finn crossed his ankles, crossed his arms over his chest. "I've seen a lot of friends bust up. Hell, I even watched Georgia and her ex call it quits."

"She's not married either?"

"Not now. In her case, I think it was more about just drifting apart and never having been right for each other in the first place. But with some of my buddies? It was like no one wanted to make an effort. Or be the one to admit they were wrong." He stopped talking for a minute, letting what he'd said sink in. "Compromise isn't such a terrible thing, Tracy."

"I'm not dumb. I know that." Ugh. He was being so nice, and she was biting off his head. "It's just that I don't know if we have any way to compromise."

"Why not?"

"Freddy wants to move my daddy into a home and sell the house since we end up stuck having to pay most of the taxes. Daddy's social security and Medicare don't go very far when he's in such bad shape."

"Would he get better care in a home?"

Her heart began to ache. "No one can care for him better than I can. Or at least no one could before Freddy left and I've been having to work so many double shifts."

"Where's Freddy now?"

"I don't even know. He's been gone a couple of weeks. I think he's staying with a hunting buddy over in Crawford."

"So, let me ask you something, Tracy." Finn tilted his head toward her. "If your father was home and had someone else looking after him, and Charlie decided to let us out of here, would you go home? Or go to Crawford?"

"You might as well ask me what I would do if the

moon turned to green cheese because the cow kept jumping back and forth stirring it up. I have enough trouble trying to figure out what to do in real life.

"I don't have time to waste imagining things that aren't ever going to happen," she said, scrambling up to her feet and heading to the bathroom where she could cry in peace.

8:15 P.M.

While Georgia was in the ladies' room messing with her hair, and after he had ordered margaritas, Harry put in a call to the private line at the SG-5 ops center belonging to Kelly John Beach.

If K.J. was in the field, the call would be routed to the main Smithson line. If he was simply out of the office, it would forward to his cell.

K.J. picked up on the second ring. "Beach."

"It's Rabbit. You busy?"

"You mean do I have time to talk to you before taking my wife to bed?" he asked, obviously at home on his cell.

Harry couldn't help but grin. Kelly John had married Emma Webster, Hank Smithson's executive assistant, in an intimate Christmas ceremony at Hank's Saratoga farm.

K.J. was the first SG-5 operative to tie the knot. The members of the Smithson Group and their significant others—for those who had them—had been the only attendees.

It was tough making friends—and keeping friends—when one spied for a living.

His grin fading at the dismal thought, Harry asked, "How about you bring yourself and Mrs. Beach down to Dallas in the morning?"

"A Sunday in April in Dallas. Nope." Harry could almost see K.J. shaking his head. "Can't think of a compelling reason."

Harry played his trump card. "Does Ezra Moore compel?"

"Fuck, yeah. You got the bastard nailed down?"

"Not yet. But I'm getting there."

"What's up?"

Harry explained the parts he and Georgia had played earlier and their need to get their hands on the lockbox without further exposure. "If you can't make it, I'll try Christian and Natasha."

"No can do. The boy just left for Alaska. And before you ask, Eli is in Turkey and Julian in Japan."

That would leave Tripp manning the ops center since Mick Savin had pretty much taken himself off the active roster while he worked in West Texas with his woman.

And with Simon already on surveillance at the diner, Tripp would have no backup at the ops center but for K.J. and Gideon Martel.

Harry frowned. "Wonder if Hank would want to make the trip?"

"Give me the specs," K.J. said. "Someone will be there."

Harry did, and had just rung off when Georgia walked up to the table, her shaggy brown waves again framing her amazingly beautiful face.

She dropped her bag onto the seat of the chair between them and pulled it close before she sat. "That's so much better. I was starting to get a headache, *and* feel like a repressed *au pair* or something."

"Something like the executive assistant you were supposed to be?" She might feel repressed, but uninhibited better described the way she looked, not to mention her actions. As harmless as it had been, he was still working to get that kiss out of his mind.

"If I'd had more shopping time and more shopping choices, not to mention more shopping money of my own, your executive assistant would have definitely been wearing something else," she said, holding the unbuttoned edges of her sweater much the same way she'd held his lapels.

He watched her eyes light up as she reached for the drink he'd ordered for her. One forearm braced on the table, he sipped at his own. "Yeah? What?"

She frowned, shaking her head as she swallowed. "Something that didn't scream church lady."

The way she fit that sweater did not make him think of church at all. "The pearls were too much?"

"Actually, I like the pearls," she said, fingering them as she spoke. He liked them, too. He wanted to see her wearing them and nothing else in his bed. "And the sweater's nice. It's just not me. I'm more into—"

"Camo?"

"I was going to say pin stripes. But really, anything would work as long as it's not bubblegum or fluffy. I'm not exactly the fluffy type."

He thought of the hellcat who'd tried to strangle Charlie Castro. She didn't fit into pin stripes or oxfords any more than she did into bubblegum or fluff. "I would never have thought that you were."

"I'm not exactly into pin stripes either," she admitted, echoing his thoughts. She dipped a tortilla chip into the bowl of warm salsa. "It's more a lesser of two evils since I don't know of any exec who would go for T-shirts and jeans."

"You know a lot of execs?" he asked, opening his menu.

"I used to be married to one."

That was interesting. "How did you fit in at the company Christmas parties?"

"The truth?" She pulled up a memory and smiled. "I was a hit. What woman doesn't want to find out the best antiques for investment?"

He laughed. "For some reason, I see you sharing that investment information with the husbands instead of the wives."

She ate a couple of chips, sipped at her drink, licked the salt from her lips. When their server arrived, she ordered a la carte, tamales and *borracho* beans.

And then she gave him her attention. "Answer me this, Mr. Engineering Firm, how you would like it if your coworkers got too friendly with your wife? Would you dump the job? Or dump the spouse?"

Harry couldn't imagine a single one of his coworkers hitting on a woman belonging to a member of the team. But he also knew that outside of the SG-5 ranks, it happened way too often.

He hated that it had happened to her. "I guess that would depend on which came with the better benefits."

She stared at him blankly for several seconds. Then she threw a chip at his chest. "You are a horrible man."

"I am," he agreed, then sobered. "And I'm also very sorry you went through that."

She shrugged. "We all have stuff in our past. I'll bet you could even think of something if you tried."

"I'd rather not. I kinda like my present." He wondered what she would think if she knew how many men he'd killed in his life.

"I don't know. Your present is pretty much a tangled mess right now. Are you going to have problems if you don't show up at work on Monday? I mean, that car you have, Morganna? I'm guessing you drove down for the auction?"

What was another lie piled on top of the rest? "I had a couple of weeks coming. Seemed like a relaxing way to spend the time."

She finished off her drink. "A man and his car and the open road. It doesn't fit any better than the engineering thing does."

"Why not?"

"You're much too . . . help me out here." She waved a hand. "I can see you parasailing or base jumping. Not driving cross-country in a fifty-year-old car."

He wanted to laugh; was that really how she saw him? And here he had thought he was doing such a good job projecting a respectable image. "Base jumping? Why? Just because I took a dive across the counter in the diner? I'm not a daredevil as a rule, you know."

She was silent while their server set their food on the table, only speaking once he'd left. "Do you think Charlie is letting Finn and the others eat?"

"I don't see why he wouldn't." He cut into his *chile rellenos*, realized her hands were still in her lap, gestured with his knife. "You. Eat. We have a busy day tomorrow, and you passing out from hunger or dehydration would put a big kink in our plans."

He shoveled his food into his mouth and watched her struggle with unimaginable emotions. More than anything, he wished he could tell her how well in hand things were.

But he couldn't give her the reassuring details. All he could give her was a nice evening out with the promise that he would not abandon her tomorrow.

So he did, and they spent the rest of the meal talking about the treasures she hunted, the treasures she'd found, the treasure hunters who hunted her.

Her knowledge impressed him, her enthusiasm,

too. He wasn't sure he knew anyone outside of SG-5 who loved their work the way she did.

It made it easy to understand why she lived as she did, a vagabond with no ties, free to pick up and go, no obligations but those she chose to take on, and what she owed to herself.

The hours moved quickly, as did her margaritas. He was driving. He'd stopped at one.

But seeing Georgia relaxed for the first time since yesterday lifted some of the tension he was feeling. He hadn't yet come up with a plan of action should the lockbox not contain the dossier. And that was weighing heavy on his mind.

He hated having to wait and pick either Hank's or K.J.'s brain, but if he didn't have some sort of Thomas Edison genius moment soon, he'd have no other choice.

And it wasn't so much the Ezra connection, the possible loss of the very thing he'd been assigned to discover that was giving Harry hell.

It was that he needed to get Finn McLain out of harm's way because of how much he was coming to care for Georgia.

His feelings were so strong, in fact, that he'd come close a couple of times to giving up caring for the outcome of his mission.

And if he didn't shape up, there was a damn good chance he'd be looking at a missionless future. Hank Smithson did not take kindly to being screwed.

"I swear, another bite and I'm going to pop like a big fat pimple."

Harry looked up from his near-empty plate and his musings. He couldn't believe what he'd just heard. "You may dress like a church lady and look like a church lady, but no one will ever accuse you of talking like one."

She groaned. "It's the pearls. I swear. I'm taking them off."

"Don't you dare," he said, his words stilling her hands at her nape.

She lowered them slowly, held onto the edge of the table, her gaze locked with his. "Harry van Zandt. That sounded like a threat."

"It was," he admitted, in for a penny, in for a pound. "You can take off anything and everything else, but the pearls stay."

She continued to hold his gaze as a sweep of color rose in her face. "You know. I'm just buzzed enough to do it. You damn well better be careful what you say."

He raised a finger and said the only thing that mattered. "Check, please."

And at that, Georgia laughed.

9:50 P.M.

Georgia hadn't been half as buzzed as she'd led Harry to believe. The margaritas weren't strong, and she was no lightweight. She was, however, still reeling from the find she'd made earlier in the day.

The booze was the most viable excuse for the smile she could not wipe from her face.

The ride back to the hotel was quiet. The trip was short, and she had a lot on her mind. Obviously, Harry did, too. She wanted to ask him what he was thinking about, but didn't. She was afraid to find out he wasn't looking ahead to tomorrow at all, but that he only had thoughts for her pearls.

And the reason she was afraid was because she hadn't been able to think of anything else since he'd walked her from the restaurant to the car.

She'd toyed with the strand through the whole of the drive. The damn things weren't even real. They were costume, fake. So much . . . paste and glass.

Yet even now they laid against her skin like balls of fire, burning her, branding her. She wanted to rip them away, to toss them out the window and into the street. But she wanted even more than that to rip away her clothes, crawl across the seat, and climb into his lap.

And that just wouldn't do.

This was a business relationship. One into which they'd both been coerced, but one now solidly forged. They had a goal; once it was met, they would have no need or occasion to ever see one another again. She could not allow herself to act on her personal feelings for Harry. Not again.

Easier said than done.

During the ride up in the elevator to their room, satchel held tight, Harry standing two feet away, she was still trying to convince herself to take off the pearls the minute they reached the room.

To store them in her duffel. To flush them down the commode. As long as she did that, temptation would not be sitting on the edge of the bed, patting the mattress, waiting for her to yield.

And oh, but she wanted to yield.

Once Harry unlocked the door and she walked into the room, she kicked her shoes off and into the closet, then headed for the chair holding her bags.

She placed her brand-new executive assistant's satchel on top, pulled out her brush and her makeup bag, dropped both into her backpack.

She then zipped the satchel tight, tucked it into the depths of the duffel, and grabbed her shorty camo pj's before securing the big bag's snaps and straps like she hadn't done since they'd checked into the room.

And it wasn't until she turned and saw the frown on Harry's face that she realized how strange—even suspicious—her actions appeared. But instead of fumbling for any explanation, she went to the bathroom to change.

The minute the door closed behind her, she collapsed, clutching her pj's close and sliding the length of the door to sit. She rested her head against the surface, closed her eyes, and soaked up the cold from the floor with her soles, fearing spontaneous combustion.

If not the fear of her deception's discovery, then it

had to be the alcohol heating her blood. Or the peppers in the salsa and the beans. Then again, it was very likely a cruel combination of the three causing sweat to bead between her breasts and in the small of her back as one single question swirled in her mind.

Why in the world had she kissed him?

What a silly thing to have done with last night still so fresh in her mind. They'd shared a bed and body heat, but he'd also made her come. Even now she could remember the feel of his fingers inside her.

He was out there now getting ready for bed. And the longer she kept the locked door between them, the thicker the tension would grow. She would wonder what he was doing, he would no doubt wonder about her.

She couldn't take it anymore. She was barely surviving now. If this thing between them built up much more, she was going to blow it. She'd give in, lose her focus, forget the reason she'd come here.

Except when she got to her feet and met her own mirrored gaze, when she saw the woman in pearls staring back, she knew that would never happen. She would not forget. Her focus was clear. She knew exactly why she was here.

But right now? At this moment? Giving in was a big part of taking care of herself—the one thing she most needed to do. If she didn't, she would never be of use to anyone. Not to her father, not to Finn. Not even to Harry.

She pulled off the cashmere twinset and hung it on the hook on the door. She did the same with the skirt. Her panty hose and bra she tossed on the marble vanity. That left her with her hair down wearing white cotton panties and pearls.

She liked the way she looked. She was thirty-four,

but she'd been active all her life. Gravity could have been kinder, but that was an observation not a complaint. She wondered if Harry would have any, if he would think her thighs too heavy, her hips too wide, her breasts too . . . unperky.

And then she thought about opening the door and asking, but that seemed like such a desperate move. Instead, she pulled on her pajamas, brushed her teeth, turned out the lights, and headed to bed.

She found Harry already there, lying on his back, propped up on both pillows, the bedside light still on, waiting. He didn't say a word. He didn't make a move. She wasn't sure what to do, which way to turn.

She reached for the spread on the second bed. Harry reached for her wrist. He wrapped her smaller bones in the larger ring of his fingers. She lifted her gaze from that point of contact to meet his eyes, her pulse jumping in his hand and in her head.

"You didn't take off the pearls."

"You told me not to."

"I didn't expect you to pay attention."

She ignored the massage of his thumb on the inside of her wrist. "I've been known to have a compliant nature."

"That falls under the category of needing to see to believe."

"I'm still wearing the necklace, aren't I?" What further proof did he want? And why was she even pretending not to know?

"Then how about you come over here and let me take it off?"

She looked down, the clock ticking, her heart pounding, taking in the shadow along his jaw, his dimples, the eyes that begged.

She thought of all the reasons she should say no.

She thought of his marble body beneath the sheet he'd pulled to his chest. She thought of the kiss in the alcove, of how no other man had ever taken her so thoroughly apart.

And then she stopped thinking and moved toward all the things she wanted to feel. The comfort and release and security she knew she'd find in Harry's arms.

She hadn't even taken a step when he tugged. She'd done no more than shift her weight, but that was enough. The sheet fell to his lap as he sat up, pulled, and tumbled her to the far side of the bed.

He leaned over her, loomed above her, pushed her hair from her face. And then he smiled his beautiful killer smile. "I like you compliant."

She searched for her voice, her hands curling into the sheet. He made her nervous in ways she couldn't even describe. She swallowed hard, hoping to dispel some of the flutter. "Does that mean you just want me to lie here?"

He chuckled. "Compliant. Not complacent."

"Oh. I thought maybe you were the type to enjoy a bump on a log." She tossed out the bait, wanting him to know what she was used to.

His only response was to shake his head. "A log, not so much. But I do like the bumps on your chest."

"You've only seen them at their best."

His fingers teased her skin along the edge of her top. "They have a worst?"

"They do. Its name is gravity," she said, and shuddered from his touch.

He stroked the swell of one breast, moved to the other. "But with gravity comes experience. It makes for the perfect trade-off."

"I don't have that much. Experience." She didn't want to tell him, but he needed to know.

"You were married."

"I don't have that much," she repeated, feeling her nipples peak, and closing her eyes to feel more.

Harry's fingers moved lower, circled the hard tips through the cotton of her top. "What was wrong with your husband?"

How was she supposed to answer when she wasn't sure what she'd done with her voice? "You're the man. You tell me."

"He was impotent, gay, or a fool."

She had an opinion or two, but none were anything she wanted to talk about here. Not when Harry pinched and tweaked and brought her up off the bed. "And all this time I thought it was me."

"You shouldn't have. Not if his coworkers showed interest."

"That was a long time ago."

"No one interested since?" He found the hem of her tank, slid his fingers beneath.

His hand was heavy, warm. She almost couldn't breathe for waiting, for wanting. "I don't know. I've been busy. I haven't met anyone. Or taken time to find out."

"Why not?" He cupped her breast. Just held her gently, skin-to-skin. "Don't you miss sex?"

"It's hard to miss what you haven't had. Or haven't had done well." And oh, but she'd never had this.

"Can you get pregnant?"

She nodded. She had assumed all men came with condoms these days. Her mistake. "I should have thought. I'm sorry."

"Georgia?"

"Harry?"

"Look at me."

She opened her eyes.

His were close. Dark. Dangerously aroused. It was

hard to hold his gaze. "Do you realize that every time we get physically close, you say you're sorry?"

"That's what happens after years of being told you do everything wrong."

"I don't see that you've done anything wrong." He rubbed his palm over her nipple in tiny circles. Over and over and over again.

The contact was so sweet and exquisite. So intense. So hot. "Could be because I haven't done anything."

"You kissed me in the restaurant earlier."

"I know." She ached. God, she ached. Her sex was so hot and so full.

"You kissed me last night at the gallery."

"I know." She wanted to come, wanted his fingers inside.

"You came all over my hand."

"That was you doing everything right. I didn't do anything at all."

"You let me."

"That's because I'm a complacent bump." She clenched her sex, swore she was going to come.

"Georgia?"

"Harry?"

"I have condoms."

"Thank God."

"Take off your shirt. But leave the pearls."

She swallowed hard as she reached for her hem, hesitating only briefly—a last, panicked no-turning-back admission—before raising up and pulling the tank over her head.

She waited, so afraid Harry would turn away. But he didn't. He didn't move at all. He didn't speak. She could barely hear him breathe. All he did was stare. Not at her breasts. At her face.

His lids lowered, his lips parted, his nostrils flared. "You're beautiful."

She tried to blow off the compliment, to hide behind humor, but the look in his eyes changed her mind. He was all business, totally serious. She couldn't make light. "I'll give you not too shabby. I don't know if I'd go as far as beautiful."

"I'd go as far as betting that you feel as good as you look. And that you taste even better."

If he didn't feel her and taste her pretty damn soon, she was going to scream. "I'm half naked, and you're not doing either."

His smile said a thousand words about what he wanted to do. "I'm waiting for you to get all the way naked."

"You didn't tell me to."

"I was hoping you might take the initiative."

She shimmied out of her panties and pj bottoms. "What about you?"

"What about me?"

"Are you wearing any clothes?"

"Crawl under the sheet and find out."

This had been so easy at the gallery. All she'd had to do was close her eyes and let go. The alcove had been cast in shadows. Harry's body had blocked the rest of the light. It wasn't like that now. Now she could see everything.

And he could see all of her. Not only her body, but her quirks and her fears, her obsessive, self-absorbed personality, every one of them a reason for him to run. Definitely reasons for her to hide.

But she couldn't hide. And he wasn't running. He was staring down at her like he truly believed she was as beautiful as he'd said. And she really couldn't take it anymore.

She reached up a hand to the pearls around her neck. "I should probably take these off. They seem to be blinding you."

He covered her hand with his. "I'm not blinded. And I'm going to kiss you now."

"Okay."

"I was just telling you so you won't bolt."

"I'm not going to bolt."

"You sure? You seem awfully skittish."

"That's just me wondering when you'll figure out I'm not such a good time."

"The best sex is had between the ears, Georgia. And I've been getting off on you since we met."

He made her feel like everything about her mattered. Her hopes, her dreams, her obsessions, her fears. She felt as if this was a new beginning. That she was bursting free from a suffocating cocoon.

She pulled back the bedcovers and slid beneath, taking that one step before she took the next and scooted her body underneath Harry's where he still loomed above.

She tangled her feet with his feet, brushed his knees with hers, pushed her hip into his groin where it was quite obvious that he was as naked as he'd wanted her to be.

Her movement elicited a groan, and she pressed a hand to his chest and said, "I'm sorry."

"Don't be." His voice rumbled beneath her hand. "That sound you heard was not a complaint."

She flicked her thumb over his nipple, threaded her fingers through the soft hair in the center of his chest, and scooted even closer, until her shoulder nudged up against him.

"Okay. I'm here. Now prove to me that this is just like riding a bike."

He laughed, and as his head came down, he murmured, "My pleasure."

She thought he was going to kiss her, and she waited for his lips to meet hers. He surprised her by opening his mouth at the base of her throat and drawing on her skin, bathing the tiny bruises he made with his tongue, turning her on.

Her eyes rolled back, and he moved over her body, shifting so that his erection prodded her hip, before he slid one knee between hers. She felt the warmth and the hardness, the sticky wetness at the tip. And then he nudged her thighs apart, pressed his thigh against her sex.

She shuddered, felt herself grow damp and hungry. His mouth drifted lower, moving from her neck and chest to the swell of one breast. He cupped her in one hand, squeezed, kneaded, finally wrapped his tongue around her nipple and sucked her between his lips.

She whimpered, arched into his mouth, rubbed herself against his leg in desperation. She *was* desperate. She could not believe the pulse of sensation sweeping her along. She tingled and she burned. And no matter how much he gave her, she could not get enough of Harry's mouth.

He'd moved to her other breast, suckling, nipping, then slid further down her body, kissing her ribs and her belly, teasing her navel with his tongue. All the while stroking his hands along her sides, over her chest, down her hips. He massaged and manipulated and played.

And she wasn't lying beneath him like a bump on a log. She was feeling. She was moving. She was trembling beneath his touch. She was loving every moment of what he was making her feel. She was involved, and she wanted him with an incredible sense of everything in her world being right.

She flexed her fingers at her sides, spreading them wide, then pulling them in to claw at the sheet. She opened her eyes and stared straight up at the darkened ceiling, conscious of nothing but Harry's heat and touch.

He held her hips, his fingers gouging her muscles, his thumbs hooked just above her bones. His beard scratched against her belly when he kissed her there. Tiny kisses. Sucking kisses. Long, slow kisses with a whole lot of tongue.

He had to know how wet she was, he had to know how ready. He had to be able to smell her, moving down her body, taking his own sweet time. His patience amazed her, as did his attention. She was so used to sex being a sprint, not a marathon.

She didn't know if her heart would survive. It felt on the verge of exploding in her chest. And then her condition worsened. Harry got up on his knees and knelt between her thighs.

She shuddered, shivered. He leaned down and kissed the crease of her thigh, one side, then the other, so close to where she wanted him, so far away. He came closer, slipped his palms beneath her buttocks, slid his thumbs into her sex on either side of her entrance, and opened her for his tongue.

He pierced her, pushed deep inside, pulled back, licked through her folds, sucked on her lips. She gasped. She panted. She drew up her knees and held her ankles at her hips, giving him better access, more room to play.

He played by using his tongue, circling the tip around the knot of her clit, pressing the flat through her folds. She arched up. He pushed her back down, moving one hand to her belly to hold her in place.

And then that hand, that thumb began to play, too, fluttering over her clit like soft butterfly wings, barely touching, teasing, causing her clit to tighten, her nipples to tingle, the moisture from her sex to flow.

It wasn't enough, and she begged, grinding against

him, flexing and clenching, widening her legs. She was ready. Surely he knew she was ready. She started to tell him exactly what she needed him to do, where she wanted him to touch, to tickle her, to soothe her ache.

But he was there, pressing along the side of her clit with his thumb and sucking her into his mouth, pulling, teething, rolling with his tongue. She cried out, thrust upward. He answered by tugging his other hand from beneath her bottom and pushing a finger inside her.

He crooked it, stroked her G-spot. The sensations brought her hips off the bed. She came then, a flood, drowning. She almost couldn't breathe. He continued to finger her, pulling back only when her muscles no longer squeezed his fingers, when her shudders faded, when she collapsed beneath him.

She couldn't even move. She knew he had reached for a condom, sensed him rolling it on, and shivered anew at the thought of his body entering hers, of how much of him she had to explore.

When he crawled over her, she took his weight gladly. He leaned to the side on one elbow, reached between their bodies and guided his cock into place. She felt that first breach of his head and moaned, drawing her knees to her chest as he pressed forward.

He filled her, stretched her, pulled out and pushed in, his head scraping over her sensitive flesh inside, his shaft grinding against her clit. She hooked her heels behind his thighs, wrapped her hands around his biceps, and held on.

As if he understood that she was giving him her body to use, he started to thrust, slowly at first, picking up speed and force, driving himself into her and nearly taking her off the bed. He pumped in and out, his elbows above her shoulders on the bed, his fists clenching the pillows on either side of her head, his face buried against her neck.

His rhythm was fierce, powerful, his thrusts hard and intense, his entire body taut. She felt the strain beneath her palms. But she felt it most of all in his center as the pressure built to a furiously full head.

And just when she thought neither of them would make it out of this alive, he came. A sound of relieved agony rolled up from his gut. He spilled it into the pillow while spilling the fluids from his body into hers. And before he had even rolled away, she fell fast asleep.

11:00 P.M.

Standing beneath the spray in the hotel room's shower, Harry let the heat of the pounding water steam the wrinkles from his mind. Some kind of operative he was, losing his way, allowing his plans to go awry, his mission to take a backseat to a woman. Her needs. His need for her.

He ducked his head, braced his hands on the tile so the water pummeled his neck and shoulders. It was the closest he could get to having the sense God gave a billy goat beat back into him.

Had he been in Manhattan, he could easily have taken on one of his SG-5 partners in the company gym's sparring ring. Or even gone a few rounds with a punching bag. Whatever it took to straighten out the kink in his obviously twisted priorities.

This was not why Hank Smithson had hired him. He was supposed to be levelheaded and on the ball, pulling tricks from a hat when his fellow operatives needed the help of his magic—not whipping his dick out of his pants because the woman he was working with had brought him to his knees.

But, hell. Look at her. And she thought she wasn't a good time. If she were any more of one, he would never have made it from the bed to the bath on his feet. As it was, leaving her behind had made him want to crawl—and bawl—like a baby.

He turned around, stepped forward, let the pulsing spray do its work on the muscles of his lower back.

Damn if she hadn't nearly killed him. What an enigma. So shy and hesitant and so . . . not. She was a hellcat, one of the most with-it women he'd ever met, yet she had no awareness of her sexual appeal. None. Zero. Zilch.

The Georgia he'd just made love to, whom he'd left sleeping in the tangle of covers they'd made, didn't fit at all with the Georgia he'd brought off at the gallery. She was no less responsive, but tonight she'd seemed vulnerable, certain of disappointing him— and of being disappointed. He knew for a fact neither of them had come anywhere close.

He didn't get it. He didn't get it at all. What he did get was that his feelings for her were about to set up a big roadblock between what they were working on together on a personal plane and what he'd been sent here to do.

He was too wrapped up in her search, and had stopped focusing on his. If he didn't start using the head he was paid to use and keep the other one tucked away, he was definitely going to be looking a pink slip in the eye.

He had his eyes closed, his head down, one hand on the wall at his side, the other wrapped around the rod holding the shower curtain. He couldn't hear anything but the running water. Not the door opening and closing, not Georgia's bare feet on the floor.

But he knew she was there. When she stepped into the tub, the hook nearest his hand slid closer. When she tugged the curtain back into place, it slid away.

It was a wide tub, luxury-sized, and if she had on her mind what her joining him in the shower brought to his, room to move was going to be a very good thing.

Still, he kept his eyes shut. He didn't want to see

her. He wanted the fantasy of simply knowing she was there, of wondering what she planned to do, of waiting. He sensed her movements, and he smelled her. She smelled like sex; his blood began flowing south, and his flagpole to rise.

The musky, earthy scents of shared fluids and sweat—hey, he wasn't exactly smelling like a rose—faded when she picked up the soap and begin to suds up the bar by rubbing it over his chest. Her hands were nimble, deft, scrubbing over his neck and shoulders, down his arms, through his armpits before moving from his ribs to his abs.

That was when she dropped to her knees. He held back a groan. Or at least he tried. It was a sound of anticipation and it echoed when he let it go. She said nothing, made no response.

All she did was run her slick soapy hands over his calves, his knees, his thighs, moving ever closer to—but never touching—the one spot where he most wanted her attention. The spot aching to feel her fingers and her tongue. The spot on his body that was the filthiest of all and needed a thorough washing.

He wanted to laugh. Instead he growled. He'd meant what he'd told her about the best sex happening between the ears. And right now, the nasty, dirty thoughts filling his head proved it needed to be cleaned.

But then she took him into her hand, and he couldn't think of anything else but her touch. She soaped him up, stroked him. He thrust against her palm. She let go, moving deeper between his legs, sudsing up his balls and sliding two fingers between the cheeks of his ass.

And if all of that wasn't enough to make him beg like a starving dog, she stayed to play, bringing along the strand of pearls as she took his cock into her mouth, one hand wrapped around his shaft just beneath the head.

She did wicked, evil things with her tongue, swirling it around the ridge and seam, running the flat over the cap of his head, piercing his slit with the tip. He had to let go of the curtain rod when it began to give beneath the strain as he tried to hold on.

He looked down then because he had to, and then he wished he hadn't. It had been bad enough feeling her hands and her lips. But seeing it . . . seeing her, her dark hair slick to her head, soap and water sliding over the pink centers of her breasts, the swell of her tummy hiding the thatch of dark hair beneath.

And then seeing her mouth wrapped around his cock, her fingers ringing him, those he couldn't see rubbing the strand of dangling pearls over his thighs, his cheeks, even his puckered rear hole.

She swirled the tiny hard beads around and around, sucking him hard as she pressed up against that sensitive spot. The combination was too much. He swore he was going to get her back. But getting her back was going to have to wait until he got off.

She rolled the pearls over his ass, the hard ridge of his erection, wrapped them like a cock ring around his sac and the base of his shaft. She held the constriction tight, loosened it, sucked him and squeezed him until he couldn't take it anymore.

He came, screwing his eyes shut as the white hot bursts pulsed free. She licked him clean, milked him with her mouth, taking it all until he hadn't a drop of cum left to give. He shuddered, felt the give of his knees, and leaned back into the wall.

She got to her feet and stepped into the spray, saying nothing, eyes closed as she reached for the small bottle of shampoo and washed her hair. He bent, reaching for the pearls she'd left on the floor of the tub, continuing to watch her bathe as he cleaned them.

She turned her back to him and rinsed her hair, her raised arms showing off the lean muscles in her shoulders and across her upper back, showing too the long line of her torso as it curved into her ass.

He was having a hell of a time keeping his hands to himself, his cock thickening again while he took her all in. She stepped around, sputtered when the water hit her in the face. He grinned because everything about her made him want to do just that.

And then he moved in. He wrapped one arm around her shoulders and brought her flush to his body. He also brought his mouth down to hers, tasting the salty hint of his own release but tasting more fully her sweetness and all the things about her that were good.

She whimpered and moaned, wrapped her arms around his neck and kissed him fiercely, her tongue tangling with his, sweeping through his mouth, her fingers kneading the muscles of his shoulders and neck. He grunted; her touch, her tongue, felt so good.

And then he slid his hand between their bodies and rubbed the pearls over one of her breasts, teasing her gumdrop nipple with the tiny little balls. She squirmed, bit at his lip, and he took the pearls lower, wrapping the strand around the fingers he slid between her pussy's folds.

He rubbed the necklace like a slick sex toy around her clit, over her lips, massaging them against her entrance until she dug her nails into his skin and tried to climb her way up his body. That was when he got serious, pushing two of his pearl-wrapped fingers into her sweet cunt, rubbing her G-spot while doing the same to her clit with his thumb.

He kissed her, fucked her with his fingers, moved

his other hand down her back to her ass, squeezing, kneading, slipping between her cheeks to press against her puckered opening the way she'd done with him. And all the while rubbing his aching cock against the warm wet skin of her belly.

The water beat down, the steam rose, and Georgia cried out, holding onto his shoulders as she came. She shook, quivered, reached down to where his thumb worked her clit and finished the job herself.

And then she reached for the bottle of conditioner, squeezed out a dollop, and grabbed his cock, slicking her palm over the head, around and around, and jerking him off.

He shouldn't have been able to come as fast as he did. He'd barely had time to recover his strength from the last two times. Didn't matter. He shot it all into her hand and over her belly, grinding against her and holding her close, his cheek next to hers, one hand cupping her head.

And then he heard her crying. Tiny sobs that he hoped to hell were either joy or exhaustion because those were the two sensations sucking him down. He held her, rinsed her, rinsed himself, turned off the water and dried them both.

Then he took her by the hand and dragged her back to bed, pulling the covers up to their heads and spooning himself around her. They would talk tomorrow. They had to. And they wouldn't talk about tonight. They would talk about business, about their plans for the day.

They would put the last few hours behind them, chalk them up to a much needed release from a hell of a day. Yeah. That's exactly what they'd do. Exactly. And he reminded himself for a third time when she sighed and snuggled against him, causing a burning, aching hitch in his heart.

Sunday

Sunday clears away the rust of the whole week.

—Joseph Addison, English essayist
(1672–1719)

March 3, 1993

Lying on his back in the bed he never turned down, Stanley McLain stared at the ceiling ten feet above his head. Ten feet, three-and-three-quarter inches if he wanted to be precise.

He'd made a ruler out of a strip of sheet one day and measured as far as he could, calculating the rest by the distance between the crevices where the cinder blocks met.

They were painted a soft yellow. A soothing color meant to remind him of butter and sunshine.

It reminded him instead of the curtains he and Sheryl had used in Georgia's room when she was born, and then again in Finn's until he got to be too much boy and protested.

Stan missed his children more than anything. He regretted that he'd ever gone to work for TotalSky when recruited by Cameron Gates. Regretted even more so requesting the transfer that had enabled him to work on the satellite contract with his friends, Arthur and Paul.

He should have thought of Georgia and Finn, and told the others what they were suggesting was impossible. But therein had lain his dilemma.

He *had* been thinking of his daughter and son, of the loss of their mother, of how his service to his country had left them with only Caroline to look after them at so many crucial times during their young lives.

One small alteration to the satellite specs was all it would take. Never again would he have to worry about his children being provided for.

After a few years, he would be able to resign his position and live for the rest of his life off the gains. Yes, they would be illegally obtained, but he'd felt it such a small crime when compared to what had been stolen from his children.

Of course he had been a fool, as most criminals were, thinking the plan infallible, not counting on the avarice of the outside party from whom he'd arranged to buy the parts.

Parts that had been the downfall of the TotalSky project, the satellites, and the lives of four men old enough and smart enough to know better than to try and pull the wool over Uncle Sam's eyes.

There was something weird going on with the trucker still broken down across the road. Finn knew it, and he was pretty damn sure Charlie knew it, too.

They were the only ones awake, the only ones who hadn't slept at all since the shutdown of the diner on Friday. Finn couldn't remember the last time he'd gone . . . how many hours *had* it been since he'd grabbed those six after arriving in Waco? Forty-two? Forty-four?

The worst part was that he didn't see himself catching any Z's for at least another thirty-six. And that was assuming Georgia made it back in one piece with the dossier, and Castro released them all to live happily ever after.

Somehow Finn didn't see that happening. Georgia might be familiar with Charlie, but Finn was familiar with Charlie's kind—the kind that did not walk away and leave evidence and witnesses behind.

The more likely scenario was that they'd all be tied to the grill and left to burn to a crisp when the diner "accidentally" caught fire.

As a private investigator, Finn was also familiar with stakeouts. And he'd be damned if that wasn't what was going on with the trucker across the road.

Sure, it was a holiday weekend, and they were all parked on a road less traveled. And yeah. There had been both state and county authorities who'd stopped. A couple of wrecker drivers, as well.

But the rig was still there, the driver in and out of the cab, tinkering with the engine, talking on his cell, gesturing and pacing like one pissed-off motherfucker. It was a hell of an act; he must have told some story to convince the cops not to tow him out of there.

Slumped down again in the booth where he'd started this really long weekend, his feet propped on the seat across from the one in which he now sat, Finn braced his elbow on the window ledge and pretended to sleep. Instead, he peered through the slit in the blinds.

The moon was up and full, the parking lot lamp shining down. If he could find a way to reflect a signal toward the truck's window, send an SOS to the driver . . . He watched the overhead light in the truck's cab come on. The man was up and awake while the thugs slept.

The timing couldn't have been better. Maybe Phil had a flashlight in the kitchen, though a penlight would work even better. A lighter or a match would do in a pinch. One of those small squeezable pocket lights would be perfect.

Unfortunately, he didn't see any way to get a full-sized light past Charlie and the thugs to actually use, and thinking further, anything involving fire would draw attention he didn't want. A smaller light he could probably manage.

He sat there for several more minutes, his gaze shifting between the big rig and the tabletop as he thought. He pulled a napkin from the holder and spread it open, then reached for a packet of sweetener, dumping the contents before folding the pink paper into an origami duck.

It was when the lamp in the lot flickered that he

realized exactly how shiny the top of the aluminum napkin case was. His heart thudded, skipping a beat.

The silver square would work as a mirror if he could pry it loose from the body and slip it between the blinds. And if he could keep Charlie from catching on while he did.

He lifted it from the table and set it next to his hip, continuing to dump sweetener packets and fold them into a whole gaggle. Fifteen minutes ticked by and not a word from the black hats, so he slumped all the way onto his spine and feigned sleep.

He moved the napkin holder into his lap and ran his fingers over the corners and edges, searching for a way to take it apart. It wasn't going to happen, not without a hacksaw and a whole lot of noise.

If he walked through the kitchen to the rest room, he might be able to pick up a spoon or a spatula. Except Charlie wouldn't let him make the trip alone.

He had to come up with something he could use here at the table, something on his person, or something in the rest room small enough to carry out in his pocket.

Eyes closed, he set the holder back beside him on the seat and began testing the flashing along the table's edge. The side facing out was corrugated and dull, but he held out hope the other side had the shine of a new penny.

Hell, at this point he was ready to try a fucking coin. Waco Phil's might be a hole in the wall but it was held together with a lot more than baling wire and spit.

As tired as he was, as bored as he was, Finn was pretty damn sure it was frustration topping his list of conditions. Tired could be solved with sleep, boredom with his origami barnyard. But frustration . . .

He scrubbed both hands down his weary face.

Phil was probably a lot more aware than Tracy of the reality of the situation they were dealing with here. There was a damn good chance his earlier prediction of an accidental kitchen fire would come true.

Getting out of here under their own steam had never seemed as much a necessity as it did now that he sat here alone in the dark. He thought about Georgia, hoped like hell she was all right, that she wasn't getting into one of her famous binds, which she'd need his help to get out of.

He hoped—hell, he even prayed—that the guy she'd gone off with was one of the good ones, that he'd stick with her, bring her back in one piece, watch over her until it was time . . .

Watch over her. Watch. Watch. Just like the big rig driver was watching over the diner. Someone knew they were there and was making sure they were safe. It was a long shot, yeah, but he was ready to lay down hard cash that's what the driver was doing.

There was no other reason that made a lick of sense for the cops to stop, then go on their merry way, for the tow truck drivers to do the same. The man had a story, one keeping him parked right where he was.

Then again, could be a case of delirium setting in. Cold cereal and no shut-eye was a recipe for mental disaster. And Finn could feel himself heading down that road.

He rested his head against the back of the booth and stared out the window through the slits between the blinds, tapping out the rhythm to the song running through his head on the tabletop with his thumbs.

He sang under his breath about trucking, about typical cities, about daydreams, rewriting the lyrics to sing about Houston being too close to Waco Phil's instead of New Orleans.

And then he saw it. The next line about New York flashed by the red lights on the rear of the rig. Same rhythm, never missing a beat.

He sang a bit louder, the line about lights shining down. And the damn truck came back with the staccato follow-up of "things lately occurring to me." He wanted to laugh. He wanted to cry. He was not losing his ever-fucking mind.

He kept singing. So did the truck. The driver was there and he was listening. Finn felt as if he'd just been rescued from a desert island by his long lost best friend.

Knowing someone had his back, that someone was listening to everything going on inside the diner, made the idea of falling asleep a whole lot easier to swallow.

Still, he ran one more test. "I'm going to take a nap. Blink once if you understand." The lights blinked, and Finn's chest expanded. "Blink twice if you'll be here in the morning." And the goddamned lights blinked twice.

Smiling, Finn closed his eyes, swearing he'd bend over, pull down his pants, and sell his soul to the devil if that's what it took to show his appreciation to the long-haired trucker for the save.

11:00 A.M.

They met Paul Valoren for brunch at an outdoor café, four hours before the auction. Georgia had made the arrangements yesterday while she'd been out of the room doing research, working out, and shopping. The weather was perfect, the sky clear, the breeze slight and cool.

Georgia was sweating like a pig. This was why she never bought nice clothes. She ruined them long before getting her money's worth. Though in this case it was Harry's money's worth he wouldn't be getting.

And, of course, he looked like a million trillion bucks. He also kissed like a million trillion bucks. Made love like a million trillion bucks. She could not believe all the things they had done.

In fact, when she woke up this morning, when she opened her eyes to find herself facing the drapes on the far side of her bed, she was certain it had all been a dream. That the time they'd spent in the shower had happened only in the privacy of her prurient imagination while she'd slept.

But then she'd stretched, feeling the ache of unused muscles in her lower back and her thighs, the burn of raw skin between her legs, and she'd cringed, rolling from one side to the other and encountering Harry's very large, very warm form.

He'd been snoring—but only lightly—and hadn't so much as budged at the contact of her shoulder to his. She hadn't asked him, even after he'd climbed out of bed an hour later, but she'd come away from those few minutes with the sense that it had been a long time since he'd let down his guard and given in to his body's need for sleep.

Real sleep. Deep sleep. Not the catnaps he'd taken since they'd checked into the room.

She didn't know what to think about the fact that he'd trusted her enough to show her that vulnerability. She'd thought about that a lot while doing her hair and makeup in the bathroom. The night before, first in bed, then in the shower, they'd both opened up; how could either of them not, in the face of such intimacy?

But this was different. Sleeping together. Baring that weakness, that basic human need rather than baring bodies. Funny how being naked together, making love together had been easier on her psyche than the time they'd spent silent in one another's company while getting dressed.

Neither had the drive from the hotel to the café been the piece of cake she was thinking of eating for brunch. Harry hadn't spoken a word. And hidden as his eyes were behind his sunglasses, she couldn't divine from them what he was thinking.

She'd stayed on her side of the massive bench seat and stared out her side of the car as they'd driven through town, getting more and more antsy as she thought of the meeting ahead and the afternoon's auction to follow.

Once they reached the café, Harry valeted Morganna, and they walked to the hostess stand with his hand in the small of Georgia's back. Where before such a gentlemanly gesture had felt like a show of good manners more than anything else, now the weight was heavy with a sense of possession, of ownership.

Her independent streak battled the idea fiercely, as did the wide swath of feminism cut into the fabric of the life she'd led. But her heart, the core of the woman she was, loved the idea of being Harry's. It made no sense. She barely knew him.

What she did know meant it was easy to go with her gut. He had her best interests at heart. He was working above and beyond to see that she didn't get hurt. He was sexy. He made her laugh. She'd been with him almost constantly for forty-eight hours and had missed him like crazy the few they'd been apart.

And now, as they approached the table where Professor Valoren had been seated, Georgia found herself slowing until Harry was at her side and she could take hold of his arm, squeezing his biceps, looking for strength. He patted her hand as they came to a stop and Valoren rose.

"Georgia. Harry. It's wonderful to see you again." He shook both of their hands, his jolly face beaming.

"Professor," Harry said, pulling out Georgia's chair and settling her in before he sat. "I hope you haven't been waiting long."

The older man returned to his chair, shaking his head as Georgia spread her napkin over her lap. "Only long enough to order a cup of hot tea. It's a quirk of mine, preferring hot to cold no matter the climate or temperature."

The server arrived then with his cup and saucer, along with a plate of lemon slices and a pitcher of cream. She took Harry's order for coffee and Georgia's for a Coke.

"My quirk," she confessed. "Sugar, caffeine, and carbonation with every meal."

Harry chuckled, reached for his own napkin, and the professor laughed. "You take after your father then. I can't remember him drinking anything except when he had a Coca-Cola can in his hand."

"I hadn't thought of that in years," Georgia said, feeling awash in wistfulness. "But you're probably right. I picked up his habit without even realizing it."

"I'd say that's not unusual, that we emulate those we love and respect." The professor stirred both sugar and cream into his tea. He placed the silver spoon on the saucer and lifted the cup to drink.

Georgia watched his lips purse, finding them thin, dry, expressionless, such a contrast to her father, who'd always been a boisterous clown. She remembered him drinking straight from a soda can, no glass, no straw, just gulping, often finishing off with a huge burp that resulted in rollicking laughter from both her and Finn.

She hadn't thought of that in so long, and missing that one little thing brought new tears to her eyes. Thankfully, Harry leaned forward, one forearm on the table, and filled the silence so she didn't have to try and find her voice.

"The symposium went well for you yesterday then," he said to the older man.

The professor nodded, sipped again. "Probably more than anyone else, I enjoy hearing myself speak. And the subject generated some excellent discussion."

"Then I'm doubly sorry we weren't there." Harry added a "thank you" to the server, who set his coffee and her glass of soda on the table.

"Are you a military man, Harry?"

"Three tours, the last spent in the Rangers." He drank his coffee black. "But I got an offer from the private sector that I couldn't refuse, so have been doing that for about a year and a half now."

"Oh?" Valoren's interest perked. "In what field?"

"Engineering."

As Georgia closed her menu and reached for her glass, the clog in her throat having cleared, the professor sat back and let his gaze drift from her to Harry. "Not that it's any of my business, but how long have you two been an item?"

"We're not," Georgia was quick to say before she even thought about the vibes they might be giving off today after last night. She could have kicked herself when Harry frowned. "We're just very close friends."

The professor nodded. "Good, good. One can never have too many."

Georgia wondered if he was thinking of her father, and could have kissed Harry for picking up the thread.

"You said you knew Georgia's father while you were in the service and working at TotalSky?"

The professor returned his cup to his saucer. "Yes. That's right. Though he was civilian and I was still in service for the duration of the contract."

The server returned then to take their orders, omelets for the men and a club sandwich for Georgia, not that she expected to eat a bite. And she lost even more of her appetite after glancing at her watch while the server picked up the menus.

Twenty-four hours. That was all the time she had to get back to Finn. She had absolutely no idea what she was going to do once they made it to the diner tomorrow. And she couldn't talk it over with Harry until after this afternoon's auction. Doing so would tip her hand.

She didn't doubt he'd be able to pull knives out of sleeves and rabbits out of hats until he found a workable solution to what was her problem, and only his by periphery. Getting started now would mean more time to do just that.

It would also mean confessing she had the dossier in her possession, and that she wasn't ready to do. Not until she was left with no other choice.

Was it fair to Harry? God, no. But she had to look at the bigger picture. He would be in and out of her life in a matter of hours. Her promise to her father, her responsibility to her brother, both of those had to come before any hurt she might cause the man she feared she was coming to love.

The thought made her sick. She felt as if her loyalties were being ripped like limbs from her body. She reached for her drink, her fingers shaking.

The glass hadn't even cleared the table before Harry's hand came down on her wrist. "Georgia?"

She smiled without meeting his eyes. "I'm fine. Professor, can I ask you a question?"

"Certainly, certainly."

She left the glass where it was, laced her hands in her lap, relishing the lingering warmth of Harry's touch. "My father would never talk to me about the case or the trial. He even made sure our nanny kept my brother and I away from the news. Since the records were sealed, I was never able to discover anything beyond the public accounts. And I've always wondered about one thing."

"What's that, my dear?"

"Did he ever give you or General Duggin any indication as to why he didn't fight harder to clear his name?"

The professor looked down, frowning as he removed his glasses and cleaned them with the napkin in his lap. "I believe the case against him was fairly compelling."

His response left Georgia taken aback. She'd expected an impassioned defense of her father, a heated condemnation of the injustice he'd suffered. And she got . . . acquiescence? "What I saw was circumstantial. As if the prosecution picked the best candidate to take the fall and didn't bother digging for the truth."

He shook his head as he returned his glasses to his face. "I hate to admit that I didn't keep up with all of the proceedings. I'd resigned my commission by then, and only flew into Washington when my testimony was required. Arthur was there through it all. Cameron came as he could—"

"Cameron?" Harry interrupted to ask.

"Cameron Gates. He worked with Stanley at Total-Sky, and was assigned along with Georgia's father to the satellite project."

"If I remember my history, the parts that failed were ones obtained from a Taiwanese manufacturer in violation of trade sanctions," Harry said.

Georgia nodded, but Valoren was the one who responded to Harry's remarks. "Those were the charges that sent Stanley to prison, yes. And he was responsible for procurement. But the testimony is not a matter of public record, and I'm afraid I cannot say more."

"Even now? All this time later?" Harry asked.

"I'm sorry. But yes. Even now," the professor said, growing quiet as their server delivered their food.

"What happened to Cameron Gates?" Georgia asked when they were once again alone, wondering why her father had never mentioned the fourth man either.

"I honestly have no idea." Valoren cut into his spinach and eggs with a vengeance. "It's been at least fifteen years since I've spoken to him. He left Total-Sky and was going into business for himself, but I don't know if the endeavor succeeded or if he's back in the corporate sector."

Georgia let Harry and the professor carry the rest of the meal's conversation and concentrated instead on all the things that weren't making sense. Surely this man, one who had worked closely with her father on the TotalSky project, knew he was innocent.

So why hadn't he fought harder to help prove it? And why was he so accepting of her father's fate?

Even though he'd denied knowing about the dossier Friday night, his reaction had her wondering if he shared the general's opinion that nothing in the file would change the public's opinion about the man her father had been.

Sandwich in hand, she started to ask if he shared the general's assessment, but stopped when she looked up and caught his gaze briefly before he returned his attention to his food. He'd left his expression open and unshielded only for a moment, but it was enough.

The hatred there, the fear, even the loathing . . . She suppressed a shudder as her queasy stomach turned. The emotion that had flashed so quickly might have been cause for a time-out, a second guess.

Except she had been the victim of retribution too many times to discount her instinct's insistence that he found her a threat.

She nibbled on her lunch and said nothing, let the conversation drift into the sort of small talk no one did better than virtual strangers.

No matter the connection Valoren may have had to her father in the past, he was nothing but a stranger, and one she was quite sure she didn't want to know.

What she did know was that at the first opportunity she needed to read the documents in the dossier and find out the part Paul Valoren had played in her father's downfall.

Because she didn't believe for a minute he was the innocent bystander he was claiming to be.

The drive from the café to the auction house took longer than Harry would've liked. He wanted to be in position early, to make contact with whichever operative had come down to get him out of this identity bind. He could bid on the lockbox himself if he had to, but didn't want to go that route.

Especially since he'd be bidding on the car. That was his cover, a collector of military memorabilia that ran to the motorized sort, not documents or photographs or stolen government files.

It had been a tough day, and his gut was telling him it was only going to get tougher. The hardest part so far had been the silence that had sprung up between him and Georgia. Last night . . . he couldn't even think about what had happened between them without getting hard.

Sitting through lunch with Valoren had been a true test of Harry's mettle. He'd listened to the conversation, participating as needed, primarily honing in on the subtext. To do that, he'd had to ignore the woman whose hidden vulnerabilities he'd taken to heart.

But something had happened during the meal. A shift in her mood that he could not overlook. It hadn't been about him. And he didn't think it had been in response to the conversation about her father.

No. It was connected to Valoren somehow. Something he'd said, a slip, a nuance. And then there was

Cameron Gates. Another name to have the SG-5 ops desk look into.

They could do that while he worked his mind around Georgia's response to Valoren's question about their relationship. Yeah, he would've denied they were a couple, too. But damn if she'd been fast on the draw.

His situation as an operative for an organization working under the radar of law enforcement, going, as Hank Smithson was known to say, where law-abiding pussies wouldn't to do what needed to be done didn't leave Harry a lot of personal time and space.

He was still relatively new to the team and feared fucking himself over by missing obvious clues, overlooking crucial intel, not keeping his head in the game. Getting involved with Georgia physically was one thing. But he couldn't—he wouldn't—bring his emotions into the mix when they were all tied up in the job.

Right. And that was why hearing her chop their relationship down to size—even though he would've done the same if he'd been the one to answer—had caused a sharp blip in his pulse.

They were involved. There was no case either of them could argue to make him believe otherwise. And as soon as her brother was safe and the Castro crew was out of commission, he and Georgia would be getting to the bottom of this thing they shared.

He pushed all of that away for now as they arrived at the auction, parking in the lot across the street from the Grace Emerald Gallery rather than giving up Morganna to a valet.

He didn't want to wait for the car to be brought around when they were ready to leave. He wanted the immediate access, the keys in his pocket, the advantage.

He turned off the ignition, hesitating before climbing from the car, glancing over at a very stoic Georgia, grinding his jaw as he asked, "Are you okay?"

A sad grin lifted both corners of her mouth. "I'm not even sure anymore. I had no idea forty-eight hours could be so exhausting."

They were bucking up against fifty-two, but he got the point, and figured correcting her would only make her feel worse. He stretched out his arm along the back of the seat. "Think you can make it through the next twenty-four?"

She shook her head, dropped it back onto the seat. "Do I have a choice?"

Smart woman to recognize that she didn't. He toyed with the strands of her hair that fell over his fingers. "I'm here, Georgia. I'm not going to make you go through this alone."

"I don't get it." She turned her head to look at him, her eyes wide, dark, damp. "Why are you here? I mean, forget last night. Why are you here?"

He would never forget last night. "Because Charlie sent me?"

Her expression said she didn't believe him. "That might be what got you here. But you didn't have to stay. I told you that."

"Yeah. You did. A whole lot of times."

"So why? I have to know." She closed her eyes, rubbed her cheek against his wrist. "It has to be about more than last night."

He looked at her face, at the stress lines bracketing her mouth, at the tiny crow's feet at the corners of her eyes. She smelled like fields of flowers, her hair, her skin, and it was as soft as petals.

They were going to have to deal with last night. And soon. He swallowed hard before he answered. "It's what I do. That's all."

Her eyes fluttered open. "Pulling rabbits out of hats?"

He shrugged. "Steak knives out of sleeves."

"Neither one seem like they have anything to do with engineering."

"They don't. They have to do with me." And that was the best he could give her right now.

Her smile softened. "A renaissance man?"

"Anything it takes."

She waited a minute before responding, smoothing down the suit skirt that cupped her ass like he wanted to do with his hands, toying with the buttons on the jacket that did God-fearing things to her cleavage.

He could hardly get his mind off her gorgeous body to listen to her question when she asked, "What is this going to take, Harry?"

"I don't know," he said honestly, because he was still working it out. He shook his head, went on to stroke her cheek. "Strange days, these last three. Strange people barging into your life."

"And one long strange trip," she said, a hitch in her voice. "Finn's always singing that song."

"He sounds like a good guy."

"He's great. The best. I don't know what I'll do if anything happens to him."

"Nothing's going to happen to him. I promise."

"How can you make a promise like that?"

"It's what I do."

"You say that a lot, you know. Makes me wonder exactly what kind of engineer you are."

"What?" Dimples appeared in the dark shadow of his beard. "I need to pull a set of blueprints out of my ass?"

She smiled, chuckled softly. "That's a start."

It was getting late. They needed to get inside.

"Hey, three or four hours from now, we'll be done, out of here, and on our way. You can hang in that long."

"We could go now."

He reached for his door handle. "I was just thinking the same thing. I need to see if my buddy made it down."

"No." She straightened, turned toward him, came alive. "We can leave. Just forget the whole thing."

Uh, okay. Where was this coming from? "Does the name Charlie Castro ring a bell?"

"You got in and out of the general's ranch without being seen," she said, gesturing animatedly. "I know for a fact there are guards, alarms, motion sensors, cameras"—she waved an encompassing hand—"all sorts of security measures in place to keep people out."

"That doesn't mean I can get into a one-room aluminum echo chamber with goons carrying live ammo holed up inside," he said more sharply than intended, but he couldn't afford for her to fall off the deep end now.

He reached across her, ignoring the feel of her body against his arm, the mingled scents that aroused him, and pushed open her door.

Then he sat back and opened his own. "We've got business to do. Let's get to it."

Georgia stood in the lobby of the Grace Emerald Gallery, people hovering all around while she waited for Harry. During her last visit here, she'd been a basket case, nervous, inept, drunk. This afternoon, she felt herself drifting in a strangely calm haze.

Conversation buzzed around her, neither words nor content sinking in. People moved to the left or to the right, dodging her where she stood in the middle of the wide walkway. She had only two things on her mind.

The fact that Harry and his friend were about to spend a whole lot of unnecessary cash, and the fact that she was going to let them.

There were words for women like her; in the past, she would have stepped up to anyone who called her such names. Now she was the one applying the labels and daring herself to deny she deserved every one.

But no amount of bitch-slapping would change the reality of the situation. She was doing what she had to do.

While still in the car, she'd tried—albeit weakly—to get Harry to forget the whole thing. To head back to Waco and find a way to get Finn and the others out of the diner without meeting Charlie's demands.

She should have known magic-hat Harry would have already realized they had no alternative but to finish what they'd set out to do. So here they were, doing just that. The calm was Georgia's only way to deal.

She glanced toward Harry where he stood talking privately with the man who'd arrived to help. She already felt like the lowest sort of scum, but learning the man was Harry's boss was enough to plunge her—and deservedly so—into a swill of bad behavior, an anchor of guilt keeping her down.

Her enjoyment at meeting Hank Smithson only compounded the fact that she felt like a shit. He was a true gentleman, boisterous and old school. A man of a different time. A man of her father's time, with the same sense of humor and love of life, and she'd taken to him immediately.

She moved out of the path of traffic and waited near the door, still watching Harry, the gestures of his hands as he talked, the way he bowed his head as he listened, hands moving to his hips, coattails flying behind him like batwings.

She took note of the way he nodded in response to whatever it was Hank said, not too much of a know-it-all to consider and appreciate the older man's input.

She hated that she and Harry had met under these circumstances because her lies and deceit meant this was it. One weekend. That was all they would ever—could ever—have. Tonight or tomorrow he would learn the truth.

She didn't see a way around the discovery. All she saw was loss. Her self-respect. His total respect, not to mention affection and companionship. She might even lose his help, though she knew he wasn't the type of man to leave a job half-done.

Her throat tightened, and she barely managed to keep tears from welling in her eyes. She was ready for the auction to get under way.

The sooner tonight and tomorrow were history, the sooner she could begin to repay the monetary debt she owed him. She would also be able to get her life back on track—a goal that three days ago held tremendous appeal but today seemed an afterthought.

But more than either of those, once the auction was over, the truth revealed, the weekend said and done, and her brother safe, she could start to work on a way to repay the rest of what she owed him. To give him the apology that was going to cut like a knife into her heart to deliver.

And then she would have to find a way to tell him good-bye.

She blinked hard and pasted on a smile as he and Hank walked toward her. And when Harry held out his arm, she stepped into the curve of his shoulder knowing it was where she was meant to be. "Are we ready?"

"Yes, ma'am," said the crusty old horseman. "Ready to kick ass and take names."

2:00 P.M.

The auction's three hours ticked by with an excruciating lack of anything resembling speed. The three hours that followed while buyers settled their accounts and picked up their goodies ticked by even more slowly.

For the actual event, Harry had chosen to stand at the rear of the crowded room rather than sit in the middle of an audience much more rabid than he was and risk falling asleep and drawing unwanted stares.

He made a lousy collector because a true Duggin fan would have reason to be all eyes and all ears and all interest. Harry was only here for a car, and even that was a sham.

Hank was the one who'd bring down the lockbox since he was the one who had Harry's back. Such was the way of the Smithson Group, one operative responding to another at the first call for help.

Harry's virgin assignment, and he drew the boss. When he'd walked into the lobby and found Hank waiting, he'd wondered whether to think of himself as a suck-up or a screw-off.

Hank had told him not to think of himself as either, that he didn't get out into the field as often as he liked, that the chance to do so now was saving him from a lot of down and dirty work at the farm that his bum hip just wasn't up to.

Harry knew from his partners that the Smithson Group principal would have traded in his horse farm for a full-fledged operative badge if he'd been physically able. Because he wasn't, he jumped at any chance that came his way to get involved in his "boys'" missions.

For the auction, Hank had sat close to the front of the room set up with rows of meeting hall chairs that faced the auctioneer and the tables of items for sale. Georgia had stuck close to Harry, looking like she'd stepped out of a fashion spread in a women's magazine.

She'd turned more than a few heads throughout the afternoon, and she didn't even seem to notice. When he'd been going over the game plan before the auction with Hank, she'd stood in the middle of the bustling crowd like a mannequin in a store display, aloof, unaware, alone.

He'd wanted to knock the teeth out of all the men who'd ogled, and tell the women who'd stared that they would look like puke wearing green. Mostly, he'd wanted to tuck her close to his body and show the world she was his.

He'd done the first at the earliest opportunity, feeling all puffy and emotionally bloated when she'd let him. He hadn't done the second because, well, he was still hung up between what was real and what was work and the responsibilities he had to the man sitting at the front of the room.

But now that the auction was over, now that he was the proud new owner of a car he had no use for, now that Hank was in possession of documents explaining Ezra Moore's identity to SG-5, Harry was ready to wrap up with Dallas and get back to Waco Phil's.

He'd settled his purchase with the cashiers, signed the legal documents the auction house and the estate required, promised his firstborn somewhere in the fine print, and walked away with the car's keys and title.

He found Georgia waiting for him beside the front door. "You look beat."

She pushed her hair out of her face with both hands. "I was trying to sleep standing up. You'll have to teach me that trick."

He swore he had never seen another woman's eyes that sizzled like this one's; even exhausted she looked like she still had another eight lives to live. "It takes time and a whole lot of practice. Think weeks at sea, days on horseback, a month of unrelieved guard duty. You learn to adapt."

She took the hand he offered and accompanied him outside. "How can you guard anything or anyone effectively if you don't get relief?"

"Good question," he hedged. "Here's another. Have you seen Hank?"

They stopped on the walkway beneath the portico, and she shook her head. "I've been watching for both of you. You made it out first."

"Not so fast with the conclusions, Miss McLain." At the sound of Hank's gravelly voice, they turned.

He walked up behind them, an unlit cigar held between two fingers, the lockbox tucked beneath his arm. "I can't abide pushing and shoving and greedy, grabbin' hands. This lot appeared to be a higher class of folk at first glance. Though bein' as old as I am, I certainly know not to judge a book by its cover."

"For some reason, whoever is managing the general's estate is in a huge hurry to settle everything this weekend," Georgia said.

She hadn't even asked about the box. As far as Harry knew, she hadn't even looked at it. Shock or exhaustion or post-traumatic stress. He didn't know which.

All he knew was that her lack of interest—after all they'd been through this weekend, after all she'd been through the last three years—raised one hell of a red flag.

He dangled the car keys in Hank's line of vision. "Trade you a 1948 Jaguar XK120 Roadster for that box you're holding."

Hank chuckled. "If not for the circumstances, I'd have a dad-blamed good time calling you sucker."

"If not for the circumstances, I wouldn't be making this fool's trade." Harry laughed, taking the lockbox from Hank's hands and passing him the keys. "We're parked across the street. I'd like to get this"— he patted the top of the metal box—"into Morganna's trunk."

Hank snickered. "You named the car Morganna?"

"Why not? She's got me under her spell."

At that, Georgia snorted and started walking toward the street. Harry watched her go, studied the set of her shoulders, the swing of her hips, wondered what he was missing because he was pretty damn sure he wasn't imagining things.

"Rabbit, my boy. I gotta say I expected a little more spark from that girl." Hank gestured with his cigar toward Georgia. "Especially if what's in this box"—he knocked his Naval Academy ring against the metal— "is as all fired important as you say. Which I'm beginning to think it ain't. And that your girl there knows it."

Hank was right. Something with Georgia's reaction just wasn't sitting right. Or maybe it was that she hadn't reacted at all. She hadn't looked at the box, hadn't mentioned it. All she'd done was walk away.

With a slap to Harry's back, Hank turned and did the same, leaving Harry standing alone on the walkway. Hefting up the lockbox, he jogged to the curb and caught up with Georgia in the middle of the street. Branches drooping low from trees on both sides met in the middle.

"Something wrong with your hands?" he asked as they made it across, stepped up onto the curb and into the parking lot on the other side.

She frowned, held out both palms, turned them down, wiggled her fingers. "No, why?"

"Because I figured they'd be all over me by now," he said, walking to the back of the car.

Georgia followed, crossed her arms over her chest. "We've had sex a couple of times, so now you think I can't keep my hands to myself?"

A couple of times. Or three or four. He dug into his pocket for his keys. "Uh, I'm talking about the lockbox, Georgia."

She didn't respond except to uncross her arms and lean a hip against the car, watching as he opened the trunk and set the box inside. He shrugged out of his suit coat, tugged his tie from his shirt collar, zipped both into his bag, lying flat on the floor of the trunk. And she still didn't speak.

He left the trunk open as he cuffed up his shirt-sleeves. "What's going on, Georgia? We haven't come this far for you to flake out on me now."

Her shoulders drooped, she shook her head. "Honestly? I think I'm numb. I don't feel . . . anything. I don't understand. I do know it doesn't make sense, because I should be jumping for joy. But there's nothing there."

He waited for a minute, then offered her the lock-box combination. "Do you want to do the honors?"

She looked from his hand to the box in the trunk and hesitated. "You know what? It's going to sound stupid to you, but I want to get out of these clothes before I do anything."

He lifted a brow. "I thought you said you weren't having trouble keeping your hands to yourself."

"I don't mean get out of my clothes for sex." She reached for her duffel bag, jerked it forward. "I mean get out of these clothes and back into my jeans and boots so I'll feel more like me."

"Then I'll wait. After three years, you deserve to be the one to let Pandora out of her box."

"I don't think that's the mythology," she said, opening her bag just enough to pull out a change of clothes. "Let me do this, I'll use the ladies' room in the gallery, and then can we get out of here? Go some place quiet?"

"Sure," he said, nodding. "I know the perfect country road. It leads from here to Waco."

"Thanks," she said, shoving her duffel deeper into the trunk. "I'll be right back."

He watched her walk back across the street, though the way she moved was more of a sexy high-heeled run, her hips swinging as she bounced from the toes of one foot to the other.

He remembered the feel of those legs wrapped around him, realized what he was about to do meant he would never have that pleasure again. Betrayal tended to do a number on passion. He reached for the duffel bag she'd shoved deep into the back of the trunk.

He loosened the cords, tossed back the flap, and pushed aside jeans and T-shirts, her camouflage pajamas, that amazing little black dress, more jeans, socks, a toiletries bag, moving to the opposite end where he found the satchel, and inside of that, the portfolio she'd used for cover during yesterday's visit to the general's estate.

He glanced toward the gallery, knowing she'd barely had time to make it into the rest room, but still feeling the need to cover his ass. He lifted the portfolio free and flipped it open. There was nothing on the first page of the legal pad but a lot of notes.

This is the ugliest excuse for a couch I've ever seen. Chair cushions with scenes from fairy tales woven into the tapestry coverings? Maybe for a six-year-old girl, but a three-star general? These lamps might bring five bucks in a garage sale.

He laughed. He couldn't help it. The woman was incorrigible, and loving that about her made what he was doing even harder to do. But he moved on, flipping through the rest of the pages, finding nothing, and only noticing the folder tucked behind the legal pad when it slipped to the side.

He pulled it out, felt a surge of adrenaline when he saw the red classified stamp on the cover. One quick glance inside, at the word TotalSky, and that was it.

He dropped the folder into the trunk, carefully returned the portfolio to the satchel inside the duffel bag, closed it up, and shoved it into the depths of the trunk.

He'd just lifted up the first layer of carpet and begun pulling back the second, which covered the third, which hid the fireproof safe built into the wheel well, when he heard the crunch of tires on gravel behind him and the unmistakable sound of an engine built over fifty years earlier.

He turned, watched Hank drive up behind the Buick, his cigar stub in the corner of his mouth, one hand on the roadster's wheel. His other hand was busy stroking the paint of the convertible's door.

"Never thought I'd be leaving Texas with something this sweet."

Harry glanced toward the gallery before picking up the TotalSky folder, walking over, and dropping it into the passenger seat. "And it only gets sweeter."

9:00 P.M.

Her expensive shoes wrapped up inside the expensive suit she'd folded as neatly as she could in a bathroom stall, Georgia looked both ways, then stepped out into the street.

In the parking lot on the other side, she could see Harry talking to Hank, who sat behind the wheel of the car Harry had purchased. She'd wondered how he was going to get it home since he already had Morganna to take care of.

She also wondered what he was going to name the Jag. It was a tight little thing. Racy. Sleek. It reminded her of Marilyn Monroe, with its perfectly balanced curves and creamy blond paint job.

Hank raised his hand in farewell just as she stepped up onto the curb; he saw her and included her in his wave. She waved back, thinking Harry had a hell of a good thing going for him.

He'd told Valoren that he'd been working in engineering for eighteen months. He'd told her that he was on vacation, having a couple of weeks coming to him.

She thought for half a second that she should give up treasure hunting and take up project consulting just for the perks because she had seriously forgotten why she loved what she did.

She used to know, back when she did it for fun and profit rather than for personal reasons, which now had her up to her eyeballs in hot water.

Harry was waiting for her to open the lockbox. She had yet to come up with another viable excuse to delay. And since she was about ten steps from being out of time, she was left with little choice but to try and act her way out of the very thing he expected her to do. She walked up to Harry just as he slammed shut the trunk. Good. A reprieve.

She put the onus back on him. "Either you opened the box without me and have bad news, or you've changed your mind."

He nodded, started walking toward the driver's side door. "The latter. This isn't the time or the place."

Relief fluttered its wings all around her. She lifted the bundle she held. "What about my clothes?"

"Toss 'em in the backseat. I'll put up the top."

She stood back and watched while he did. "I like your boss."

"Yeah. He's a great guy."

"Nice of you to let him take off in your ninety-thousand-dollar car."

Harry unsnapped the cover locking the car top in its well and began to unfold the accordion-like frame. "I know where to find him."

"Not a bad trade-off, I guess. A long vacation after less than two years on the job in exchange for use of the Jag."

That shut him up. She went on. "Makes me wonder if what you do for him has anything to do with engineering at all. Especially if he recruited you out of the Rangers."

He finished hooking the top into place. "Are you ready to go?"

Since he wasn't going to address her observations, she supposed she was. She'd gotten the breathing room she needed and—

"Ms. McLain? Georgia McLain?"

She turned to see an older man hopping onto the curb and walking toward them. "Who's asking?"

"My name is Marvin Katz. I am, or I was, Arthur's attorney." He held out his hand.

She shook it as Harry walked up behind her. "Can I help you with something?"

Katz referred to a business-size envelope he held in his hand where he'd apparently jotted his crib notes. "You are Georgia Tillie McLain? Daughter of Stanley Dean and Sheryl Annette McLain? Sister to Finneas Scott?"

All she could think of was how funny it was to hear her brother called Finneas. Until she heard Harry snicker and ask, "Tillie?" She elbowed him in the stomach. "That's me."

Nodding, the attorney reached into his coat pocket and handed her a business card. "I need to get in touch with your brother, as well."

She was still wondering how he'd found her, but her stomach churned thinking of Finn. "Finn's not available. It may be several days before I can get in touch with him."

"Hmm. Well, if the delay can't be avoided—"

"Sorry. It can't."

"Then could you be at my office tomorrow morning at nine? I'll have to speak with your brother at a later date."

Frowning, Georgia stared down at the business card. "What's this about, Mr. Katz?"

He glanced over her shoulder at Harry, who started to back away. She reached out and grabbed him by his shirt. "Harry's a friend of mine. I don't mind him hearing whatever you have to say."

"It's in regard to the reading of Arthur Duggin's will."

"And that affects me how?"

"He has made a bequest to you."

A bequest? To her? She didn't understand. She already had the dossier. "Is it the correspondence from my father?"

"The paperwork that outlines the bequest is at my office."

Harry stepped up then. "But you don't need the paperwork to tell Miss McLain what it is."

"No, but I do have a letter from the general that I'm required to give you at the time the will is read."

Georgia couldn't even focus. She only knew one thing. "I can't be there in the morning. It's impossible."

"Hmm. That does complicate things."

"Give her the letter tonight," Harry put in. "We can go to your office now."

"It is rather late, but I suppose that solution would work."

"Then let's go." Harry took both the business card and the clothes Georgia was still holding from her hands. The clothes he dropped through the open window into the backseat.

The card he simply flicked once. "We've got the address, we'll meet you there."

Katz's office was a short drive from the gallery in Oak Lawn, a trendy neighborhood of old homes converted into creative studios and office space.

Harry pulled into the driveway behind Katz's Volvo and stayed in the car while Georgia and the attorney went inside.

He could have insisted on joining her, but she hadn't asked, and he was glad. He needed to contact Simon and let his partner know that he and Georgia were on the way back.

The lockbox content was now a moot point. And a big fat albatross of one at that. Georgia wasn't going to want to open it since doing so would put her in the position of having to feign distress she obviously didn't have energy to feign.

And he wasn't too thrilled about having to falsely console her false angst and swear to find another way to take Charlie down. Harry's energy was better spent working to do just that.

He waited until he saw lights inside come on with a warm golden glow before reaching beneath his seat into the compartment that held his satellite phone. He dialed the ops center, asked to be put through to Simon.

"And it's a goddamn boring night here at Waco Phil's, so give me something to talk about lest I start dreamin' about your mama."

Harry rolled his eyes. "Guess a trucker's life's not for everyone."

"Rabbit, that is a mouthful and a half. Though I have caught up on my *Buffy* DVDs. I'm up to season four."

Harry tried not to laugh. He figured he didn't have a lot of time. "I'll be there before dawn. What's the plan?"

"Lose your car at the airport. There's a beater there with your name on it." He told Harry where to find it parked and where the key was stashed. "Remember the wrecking yard?"

"Half a click south."

"Right. Leave the car there and then use the brush along the road for cover. Oh, and there's a shield and ID stashed with the key."

"Yeah? Who am I?"

"FBI, boo. We're staking out the lot. Top secret. Locals are probably waiting for a heroin bust."

This time Harry did laugh. "You're a mean man, Baptiste."

"Just dumping another load of bad shit onto the rep of my favorite agency."

Simon definitely had tales to tell. But old home week was over. The light inside the house had gone off. "Look for us around one."

"Just don't forget the secret knock," Simon said, and rang off.

Harry had just shoved the phone away when he looked up to see Georgia coming down the front porch steps two at a time. He pushed open his door and got out, meeting her halfway across the yard and walking her to her side of the car.

She didn't say anything. She didn't reach out, didn't respond when he touched her shoulder, when he reached for her hand. All she did once he'd opened her door was slide into her seat.

She clutched an envelope in one hand. "Can we go, please?"

"Sure," he said, closing her door and heading back to his. He cast her a quick glance as he backed out of the driveway, his arm along the seat. "You okay?"

She nodded, shook her head, let it fall back against his hand. "I don't know. Is shock good or bad?"

"Depends. Is it the kind of shock where I need to grab a blanket from the trunk, lay you down, elevate your legs? Maybe loosen your jeans, since they look pretty tight?" He caught the hint of a smile and it lightened the weight of worry on his heart. "Or is it something you'll get over here in a few and can then tell me about?"

"The latter. Just . . . give me a few minutes."

He did, maneuvering his way through the neighborhood, into the city and out again, picking up the main artery south to Waco, then cutting east on a lesser traveled road. He couldn't say he'd ever been happier to leave a place behind, and had to imagine Georgia felt much the same.

She waited until they'd been on the road for fifteen minutes before she said anything about what had happened. And then what she said left him speechless. "He willed me everything. Well, half of everything. I'm assuming he left the rest to Finn."

"Everything? As in, everything?"

"Yep. The proceeds from the sale of his properties. His investment portfolio. His liquid assets. I quit counting the zeros at seven."

"This is the general you're talking about?"

"No. Mr. Katz." She propped her boots on the dash, a really bad habit that was hell on Morganna's interior. "Yes, the general. I met the man once. Finn's never met him at all. And *I* wouldn't have had reason to if not for my father's insistence that I find out the truth about TotalSky."

Harry frowned, his thoughts clicking. Nothing he knew about Arthur Duggin's life would lead him to believe the man's net worth had reason to run that high. Granted, he didn't know much. And seeing the spread south of Waco and the Highland Park estate had sent his rabbit ears twitching.

It was obviously a clue he should have followed up on. Either the general had been living above his means, or he had a means Harry needed to look into. "So what's with the envelope?"

She held her fists wedged between her knees. "It's a letter. Supposedly explaining everything."

"Are you going to read it?"

"It's too dark."

He reached beneath her raised thighs and opened the glove box. The light came on automatically, shining down on the Mediterranean blue carpet. "It's a map light. Bright enough to use to read anything."

She didn't move. She just stared ahead into the darkness. "I don't know if I want to."

"You're not curious?" He sure as hell was.

"I don't like it. The whole thing. It's not right."

"That you're suddenly a millionaire?"

She gave a hoarse cackle. "It's a joke, you know. It has to be. I'll open this letter and there will be all sorts of stipulations attached."

"Did Katz tell you there were any?"

"No."

"Then there aren't." Harry flashed on his high beams, illuminating the long dark road ahead. "He would've been legally bound to spell it all out."

"Are you suddenly an attorney as well as a mysteriously well-compensated engineer?"

"No. I'm someone with enough common sense to see that you're putting off the inevitable because you're afraid you won't like what you find out." And if that wasn't an identifiable human trait, he didn't know what was. "Just rip off the bandage and get it over with."

And she did.

Georgia's hands shook as she unfolded the two hand-written sheets. She dropped her feet to the floor and hunched forward, glad that Harry had put up the car's top. She was quite sure the wind would've whipped the reasons for her new tax bracket right out of her grasp had he not.

She shoved the envelope into the glove box and ran her index fingers over the back side of the fold to straighten the paper. The general's handwriting was bold, the letters formed with large loops and sharp slashes. "*Dear Georgia. I hope you don't mind me calling you Georgia even though we don't know one another well.*' Hey, Arthur, whatever floats your boat."

Harry chuckled. "You never mentioned you two were on a first name basis."

Georgia spared a quick glare for Harry. "My world is upside down. I have no time for what you try to pass off as humor." She took another breath and forged on. "*You are, after all, the closest thing I have to a family of my own.*' What a load of crap."

"How many times did you say you visited him?"

"One. Just one. When I went to ask him for the dossier." When she had pleaded her father's case and received a lecture suggesting an attitude adjustment in response. "I don't even get where he's coming from."

Harry rolled his window up an inch. "Uh, maybe

you should read further before jumping to that conclusion? Just consider it another bandage, and rip."

She rolled her eyes. She hated it when Harry made sense. Hated it even more when he saw through her delay tactics. She smoothed her fingers over the crease again. "*I know you're doubting my sincerity, and I don't blame you. We never did come to a meeting of the minds. That's something I regret, but which I also fully understand. Were I in your position now, I would no doubt find my affection for you rather odd.'*"

She lifted her gaze, stared straight ahead into the darkness beyond the reach of Morganna's lights. Great. Now *she* was referring to the car by the name Harry had christened her. That seemed even more twisted than using the gender specific pronoun. Cars were objects, not people—

"Georgia?"

She squeezed her eyes closed. "I don't want to know about his affection for me. I want to know about his betrayal of my father."

Harry held out his hand. "Give it here. I'll read it."

"You can't read and drive at the same time."

"So you do know all my deep dark secrets."

It was more like she didn't want him knowing hers. "I'll read it. You keep your eyes on the road so you don't hit any bunnies or skunks or puppies or anything."

"Puppies?"

She ignored him and cleared her throat. "*When you came to me three years ago after your father's death, I wasn't surprised. Stanley was the last to agree to our proposal, and was never completely gung-ho once our alliance set things into motion.'*"

A sickening sensation settled in her stomach, but

she continued to read, drawn toward the oncoming train. "*He told me that you and your brother were the reason for his decision to go forward with our plan. He felt it was his only way to give back all that had been taken from the two of you. I promised him then that I would see to your future should anything happen to him. As we both know, it did.*

"*'By now, you're wishing I would get to the point. Once I explain, you'll understand why I could not give you the dossier when you asked. You see, Stanley was as much a part of the TotalSky scandal as I was. But we were not alone. As I swore to your father to look after you, I swore to the others I would never speak to anyone of the deal we had made.*

"*'I was honest with you about the file's contents. Nothing inside would change the public's perception of your father. The extent of your father's involvement was spelled out in the charges against him, though the details are not mine to reveal. I give you that much only to explain my bequest. I hope that knowing he was looking out for your well-being will ease the sense of betrayal you must feel.'* "

Betrayal? Was he kidding? What she was feeling was rage. The man was a fucking liar. Her father had told her not to let the truth go unknown. He had to have known what Duggin would try to pull.

She slammed her feet against the floor, looking for the brakes. "Stop the car. Now." Harry began to slow, edging toward the shoulder at a snail's pace. "Hurry up. Stop the car."

"I'm stopping as fast as I can, sweetheart. Morganna needs more than a dime."

By the time he had the car off the road, she had her door open and was running around to the trunk. Ugh. She didn't have keys! She scrambled around the side, slipping and sliding on gravel, reaching his door just as he opened it.

"Open the trunk. I need my duffel."

"Georgia. We need to talk."

They could talk later. She had three years of her life, her father's reputation, her brother's head on the line. "Harry, please. This is important."

"So is what I need to tell you," he said, sliding the key into the lock, turning it, lifting the trunk's heavy lid as if purposefully moving in slow motion.

"Tell me later," she said, shoving the lid up and out of his hand and diving for her duffel. She loosened the straps, pulled back the flap, opened the bag wide, and reached for the satchel containing the portfolio and the dossier inside.

She came out with the first and the second. She was missing the third. She tossed the satchel and leather binder to the road and dragged her bag closer, rifling through T-shirts and jeans and undies and the dress for which she still needed to repay Harry and . . . nothing. It wasn't there.

"It's not here," she cried, turning to look up at him. "I had it. I found it. It's gone."·

"I know," he said. And he didn't even ask what she was talking about.

"What the hell do you mean, you know? How can you know? When—" She cut herself off. She'd left the bag in the trunk, left Harry at the car when she'd gone into the gallery's rest room to change. He'd fucking searched her things?

How dare he! How *dare* he. How dare he take what was hers! It didn't matter that she'd stolen it, never told him, deceived him into having his boss spend thousands of dollars on a box full of worthless papers because it *might* be there.

What mattered was that he'd been equally dishonest with her . . . and she'd never suspected. Except she had, hadn't she? She'd suspected more than once that he wasn't the engineer he said he was.

She rubbed her fingers over her forehead, squeezing her headache out through her ears. "Where is it? No, wait." She held up one hand. "That's not what I want to know. Why, Harry? Tell me why."

He stepped back, snagged the portfolio and satchel from the ground, tossed it on top of her things, then slammed shut the trunk. "I told you, Georgia. We need to talk."

Monday

*On Monday mornings I am dedicated to the proposition
that all men are created jerks.*

—H. Allen Smith, American writer
(1906–1976)

Harry stared down at his hellcat. She was livid. In tears. Shaking. He couldn't blame her for a single one of the reactions. And after seeing her dive across the table at Charlie Castro, he'd expected a whole lot worse.

He shoved his hands to his hips, studied the gravel and concrete beneath his feet, seeing only what was illuminated by the light from the moon.

He still wasn't sure how much to tell her, whether to bring her in or keep her on a need-to-know basis. Problem with that argument was that she was already in, and her need to know was critical.

"Harry?"

He looked up. She stood in front of him, small, shivering, her arms wrapped around her middle. He started with the simple truth. "It's what I do, Georgia. That's all."

"That's not all. And it sure as hell isn't enough." She advanced, slammed a hand down on the trunk. "And what the hell is it that you do? You've said that all weekend."

"Let's get in the car."

"No. I want to know what you did with my dossier."

"It's not yours. Not anymore."

She spun where she stood, came back around and stomped her foot. "What are you saying? Where is it?"

"Georgia—"

"No, Harry." She was crying now, sobbing, scream-ing. "I need those papers. I need them. I have spent three years hunting them down. You can't just take them away."

He took her by the arm then, brought her around to the driver's side of the car and urged her in. She didn't fight him, but scrambled back into her seat and collapsed. Neither did she pick up the letter she'd dropped to the floor without having finished reading.

He turned toward her, made sure he had her at-tention. Her eyes were wet and wild, and more angry than hurt. "I'll tell you what I can, but we've got to get back on the road."

"Afraid you'll be late for a consulting appoint-ment?" she practically sneered.

"Yes." He put the car back into gear and spun the tires pulling onto the road. "There's only one thing that matters here. And that's getting those people out of the diner."

"Right. And how are you going to do that since you have nothing to bargain with?"

"Who says I have nothing? I have the lockbox you were sent to find."

"With nothing inside."

"Charlie doesn't know that."

Georgia jammed her crossed arms tightly against her chest. "You don't really think he's going to let everyone go without looking to see what's inside."

"I never said that he would."

"Then what are you going to do?"

"Make him an offer he can't refuse."

At that, she hopped around on the seat, her exas-peration evident. She couldn't sit still. And then there was her tone of voice.

Strident, with just a hint of condescension. "He's

got manpower you don't have, Harry. Manpower with big bad guns. This isn't some game you've been pulled into playing."

"I've told you before. There's a reason they call me Rabbit." Though he doubted she found anything in the reminder reassuring.

"So what? You took the dossier to pull out of your magic hat and use against Charlie somehow?"

He draped one wrist over the steering wheel and cast a glance toward her. "Aren't you at all interested in who hired Charlie to find it? And why?"

"If I had a way of finding that out, I might bc. I don't. I'm a treasure hunter. Not a cotton-tailed spy." She ran both hands through her hair and sighed. "Anyway, right now my main interest is why the hell you took my property and when you're going to return it."

He was stuck thinking about her cotton tail and took a moment to respond. "You mean the general's property, which you stole over twenty-four hours ago and never bothered to mention?"

"If you had known I had it, you would've turned it over to Charlie. I couldn't let that happen." She drew her knees up into the seat and turned to face him. "At least that's what I thought then. I'm not sure what I think now."

He wasn't quite ready to make things any clearer, which it appeared she was waiting for him to do. "So you let me use my resources to find you another way out of your mess?"

"Yes. I did. And you can't tell me you wouldn't have done the same thing in my shoes."

"You're right. I don't know what I would have done if I were you. But I do know what I had to do as me."

Another few miles rolled by, another few minutes

ticked along with the sound of the tires on the road. It was dark, the light from the moon all that was left since Georgia had closed the glove box.

He felt her gaze moving over him as she tried to figure him out. He weighed giving her a brief explanation. It wasn't like she would ever know what she would need to find him again.

And taking what she did know to the authorities wouldn't be in her best interest any more than his. But he didn't like the idea of disappearing from her life and leaving her in limbo.

Hell, he didn't like the idea of disappearing from her life at all. In fact, it didn't take much imagination for him to picture the two of them driving until they hit the beach in Venice and never going home.

"Who are you, Harry?" she asked, her voice soft, wounded, sad. "Tell me. I'm hardly in a position to reveal your deep dark secrets to anyone unless I want to end up in jail again."

Same train of thought he'd been traveling. Still, he pressed. "For what?"

"Let's see. Impersonating whoever I impersonated and stealing the file from the general's house. Not going to the cops about the siege at the diner and letting Charlie get away with his crime."

"He hasn't gotten away with anything yet," he reminded her.

She snorted. "Unless you're going to pull a supernatural SWAT team out of your hat and morph through the walls in energy particles, I don't see any way around it. Which means I'm up shit creek for being an accomplice or an accessory or just a really bad American citizen."

Oh, ye of little faith. Though he did like the *Star Trek* concept. "You think I'd let that happen? Let you take the fall for doing what you had to do to save your brother?"

"You took my dossier."

"That's business."

"What sort of business? Because I'm pretty damn sure there are no blueprints of any kind in that file."

This was where things got sticky. Staring into the darkness at the long stretch of road, he said, "I'm not an engineer."

"Now there's a surprise. Or not."

He ignored her sarcasm. "I work for a private organization. We help people in trouble, and we do what we can to make sure the bad guys pay."

"Bad guys like Charlie?"

"Usually we work on a larger scale. But, yeah. Bad guys like Charlie."

She was quiet for several minutes, several miles. He could almost see the scales moving as she weighed his admission against her suspicions. "It wasn't an accident that you came into the diner, was it? You were looking for Charlie."

Half-right anyway. "It wasn't an accident, no. But I wasn't looking for Charlie."

"You were looking for me?"

"I was looking for the dossier. You just happened to be my connection."

"How? How did you make it? No one but Finn knew that I was chasing it down."

"Charlie did," he said, listening to the gears click in her mind.

"If you and Charlie both thought you'd find the dossier through me, then you've got to know who sent him to find it."

"I'm getting close to figuring it out." He was, in fact, down to two names. Paul Valoren and Cameron Gates.

"I can't believe this. I cannot believe this," Georgia said, collapsing against the corner where the seat met the door. "I've been beating myself up about taking advantage of you—"

"And I've been the one doing the taking all this time."

She turned her head, stared out the windshield. "So what now? Are you going to give it back to me?"

"Do you want it back?"

"Why wouldn't I?"

"After reading the general's letter, I wasn't sure you would want to know what's inside."

"I have to know what's inside," she said, toying with the frayed edge of a hole in the knee of her jeans. "It's the only way to find out the truth about my father."

"Even if it's not what you're expecting to find?"

Her head whipped around. "Why? What will I find?"

"I don't know yet. It's on its way to our ops center to be analyzed."

"Ops center? What? You really are James Bond or something?"

"Or something, yeah."

"Where is your ops center?"

"New York."

"Did your personal carrier pigeon swoop down from the trees at the gallery and carry it off?"

He laughed to himself. "I wondered if you would figure out when I took it."

"It's the only time you could have. I haven't let you and the dossier out of my sight at the same time since finding it."

"Since stealing it, you mean."

"Semantics. And since that was only a few hours

ago . . ." She sat up straighter, shook her head in disbelief. "You gave it to Hank, didn't you?"

"He's the boss."

"Does that mean you didn't lie to me about everything?"

"I didn't lie to you about a lot of things, Georgia. Only about the job."

"Yeah," she said with a snort. "Your whole reason for being here."

She was right. This entire weekend past had been a lie. Sixty or so hours' worth of deception. Except for their time in bed. Every one of those minutes of intimacy had been real.

Nothing in his life had ever been more so, and that much she needed to know. "I didn't lie about us."

She tried to huff, but he heard her voice quaver. "You mean the sex."

"I mean us. Making love. Being with you that way was as real as it gets. You have to know that."

"Does it matter?"

It mattered almost more than his job—a realization that had been eating him up since last night. He didn't want to screw up his position with SG-5, but neither did he want to lose Georgia.

Not when everything he felt for her seemed so damn real, so damn right. "It matters. More than anything."

"That's not so easy to believe when you took away the one thing I valued most in the world."

"More than your brother's life."

"No. Of course not."

"More than your own?"

"No."

"I can't begin to know what your life has been like,

Georgia. But I do know it will go on no matter what your father did or did not do."

She let that sink in, riding in silence as they approached the Waco city limits. "So why are you sticking around?"

"What do you mean?"

"You have what you want. Why not go on your merry way? Move on to the next bad guy. Leave me to deal with Charlie. You have no real stake in what happens."

"That's not who I am, Georgia. And I'm pretty damn sure you know that by now."

She blew out a heavy breath. "I don't like being kept in the dark, Harry. I don't like being deceived."

He wasn't sure how much of her statement was directed at him and how much toward her father. He gave her what he could while making the turn into the airport and following Simon's instructions on where to find the car.

"Right now, there is a tractor-trailer rig parked on the side of the road across from the diner. It's been there since Friday night."

"What? I don't understand. And what are we doing at the airport?"

"Patience, grasshopper," Harry teased, pulling into the space nearest to the old pickup Simon had described. He turned off the car and climbed out, heading for the trunk and his bag there.

Georgia slammed her door and followed him to the rear of the car, watched while he stripped off his dress shirt and pulled on a long-sleeved black tee.

He tossed her one, too. "Here. Put this on."

She moved her gaze from his chest to the shirt she held. "I'm not stripping in a parking lot."

"Put it on over what you're wearing. You can take it off when we get there."

"Get where?" she asked, tugging the shirt over her head.

"To where we're going." He toed off his dress shoes, pulled on combat boots, laced up the legs of his suit pants inside. "Anything in here you need between now and tomorrow?"

"Between now and later today, you mean?" He nodded. She shook her head. "Nothing as valuable as there was a few hours ago."

"I'll get it back to you. I promise." He slammed the trunk. And then, because he loved the way she looked swallowed up in his shirt, he hooked his elbow around her neck and pulled her close for a kiss.

It was a kiss long overdue, and he made sure she knew it, opening his mouth over hers and sliding his tongue inside the minute she parted her lips.

He made it fast, made it hard, and then stepped away, taking her by the hand and hauling her cute little ass to the truck.

1:30 A.M.

They drove the rust bucket of a pickup back toward Waco Phil's, stopping a third of a mile away at a wrecking yard filled with similarly disreputable vehicles.

Harry warned her on the drive that they'd be making the last leg of the return journey on foot. She was in shape. The night was cool. She didn't mind.

What she did mind was still not knowing what was going on. Harry seemed more into giving orders than sharing the steps he'd mapped for her to follow.

Focusing on the moment had to be her priority. She'd think about the general's letter and bequest, about the truth surrounding her father, when Finn's life was no longer on the line. For now, getting him back in one piece was all that mattered.

Harry was right about that. Harry was right—an expert, even—about a lot of things. And no wonder.

The man spied for a living. He had resources and contacts and who knew what else at his disposal—obviously not everything on the right side of the law.

She couldn't compete with that. She was surprised he was even letting her tag along. He was in survival mode now, silent, intense, a man apart.

And she swore standing there in the airport parking lot that she could have kissed him forever.

As much as he had taken from her, he had given back—was still giving back—even more. He didn't have to be here. She'd told him so many times that he could have left her in Dallas to fend for herself.

What she hadn't known until tonight was that he'd stayed even after his own job was done. He hadn't returned to his mysterious ops center along with Hank and the dossier. He'd remained behind. With her. For her.

Then he'd pulled her close and kissed her as if needing her at his side, as if finding his own strength in having her with him as his partner, his lover, his woman. She'd felt drawn to be every one, almost as if she'd found everything she'd been searching for all of her life in Harry.

It was ridiculous. Attraction and lust, sure. Those she understood; they took no time, struck like lightning. But not honest affection and the sort of emotional hunger she felt for Harry. Surely true love didn't happen over a weekend. Especially not a weekend rampant with lies.

Walking ahead of her by three or four steps, Harry glanced back, smiled, urged her on. He made it easy for her to push herself, trusting her, encouraging her, slowing when his long legs took him too far ahead.

But really? Walking behind him, watching his body in motion—the roll of his hips, the reach of his legs, the determined set of his shoulders—was where she wanted to be.

They'd moved to the far side of the road once they'd left the cover of the hulking wrecks in the junk-yard, and were now using the brush along the fence line for cover.

There had been very little traffic; the few times cars had passed, they'd simply dropped flat to the ground in the shoulder's overgrown weeds.

She imagined she'd arrive at their destination with

cockleburs in her hair and smears of green across her knees, chest, and palms. But she could hardly complain. Reaching the tractor-trailer rig meant they were that much closer to freeing her brother.

Of course, it also meant she was that much closer to having to tell Harry good-bye. And unlike earlier in the day—last night, yesterday, whenever it had been—she wasn't quite as right with this being the end of their line.

What she wanted was to know Harry in real time, not spy time, not lie time.

She wanted to sit back with a cold beer while he grilled burgers on the patio, and baseball played in the background on Finn's big-screen TV. She wanted to drag him through her favorite junk shops and flea markets, sharing the fun of an unexpected find.

She wanted to eat out of his popcorn tub at the movies, his arm draped over her shoulder holding her close. She wanted to sit beside him on the beach on Padre Island, stare across the gray-blue water and talk about life—or not talk at all. Just sit and enjoy being with him.

She wanted for one week, for even one day, for both of them to lead the sort of lives that allowed for simple joys and normalcy. She was tired of fighting bad guys like Charlie Castro and Arthur Duggin. She wanted her life back, and to see how it fit with Harry's.

It wouldn't, of course. The man worked in espionage or intelligence. He was an agent or a spy or an undercover operative of sorts. The specifics really didn't matter. None of the possibilities would mesh with her days spent searching out treasures in attics and barns.

That didn't mean she was ready to have him walk out of her life completely. Not yet, with so much about him to learn and explore. She took that airport kiss as a sign. If he felt the same way, if he had thought at all about taking the rest of his vacation time and spending it with her . . . Except he wasn't on vacation, was he?

She scurried forward when Harry slowed and waved her on, the bulky, boxy outline of the big rig now in view. Even his vacation had been a fabricated story enabling him to worm his way closer to her and the dossier. Ugh, was there anything real between them?

Had he been telling her the truth when he said their intimacy had been anything but a lie? That it had been as real as it could possibly get? Believing that would go a long way toward easing future regrets. Because coming out of this with long-term misgivings was the last thing she wanted to do.

She shook off the thoughts and looked up to find him waiting for her at the corner of the rig's cab. Once she'd reached him, he knocked, the sound seeming louder than it probably was. She was tense, nervous, wondering what the hell she was getting herself into.

The door pushed open from the inside. The cab was dark, but when a hand came down to help her up, she took it. Harry boosted her from the backside and followed her into the cramped space. Or so it seemed cramped until the other man inside slid back a panel to reveal what in any other rig would have been a sleeping compartment.

She swore she had just stepped onto the stage of a movie set. An outpost in space. Or a high-tech military headquarters. A scaled down operations center, she supposed. The sort of environment Harry was used to working in. It was nothing like she had ever seen.

The door closed behind her. She glanced back at

Harry and, as she did, realized the cab's windows were blacked out. Even with the red and green and blue lights burning in tiny pinpoints and larger rings, no one outside would be able to see in. Clever. Ingenious. She was definitely impressed.

"Simon Baptiste, meet Georgia McLain," Harry said, wedging past her into the sleeper-cum-instrument console room. She backed up to sit in the driver side captain's chair and swiveled it around.

The man Harry had introduced her to was big and gorgeous in that way of quarterbacks. Muscled, but not bound. Rangy and long. Before he turned, she saw that his hair was pulled back with a matching black rubber band. The thick tail hit his shoulder blades.

And then he smiled. A wide, welcoming smile full of deep set dimples and white teeth. Georgia responded in kind. "It's nice to meet you. I would say I've been looking forward to meeting you since hearing so much from Harry, except he hasn't said a thing."

"Nice to know the boy has a proper respect for the rules," Simon said, a hint of a Cajun accent in his voice, his bright green eyes cutting up to Harry. "I gotta say it's good to see you, boo. As much as I dig on Willow and on Oz being a werewolf, I miss the human conversation."

Harry turned to Georgia. "He's on a forty-eight-hour *Buffy* marathon. You'll have to excuse him."

"There is no excuse for me," Simon said, and laughed. "Or so everyone's been telling me since the day my mama shoved me into the world and slapped me for taking so long."

Georgia grinned. She had to. It was the only way to deal with the madness, even as her thoughts turned to her brother. "Do you know what's happening in the diner? Are Finn and the others okay?"

"Had a nice chat with your brother last night." Simon settled the headset he'd obviously removed earlier back into place and straddled the stool in front of the board. "One-sided, to be sure. But a nice change from listening to Xander piss and moan."

She plowed past his *Buffy* comparison. "You talked to Finn? How?"

"Not talked, *cher*. Listened in." He tapped the receiver in his ear. "He was singing The Grateful Dead."

"Wait. I'm lost. How are you able to hear Finn?" A stupid question to ask considering she was sitting inside a spymobile. But knowing that Finn was upbeat enough to be singing was music to her ears. "I mean, I'm sure you have the equipment . . . but how?"

"Trade secrets." Harry held out a hand. "C'mon. Simon and I need to discuss man business. I'll get you settled in the trailer."

"Fine. Be that way." She stuck out her tongue while letting Harry tug her up from her seat. "I hope it's refrigerated at least."

"Ah, you just wait," Simon said. "Boo here may try and convince you that car of his is riding in style, but you see my trailer? You know the truth."

Harry shook his head and, ignoring Simon's laughter, pressed his thumb against what looked like a two-inch-square television screen on the sleeper cab's back wall. A red light glowed, a line scanned down, then up, and another panel slid open, this one revealing what appeared to be a fully furnished apartment.

She followed Harry inside. The door closed behind them. He let go of her hand and let her explore. Obviously all the widgets and gadgets of their trade were within Simon's reach, while the state-of-the-art trailer gave new meaning to the term mobile home.

Georgia could've lived here without complaint for the rest of her life. And take this on the road while antiquing? She walked deeper into the interior, moving slowly until Harry turned up the track lighting. And then she stopped.

The walls were papered to appear as red brick, the furnishings painted white in a style she thought of as Scandinavian spare. But the accent colors of fire engine red and Christmas green and bright banana yellow gave it personality, brought it to life.

She loved it, and almost forgot why she was here. Until she turned and saw Harry standing at the door, ready to leave her, to return to the world where she didn't belong. It was hard not to be hurt when it was her brother sitting in the tin can across the street.

She didn't show it. She just raised a hand. "See ya."

"Getting the hang of blowing me off?"

"Just don't want you to worry about me while I'm in here with the womenfolk."

"It's just for a few minutes, Georgia. While I get a briefing from Simon. I won't be gone long."

A briefing. Two little words. Simple words. Words that accentuated the cavernous gulf between their two worlds. She'd never been to a briefing in her life.

She reached for the hem of Harry's shirt and tugged it over her head. "I'm fine. Do what you need to do."

"Twenty minutes. Thirty max."

"It's not like I have anywhere to be. Just go." She fluttered one hand dismissively. "Do."

He looked so crestfallen, so certain he was in the wrong to leave her alone, that she softened, her heart turning to mush. "Oh, Harry. We'll figure out the rest of this stuff later. I swear to you, boo. We will."

3:00 A.M.

When Harry finally made it into the trailer, it was to find Georgia huddled cross-legged in the middle of the bed. He'd expected to find her asleep, curled up in the oversized twin bed.

Instead, she sat with the red, green, and yellow checkerboard comforter pulled to her chin while staring at the kitchen nook's tabletop TV. The sound was off. The picture was nothing but snow.

"Georgia?" he asked softly, not sure if she was dozing or awake.

He'd been known to nap with his eyes open. He also knew it wasn't something everyone could do, though it was a shared skill among the men with whom he had the pleasure to work.

She wasn't asleep. She turned her head slowly and, exhausted, watched him approach. Her eyes were bloodshot, her lids droopy, the half-moon bags beneath her lower lashes the color of a bruise.

"Hey," she said, and she managed a weak smile.

"Why aren't you sleeping?" He crossed to where she sat, scrubbed both hands over his face and turned to sit beside her with his own exhausted sigh. "You're going on twenty-four hours without. And you didn't get much the night before."

"And whose fault is that?" she asked, her bleary gaze cutting up to meet his, a weak attempt at flirtation.

Nope. He wasn't having any of it. Not of the blame,

or of his body's response to the plea in her eyes. His heart, however, was having the fight of its life. "I'd have to say yours since you followed me to the shower."

"I did, didn't I?" Her smile was dreamy, and only then did he begin to understand how much trouble he was in.

He wanted to ask if it had been worth it, a question that was nothing but an ego-stroking waste of time. They had more important things here to deal with than whether or not he was good in bed.

Things that reached beyond the way he wanted to cradle her tenderly and keep the ugliness away. He took the first step. "Simon showed me the preliminary report that came in on the dossier."

He didn't explain. Neither did he ask if she wanted him to tell her what he had learned. He just waited. He wanted her to be the one to put the discussion into play. He didn't want to blurt out the news and cause her more distress.

But she didn't ask anything about it at all. She shook her head, thinking. "Do you think if Simon hears Finn again, I can listen? I know three days isn't a very long time. It's just that we talk constantly. I miss him. And I'm worried."

Harry felt as if he'd swallowed a big rubber ball. He scooted back, rested against the faux brick wall, wrapped his arm around her shoulders and brought her with him. "The diner's quiet now, but yeah. I don't see why not."

"Thanks," she said, snuggling close. "It would mean a lot."

It would mean a lot to him if she would get some goddamned rest. "Thing is, sun's up in less than three hours, and you'll be seeing your brother not long after that."

"God, I hope so."

"Consider it guaranteed."

"Promises, promises," she teased, but there was a joyful hope in her voice.

He teased right back. "Have I broken one yet?"

She pulled her knees to her chest, rubbed the comforter against her cheek. "If I had a working brain cell, I might could come up with one."

"If you would get some sleep, you might have a better shot at a working brain cell."

"You haven't slept either. And you're not poured out like soup on the ground."

Soup? Where did she come up with this stuff? "Part of the training. Besides, your exhaustion's not the result of keeping a long and boring twelve-hour watch. It has a large emotional component."

"One named Finneas Scott."

He reached for the remote, clicked off the television. "That's only a part of it, Georgia. What you're feeling is bigger than Finn."

She waved off his concern with one hand. "I'm not going to turn all weepy and clingy just because we had sex."

He'd never expected her to. But that wasn't what he was talking about. And she knew it. She was just avoiding the subject like a seasoned pro. "I'm talking about your father. Not about your brother. Not about us."

She was silent for several moments, then curled her whole body into his, her knees resting against his thigh, her cheek on his bicep where his arm was still draped over her back.

She pulled the comforter around to cover his lap, too. And her fingers, which clutched it at her chest, began to wander and play with his.

He didn't stop her. If this was what she needed,

how could he deny her? It wasn't like it was costing him anything. At least nothing he had the least idea of how to measure.

A cup of heart, a spoon of soul, was that about right?

Georgia flexed her fingers against the muscles of his chest, and all he wanted to do was take off his shirt, feel her against his skin. But he didn't even move since he could tell by the shift in her breathing she was finally ready to talk.

"You've got to know that my father's been on my mind since I read the general's letter," she said, her voice soft but steady.

He took that as a good sign. "I was pretty sure that he had been."

She scoffed. "That's not even half of what's true. There's not a day that goes by that he's out of my mind. But right now?" She shuddered, snuggled closer. "I don't have the strength or the energy to process anything. So if you tell me what you found out? It'll be all over for me. If I don't focus on my brother, I'm afraid I'll go 'round the bend."

He kissed her forehead. She smiled, looked up with imploring eyes. "You're welcome to join me, of course, though I doubt anything leaves you flustered. You've got that perpetual James Bond cool about you."

"I've got that duck's back thing going on. Most of the time stuff rolls right off."

"So tell me something that hasn't."

"If I tell you anything, I'd rather it be a bedtime story than some tale of horror to keep you awake."

She waited for several seconds, her fingertips circling his nipple, the burn at the base of his spine getting way damn close to making itself known in his lap. But he kept it at bay, wondering what she was thinking, waiting to hear.

"Is that how you view the work that you do? As a horror story?"

Well, if he told her everything he'd seen, everything he'd done . . . "Not the Stephen King brand, but yeah. The job does have its gory moments."

"Can you talk about it?"

Did he want to talk about it was the better question. "The specifics? No. The fact that I went undercover for months with a group running a child prostitution ring? That much I can gloss over."

"You glossed well. I don't need to hear more."

"Good," he said, with a harsh laugh. "Because I don't want to talk more."

Her fingers had stilled, but now they started to move, rubbing, stroking, soothing. He growled and sat forward, whipping off his shirt. "There. That's better. If you're going to torture me, at least do a full-fledged job."

"As opposed to half-assed?" she asked with a laugh.

He doubted there was anything about her approach to life that qualified as half-assed. "I'm definitely more the all or nothing type."

"And I'm definitely appreciative for the way you throw yourself into your work." She tugged at the hair in the center of his chest. "At least most of it."

"What's that supposed to mean?" he asked, certain he could figure it out on his own if it was only his mind involved in the moment. But his body was proving rapidly that it was in charge.

"You took my dossier."

"I recovered a stolen government file." He grabbed hold of her hand before she could move. "And don't give me that semantics crap because I'm not talking about your theft."

"You're talking about General Duggin's."

He was, but since she didn't want to talk about her

father, he doubted she wanted to have this conversation either. "Yeah. I am."

"A pretty drastic, not to mention criminal, example of covering one's ass." She tossed back the comforter and stretched out her legs, reaching down to unlace her boots.

"From the sound of his letter, I'd say it wasn't just his own he was covering."

Her first boot hit the floor. She went to work on the second. "Yeah. Try everyone's in this little consortium of his except for my father's. Ugh, my feet are killing me."

Before she'd finished tugging off boot number two, he offered her a third. "Take mine off while you're down there, and I'll rub your feet."

She gave him an eye-rolling glare, but started in on his laces. "I can't believe you just ruined a pair of designer suit pants."

"Expense account, sweetheart. Expense account."

"Did you keep the receipts for my outfits? Since I suppose you'll be writing off those, too."

He wiggled his freed toes, calling himself all kinds of stupid for not switching out his dress socks for a pair better suited for their hike. "Got 'em tucked safely away."

"I'm about ready to apply for your job," she said, lying down and propping her feet in his lap.

He ditched her socks to get to her skin, and started in on her toes. "It's not all time off and shopping. I do work."

"And you do good work," she said, eyes closed, moaning. "Do some more."

He moved to her other foot, hoping the massage would put her to sleep. That it wouldn't have a similar effect on her that it was having on him. Because being in bed was on his mind, but sleep wasn't.

He moved up to her ankles beneath the hem of her jeans, pressing his thumbs behind the bones, squeezing there, doing the same with her heels, closing his eyes and trying to pretend he wasn't about to burst his own seam.

"That feels so good," she said, and moaned. "You have no idea."

No, but he could imagine. "Good. Relax."

"Want me to do you?"

And because he had seriously reached the end of his rope, a rope ragged from his clawing efforts to hang on, he gave her the only response that came to mind. "Yeah. But it's not my feet I want you to do."

He thought his heart and his head and his swollen body parts would explode before she answered. When she did, it was to toss off the comforter and get to her feet.

She stood in front of him, her eyes still wickedly weary, her smile just plain wicked, and took off her pink camo T-shirt. Her jeans followed. She shoved them to her ankles and kicked them away.

That left her wearing only her bra and her panties, both simple athletic gray. They couldn't have done more for his imagination had they been see-through lace. It was the woman he was interested in, her body, yes, but even more so her mind.

She climbed back onto the bed but this time it was more a case of climbing onto him. She straddled his lap, planted her palms on his pectorals, her mouth on his mouth.

He kissed her with his tongue, slid his hands from her knees up her thighs to her hips, wanting to take off her panties, waiting instead.

Her fingers took a long, slow, meandering trip south, toying with his nipples and his navel, playing with his hair, finally getting busy with his belt buckle and the goods. He slouched onto his spine to help her, pulling away from all the things her mouth was doing to his.

Once she had his zipper down, she reached into his shorts and leaned in, sprinkling tiny kisses over his collarbone while rubbing her thumb in circles over the head of his cock.

She used his first ooze of clear fluid for lube, smearing around and around, and going back for more. He thrust into her hand. She ringed her fingers around his shaft and stroked.

"Is that what you want?" she asked, whispering the question against the corner of his mouth, her tongue wetting, her teeth catching and nibbling.

He wanted more than her hand. He wanted to slide into her mouth, between her breasts. He wanted her on her hands and knees. He wanted her pussy on his face.

"I want you naked." He ground out the words, loosened his grip on her hips, and pulled aside her panties, cupping her, thumbing her, pushing inside.

She was wet and open. She was warm. She gripped his fingers, squeezed, panted against his mouth. "I love to hear you talk dirty."

"I love it when you come in my mouth."

"I love it when you come in mine."

"So get naked. Let's do it. I'm about to pop."

"I know the feeling." Her mouth open at the corner of his, her breath hot on his skin, she squeezed him, stroked him.

He fingered her right back, pulled free and spread her moisture over her ass. "I can't believe I'm saying this, but would you please get the hell outta my lap."

She scrambled away and was out of her underwear before he'd even managed to get to his feet. And

then, as if watching him strip was the greatest pleasure ever known, she stretched out on the bed while
he did.

Seeing her like that, naked, waiting . . . he didn't
know whether to take it fast or go slow.

His head and his heart were telling him to enjoy,
to cherish her, to indulge. His snake, when he finally
got it out of his trousers, was ready for action. And
since action was a rabbit's middle name, his decision
was made.

He kicked his pants across the floor. Georgia sat
up, scooted to the foot of the bed, waited for him to
join her, and pushed him down on his back.

Since he took up most of the mattress, he let her
do all the work. All he did was watch the sway of her
breasts as she moved, crawling around on her hands
and knees to straddle him in reverse.

He hadn't even begun to look his fill when her
mouth came down on his cock. He slid his hands up
the backs of her thighs and held on, squeezing, closing his eyes to get a grip.

It wasn't happening. She'd cupped his balls in
one palm and ringed the base of his cock with a finger and thumb. Her other thumb slicked and circled
and teased the head, the seam, the ridge. And her
tongue followed, even dipping into his slit when he
opened and leaked.

All he wanted to do was lie back like a big fat
hairy pig and let her suck him into oblivion. But he
could smell her. He could feel her heat. She was so
close, he had to taste.

He dug his thumbs into her cheeks and pulled
her open, then lifted his head and licked her juice.
She groaned. He felt the vibrations in her tongue
where she'd cupped it over the head of his cock.

He played his thumbs through her damp folds

and over her pussy's downy soft lips, rolling her clit with his tongue. Her mouth was doing little more than blowing her heated, panting breaths against him. He budged his hips upward to remind her he was there.

She flexed her abs; the motion drew her hips forward and down, bringing her slit even closer. He pierced her with his tongue, in and out, thumbing her clit with one hand, the bud of her ass with the other.

She let go of his cock, planted her hands on the mattress on either side of his knees and tossed back her head. He grinned to himself—not an easy task with his mouth full.

He loved giving her pleasure, loved her response. She was wet, swollen. The tips of her breasts were hard; he could see them when he looked between her legs.

When she begged, "Harry. Oh Harry, please," he crooked his middle finger and slipped it inside of her, stroking the plump pillow of her G-spot while pressing his tongue to the side of her clit.

She cried out, shuddered, squeezed and flexed as she came, dropping her forehead to his belly, her hair falling between his legs. He pulled his hands and mouth from her sex, kissed her thighs, nipped at the curves of her ass.

She trembled, chuckled, shook. And before she could go down on him and finish him off, he reached for his pants, his wallet, and a condom. As talented as her lips and tongue were, he wanted to be inside her, and tossed the packet to the mattress between his legs.

Straddling his chest, she sat up and sheathed him, then crawled down his body to the end of the bed and took him into her hand. She positioned him, lowered herself slowly, still facing away.

He propped up on his elbows so he could watch her ride. With her hands braced on his ankles, she did just that, lifting her hips, lowering them, raising up on her knees, leaning forward.

She swiveled. She danced. He watched it all. The swing of her hair down her back.

But most of all, he watched the wet slide of his cock as it disappeared between the sweet folds of her sex. In and out. Up and down. Her pussy spread wide, her moisture coating him, slicking the way.

He dropped back to the bed, grunted as he surged upward, once, twice, feeling her tight grip contracting in a shuddering rhythm, milking him dry.

He burst. He turned inside out. He thought he was going to die. He closed his eyes and gave up the ghost, the sensation fiery hot and ripping him to shreds.

It was like nothing he'd known, the way she used him, the demands she made, the way she gave and didn't stop until he was spent. He slowed his pumping thrusts, and she eased herself from his body, turning around, crawling up, settling against his side, her back to the wall.

He rolled away only long enough to dispose of the condom, then pulled the comforter up over the both of them. Doing those two things took the rest of his strength.

And that was it. Lights out.

Georgia dressed quietly in the near dark of the trailer. Harry did the same, standing in front of her and facing away. They'd slept less than two hours. Barely worth calling a nap. They hadn't spoken a word since getting out of bed.

But now the silence was getting to her. She hadn't asked him when he'd finally joined her earlier what he and Simon had discussed. Their business wasn't hers. And, quite frankly, she was too overwhelmed with the truth about Harry to even know what to ask.

This, however, was her business. This morning, today, was about her brother. After that, it was about her father, the dossier, and the rest of her life. She wasn't going to be kept in the dark any longer, and once she finished lacing up her boots she stood.

"Harry?"

He turned at her softly spoken question. The whites of his eyes were the only thing bright in his face. His expression was grim, as if he knew they were going into a situation with little guarantee of success. As if he was expecting the worst to happen no matter his plans.

She didn't even want to know what he thought the worst might be. Her worst was already eating her alive. "I'm sorry. I just—"

He shook his head, gave her a hint of a smile. "You just have nothing to apologize for."

His smile killed her. She'd distracted him. She

should have left him alone, let him be the warrior he was, going in to do battle. "You lost your game face pretty quickly. Have I screwed you up for the day?"

His smile narrowed. "This is what I do, remember? The face is all for show."

Or so he wanted her to believe. "Can I thank you now? Before anything happens? In case it doesn't go the way you want? I don't want you to think that I would ever blame you if anything goes wrong. If Finn gets hurt. Or if I do."

"Georgia, listen—"

She shook her head, cutting him off. "I deserve the blame. I'm the one responsible. Six innocent people are in danger because of me and my stupid quest and my lies."

He came closer, slid his arm around her shoulders, brought her to his chest. "What you've been doing, working to clear your father's name . . . It's not stupid if it's important to you. And trust me. There are at the most four innocents here. Simon and I make a living putting people in danger."

She rubbed her cheek against him, wrapped her arms around his waist. His warmth was so comforting, his muscles so solid. His heart beating beneath her face an affirmation of life. The thought that his life might end today left her cold, shaking, scared.

She loved him, and closed her eyes at the realization. "I can't think of this as just another day at the office. I know that's what it is for you—"

"Trust me. It's not." He held her tighter, closer, cupped the back of her head with his other hand, lovingly stroked her hair. "This one is too close to home, and that fact is giving me hell."

Home? She wanted to know, was afraid to ask, couldn't put what she was feeling into words. Later. Once Finn was safe, once the day was finished, once

Harry wasn't looking down both barrels of Charlie Castro's guns, then she would tie him down and make him explain what he meant.

If he thought of her as home, as she was coming to think of him. She hugged him one last time, then stepped from his embrace, giving him the space and the freedom to do what he needed to do. "Are we ready for this?"

Emotion flashed through his eyes and he swallowed, regained his cool just as quickly. "You tell me. You know the hike we have to make."

She was talking about more than the return trek to the wrecking yard for the pickup. More than the drive to the airport to switch out the bucket for Morganna. Even more than the trip back and the confrontation to follow.

She was talking about where she and Harry were going to go from here. "Just tell me what you want me to do. I'm with you all the way."

Charlie Castro was ready for sleep. He didn't consider it a priority. He caught up when he could. Cat-
napped the rest of the time. Always too much going
on, too much to do.

He was close to seventy hours of doing nothing.
He was stiff, not on his mark. He was no longer look-
ing forward to the return of Georgia McLain and
Harry van Zandt.

That was a sure sign that the dynamic of the day
had shifted. His men were tired, too. They'd taken
turns resting, one spelling the other.

He was more concerned that he wasn't in control.
He'd missed something. He didn't know when. He
didn't know what. So little had happened.

All he knew was the tension during the last twenty-
four hours had waned. It should have heightened.
The end was in sight. The sun was coming up.

Georgia would be arriving soon. He knew she would
come for her brother. He did not know if she had met
with success. He had no plan for what he would do if
she hadn't.

That was where he had failed. He had quit playing
the game. His interest had turned to the players.
Specifically, to the only one worth his time.

This was the first time he'd worked with Georgia
McLain. He knew of her reputation. Anyone dealing
in antiquities did. She was loved for her cunning success.

She was hated for the same. She could have been hated for other things. No one seemed to know who she was. The man who had hired him knew. Now he did, too.

Charlie would make the connection between those two soon. His move would follow. One move if she delivered the dossier. One move if she failed. When the time was right, he would know.

At the sound of wheels churning gravel, he turned his head. Outside, Harry van Zandt pulled his big blue car to a stop at the door. He got out first. Georgia followed.

Charlie signaled for his man closest to the entrance to be ready. His other man ordered the three hostages to sit behind the counter on the floor.

The door opened. Georgia walked in. Harry followed. Neither carried anything in their hands. Leave the dossier in the car. Charlie would have done the same thing.

Harry was the one who walked to the table and sat. "Do we get points for being early?"

The man was too cocky. Charlie didn't like his attitude. He nodded for his man to hold Georgia, and propped his elbow on the back of the booth. "This isn't a competition."

Harry waited. He stared, his eyes dark. "But it is a game, isn't it? And the man with the big prize wins in the end?"

"Where is the prize?" Charlie cast his gaze toward Georgia. "Neither of you have it."

Harry lifted his chin. "Tell your man to let her go."

Charlie's gaze flicked to Georgia and back. He shook his head. "I see no need."

Harry held his gaze. "Georgia?"

"I'm coming."

Her guard stopped her with the barrel of his gun. "You're not going anywhere."

Harry paused, nodded, called out, "Finn? You okay?"

"Short on sleep, long on Wheaties, but yeah."

Charlie's pulse picked up. "No one's hurt. No need for a roll call."

"Phil?" Harry called out anyway.

The cook answered. "Here."

Harry's gaze sharpened. The corners of his mouth lifted. "Can I get you to help me with something?"

Charlie heard Phil scramble behind him. He heard his own man order the other, "Sit down, Grandpa."

"Thanks, Phil. That was all I needed," Harry said, his smile widening.

"What the hell's that supposed to mean?"

Charlie lifted a hand to silence both of his men. "Our friend here is playing a game. One that has failed to hold my interest."

"Your interest isn't what I was after, Charlie ol' boy." Harry hooked both elbows back over his seat. "I only wanted voices. Yours, thug one's, and thug two's."

Charlie sat forward slowly. He didn't like this.

Harry turned his gaze up to the ceiling. "Simon? You get all that?"

The answer caught Charlie off guard. The red point from a laser beam glowed between the eyes of his man who held Georgia. He stared for a moment, then turned in his seat.

Another danced on the forehead of his man who held Finn. Charlie assumed there was a third on his. "Is this parlor trick part of your game?"

"Take a look out the window, Charlie." Harry jerked his chin that way. "See the dishes on top of the rig across the street?"

Charlie hooked a finger in one blind and pulled down.

Harry laced his hands behind his neck. "Yeah. Those."

The blind popped into place. Charlie sat back. He'd known the truck was bad news. He'd been too caught up in Georgia to act. "Impressive. But all I see is a trick."

Harry's grin was wide and all teeth. "I can give you a demonstration if you'd like."

At this point, he had nothing to lose. "Be my guest."

"Finn?"

"Yo."

"That cake plate on the counter. Can you give it a whack?"

"Not a problem," McLain answered, tapping his knuckles on the glass top. The crystal ring sang like a bell.

"One more, Simon."

Charlie watched a fourth red light sparkle against the glass. He shrugged. He had yet to see an upper hand.

"Is everyone ready?" Harry glanced around the room. "Simon? One, two, three."

The cake plate exploded. Cake bits scattered. Finn howled. Phil applauded. Tracy screamed.

Charlie closed his eyes and sighed.

Tracy couldn't breathe. She was going to pass out any minute. First she spends three days as a hostage, and now she ends up in the middle of laser beams and exploding cake.

"What do you want?" she heard Charlie ask.

"A couple of things," Harry answered. "Finn, you and Phil frisk these three and gather their weapons. Georgia, you and Tracy find rope or whatever you can so we can put Charlie and crew in a bind."

Rope. Did they have rope? Tracy hurried out of the alley, seeing Phil grab the guard's shotgun from his hands as she passed. She heard Georgia behind her, and called back in a whisper, "What is going on?"

"A rescue like you've never seen." Georgia stopped in the middle of the kitchen and looked around. "Do you have string or twine or anything?"

"No, but we've got duct tape." Tracy headed for the supply cabinet in the add-on room behind the kitchen. "So that guy you went off with? Harry? Is he a cop or something?"

"He's an agent, yeah," Georgia answered, and grabbed two rolls from the shelf.

Tracy grabbed another, then closed the cabinet door. "And the guy in the truck is his partner?"

"Something like that."

"He had the driver watching over us the whole time, didn't he?" When Georgia nodded, Tracy laughed and followed her back through the kitchen. She could not believe how light her heart felt. "Charlie must be about to croak, finding out he sent you off with a cop."

"The look on his face when that plate exploded? God, I wish I'd had a camera." Georgia started to push through the kitchen door back into the dining room.

Tracy stopped her. "I want to tell you something. I know this is an emergency, but before things get any crazier, I want you to know what a wonderful brother you have."

"Oh, you don't have to tell me—"

"No. I do. He held my hand when I was scared and he made me laugh." She swallowed, tears welling. "He made me miss my husband, and realize how much I want him to come back."

Georgia's own eyes were damp and happy as she came close for a hug. Tracy wrapped her arms around Finn's sister as if she were her own, then they both wiped their eyes, laughed at how silly they were being, and pushed through the door and into the dining room.

Tracy handed one roll of tape to Finn and one to Phil. Georgia handed hers to Harry. The three bad guys were sitting on the floor, each one with his arms and legs wrapped around the posts of the stools. The tape made sure none of them would be going anywhere for a very long time.

"Here's what's going to happen, Phil," Harry said, standing up after taping Charlie's mouth. Tracy listened, watching Finn and Phil finish with the others.

"I'm going to send Georgia and Finn on their way, and I'm heading out. You can make up any story you want about disarming this bunch. Just mention heroin smuggling and the wrecking yard down the road. You'll be a local hero."

Phil didn't question anything Harry said. He shoved the three handguns into his waistband, and hooked both shotguns over his shoulder as he headed for the phone. Tracy looked from Phil to Harry to Finn.

"What am I supposed to do?" she asked, and Harry started to answer. But at the sound of wheels screaming into the parking lot outside, he stopped, reached over, peered out through the blinds.

Tracy caught a quick glimpse of red flames licking over shiny black fenders. It was enough. "That's Freddy."

Gravel spewed. A door slammed. Boots clomped across the ground. "Trac-eeeee!"

"Oh, Freddy, Freddy." She didn't wait to hear if she was supposed to stay put because a million bucks wouldn't have kept her inside. She yanked open the door and ran out.

Freddy opened his arms and caught her. "Tracy May Dunn, where the ever-lovin' hell have you been? I've been to the house, to the hospital. No one has seen you for days, baby. What's going on?"

She wrapped her arms around her husband's neck and sobbed. "You'll never believe me. I've been right here all this time held hostage."

"Hostage? Baby, what are you talkin'—" Freddy stopped, looked up over Tracy's shoulder.

She'd heard the door open and figured Finn and the others were on their way out. She didn't want to let Freddy go, so she kept hold of his hand. "C'mon. I've got to go back inside. Phil's waiting for the cops."

"Wait a minute. Cops. Tracy, girl, you're not making any sense."

"I'll tell you everything, I promise." But then it hit her. She didn't even know if he was staying. "I mean, if you want to know. If you'll be sticking around."

"I'm not going anywhere, baby. When I started getting calls asking where you were, and then when I couldn't find you anywhere . . ." His big blue eyes grew wet and wide, and he pulled down the brim of his Peterbilt cap.

She reached up a hand to his cheek, her heart bursting. "I love you, Freddy. I love you so much."

"I swear, Tracy." He stopped for a minute because he almost choked. "The house and the taxes don't matter to me. You're the only thing that's important. The only thing that means a damn in my life."

She smiled up at him and told him with her kiss that he was the only thing that meant a damn in hers.

Walking outside with Georgia and Harry, Finn grabbed up his sister and swung her around the minute they cleared the door.

"I swear, if you ever scare me like that again . . ." He couldn't even finish the thought. All he did was hold her as long as he could.

When he finally set her down and away, her response was typical Georgia. "You're the one who wanted to stop for burgers in the middle of nowhere."

He had to laugh. "So, this is all my fault then?"

"I'll let you know in a minute," she said, her dark eyes growing round and sober. "First, I need to tell Harry good-bye."

He nodded. She wouldn't have a chance again. Once Harry dropped them off at wherever Castro had stashed Finn's truck, the other man would be hitting the road.

This was the couple's only private time, and it was hardly private at that. Finn couldn't deny his sister the desperate need he saw in her eyes.

He climbed into the backseat of the Buick, waving at Tracy as she followed Freddy through the diner's door, turning as the big rig across the street rumbled to life.

He understood that these two—Harry and Simon—weren't law enforcement, and being here when the authorities did arrive wasn't an option for either.

He understood, but he still would have liked to

meet the truck driver. To thank Simon Baptiste for saving his sanity as well as his life. And for being a fellow Deadhead.

The memory of their impromptu concert caused Finn to smile. And when Simon pulled out onto the road moments later, Finn waved, laughing like a fool when Simon honked back, his horn playing the very tune they'd sung.

One Month Later

Don't wait. The time will never be just right.

—Napoleon Hill, American author
(1883–1970)

"Can I tell you how happy I am right now and not have you ream me a new one for being in insensitive jerk?"

Georgia pouted. Her brother was not insensitive or a jerk. He was just too depressingly well-adjusted. Too balanced, secure, normal. He'd bounced back from his seventy-two-hour hostage ordeal like he was made of Spandex while she was still dragging ass.

"You can tell me," she said as he pulled into the post office parking lot. "Just don't expect me to share your Christmas morning moment."

He laughed, chose a space, put the truck into park. "No expectations whatsoever. It's just nice seeing you make a fresh start. Hand me my checkbook out of the glove box, will you?"

She dropped her feet from the dash to the floor and sat forward. "It's only a change of location. Not a fresh start."

"Bullshit." Finn took the checkbook from her hand and pulled a pen from his visor. "It's a new beginning, and you know it. Otherwise you wouldn't have thrown everything you own into the bed of the truck."

Did it count that she'd done it at the last minute? The moving crew had packed up Finn's place two days ago and the van pulled out for the trip to the Keys then.

Georgia had only come over this morning to say

good-bye, to help Finn clean, to stow the things he needed for the trip in his truck's covered bed, and to load her boxes into the backseat of the rental she was driving.

Sometime during all of that bending and lifting and scrubbing she'd hit a brick wall. Harry was gone, everything she'd always believed about her father was gone. She couldn't lose Finn, too.

So here she was on her way from Houston to Key Largo, in no hurry, with no plans. She glanced over at her brother as he tore the check from the pad. And then she frowned.

The only time she'd seen that many zeroes was when she'd received her share of Duggin's estate. As he unfolded a pre-addressed envelope from the back pocket of his jeans, she grabbed the check out of his hand.

"Tracy Dunn? You're giving your money to the waitress?"

He shrugged, grabbed for the check. "Why not?"

"Why not? That much money means you can do anything you want for the rest of your life."

"And now so can Tracy," he said, licking the envelope closed and climbing from the truck to buy a stamp.

See? This was why she was a horrible person. She knew nothing about Tracy beyond the fact that the woman waited tables at Waco Phil's, and yet she was questioning her brother's actions.

Hadn't she learned her lesson about people being more than they seemed? Or being less than she'd made them out to be? Her time spent with Harry had taught her more about snap judgments and misconceptions than had her previous thirty-four years.

The truth the general's letter revealed about her father had been a huge blow, one she dealt with day by day, reminding herself of his motives and looking past the damage he'd caused.

She couldn't say she wouldn't have done the same in his shoes; after all, look at the lies she'd told, the hurt she'd been a part of, the deception she'd perpetrated because of her love for him and for Finn.

She didn't know the specifics of what had happened with the men who'd given life—and apparently death—to the TotalSky project. She doubted she ever would. But she had to move on, to get beyond the standstill her life had become while working to clear his name.

When he'd told her not to let the truth of the scandal die, she'd assumed he was talking about just that, about proving his innocence. Now she was certain he didn't want the others to get away with what they'd done.

He'd been their fall guy, had borne the brunt of the blame for thirteen years of his life. In death, he wanted the truth to be known, the others to pay.

Only now she couldn't do anything. The single piece of existing evidence had been snatched from her hands—obviously never to be returned as promised. She'd thought better of Harry. And because of that, she still hadn't given up hope; spy stuff probably happened on its own timetable.

She looked toward the post office's door, her gaze snagged by the reflection of the vehicle pulling into the space next to Finn's truck. She glanced in her side view mirror and saw bright metallic aqua.

It was enough to cause her heart to miss a beat.

Swallowing hard, she pulled her feet from the dash and sat forward, looking down into the open car and Harry's face. She tried to smile, got off to a shaky start. "Hi. Really long time no see."

His eyes were hidden behind dark sunglasses, but

she had no trouble seeing the dimples in the sexy
stubble on his cheeks. "You look so good. You look
great. You look better than I remember."

She pretty much looked like warmed-up crap and
knew it. "Try that line on someone with the cash to
buy what you're selling."

"Don't tell me. You've already burned up all
those zeroes." He put the big Buick into reverse and
started backing out of the spot. Then he pulled his
glasses down his nose and winked, shifting into park.
"Ah, well. Shop till you drop, I always say."

"That from the man who spent more on clothes
in one weekend than I've spent on myself in the last
five years."

"Then you deserve a bit of spoiling."

"Is that what you call it?"

"Damn, I've missed you, woman."

Her heart fluttered, traitorous organ that it was.
"Couldn't prove it by me. No phone calls. No e-mail.
No dossier."

He opened his door, climbed from the car, and
stepped up to her window. "I'm here now. And I
come bearing gifts."

He looked even better up close, so near all she
had to do to kiss him was lean a few inches to the
side. Instead, she said, "Looks to me like your hands
are empty. Wait. Don't tell me. You're going to pull
my file out of a magic hat."

He ignored her sarcasm and the subject, glancing
first at the cover over the pickup's bed, then at the
boxes and bags stuffed in the extended cab behind
her seat. "Finn loaded up and headed out?"

Observant, this one. She nodded. "We both are."

Harry raised a brow. "What? He managed to get
you to pull up your roots?"

"Hard to believe, isn't it?" She looked at the glass

doors, willing her brother to hurry. She needed to get out of here before she did something as reckless as forgiving Harry for everything. "Being as they were so deep and all, I'll probably never recover."

"You'll blossom wherever you land." He swallowed; Georgia watched his throat work, watched the tic pop in his jaw. "But I'd like you to consider landing in New York."

"What's in New York?" she asked, her breath held tight in her chest.

"Me," he said, the one word changing her world forever.

11:00 A.M.

Harry still couldn't believe Georgia had come with him, but he'd been as happy as a shrimp at a lobster boil when she'd scrambled down from Finn's truck.

She grabbed a couple of her bags and tossed them into Morganna's backseat, running into the post office to tell her brother good-bye, running back out as if she couldn't wait to get on the road.

He liked knowing he wasn't the only one who'd hated their separation.

The last thirty days had been nothing but work, and work had been hell not having Georgia around. They made a damn good team, and he told her so. "You know it's been hell not having you around. One long weekend of working with a partner, and I'm worthless on my own."

She turned sideways and smiled, propping an elbow on the seat back and catching the flying strands of her hair. "If it makes you feel any better, I haven't even looked at an ántique in weeks."

He couldn't say that didn't make him happy. "Sounds like misery really does love company."

She leaned close enough to smack him on the shoulder. "If you'd showed up sooner, neither one of us would have had to spend the time being miserable."

"Were you miserable?" God, but being with her made him feel good, even if they were doing nothing but talking about feeling bad.

"Oh, Harry." Her voice broke, her eyes grew misty. "I love you. Of course I was."

She loved him. She loved him. He wanted to shout it from the rooftops. He wanted her to reach over and feel how his heart was bursting. He wanted to admit to all of his feelings for her.

But he couldn't. Not yet. He had something here to finish, so he pushed the rest of the thoughts away. "Georgia, we need to talk."

"I thought that's what we were doing," she said, and he heard the "uh-oh" in her voice.

He went ahead and confirmed her worst fears. "We need to talk about the dossier."

"Oh." One word. Myriad emotions.

He slowed the car, suddenly feeling less of a need to rush, and more of one to do this right. "The file held more than government records. There were notes. Handwritten. Duggin's. Valoren's. One we've assumed to be Gates's."

"And my father's," she said before he could get out the words.

"He was involved, Georgia. He was guilty. He wasn't the only one, but the verdict at his trial was sound."

She didn't say anything for several minutes, and then only a quiet, "I know."

He was pretty sure that she had known, that she'd had time to let the contents of the general's letter sink in. But there was more that he needed to tell her. "Valoren is the one who hired Charlie."

"I knew it!" She let go of her hair and sat up straight. "I knew from the beginning there was something off with that man. When we had brunch? He gave me this look that seriously creeped me out."

Harry had wondered about that, the shift in her demeanor that day. "Obviously, he didn't want it to come out that he'd been involved in the scandal. He suspected you might know Duggin had the dossier, and found an expert in antiquities theft to find it before you did."

She shook her head, shuddered. "Those two deserve each other. May they rot in hell holding hands."

And what a picture *that* made, one Harry was really going to have fun with. "Unfortunately, the professor may not meet his fate until then. He sold everything he had years ago, cutting his ties to future gains, making previous ones impossible to trace."

"God, I hate loopholes." Georgia sighed, sat back, and propped her feet on the dash, didn't say anything for another two miles.

He'd thought she'd fallen asleep, and was surprised when she asked, "What happens now? Do you and your group go after them?"

This was the tricky part. "No. At least, not publicly."

"Then it's up to me to reveal the truth?"

Tricky part number two. "It would be best if you didn't."

"Best for who?"

The citizens of the world. That was the real answer. But before he found a version of that not requiring copious explanation, she cut him off.

"So you're saying that everyone gets away with what they did except for my father."

"For now. Not forever." It still sucked.

"And how does that work?" she asked, her cynicism more than clear.

Harry checked his rearview for traffic before pulling into a rest area and stopping the car. He turned to the side, cocked his knee up onto the seat. "If Duggin's involvement in TotalSky is revealed, you'll have to surrender your money. It was illegally gained."

She was already shaking her head. "I don't care about the money."

"I know you don't. But you might care to know that you could use it to help bring down the final man."

She considered what he'd said. "You mean Gates?"

Harry nodded. "We think he's used his money for a lot of really bad things."

"So I'd be working with your group?" she asked, glancing over.

If that made her feel better about it . . . "As a project consultant."

She rolled her eyes. "How long can I have to think about it?"

He breathed a sigh that felt like relief when he hadn't even known he was tense. "As long as you need."

"I have to know something first."

"Anything." He reached for her fingers. They were icy cold, and his gut knotted. He hadn't even stopped to consider how worried she must be.

"Is this why you wanted me to come to New York?" she asked, her expression guarded.

"Oh, no. No. I want you in New York because I love you."

"You do?"

"I do. I figure you can hunt for treasure anywhere. But I'm going to only find it once in my life." He reached out to cup her cheek. "I love you, Georgia McLain. Even if your middle name *is* Tillie."

And then he pulled her into his lap and kissed her, the only woman he'd ever loved. The woman who was his life.

Current day—a private island in the Bahamas

Cameron Gates stood against the rooftop railing of his compound, looking across the wide swath of jungle that fanned out to the beach beyond. Of all the spots on the property, this was his favorite view.

If he turned, he saw too much of the infrastructure that supported the island. Antennae towers, generator stations, supply depots. All the things that allowed him to be king of all he surveyed.

Not that he considered himself to be a true head of state. This was his domain. He'd founded it, funded it. But he knew it took a small international army to run the organization's individual arms.

The island was more of a sanctuary. He had lived here many years. He would die here as well. He was in fairly good health for a man of seventy, an age that came with insomnia and joint pains and arteries thicker now than they'd been even fifteen years before.

He had no plans to retire. That didn't mean he had no plans to make. He ran a multibillion-dollar organization, one that would continue to thrive after he was gone—as long as he saw to its future now.

That was why he was up here. He'd watched his private helicopter arrive ten minutes ago and was waiting for good news. His own right-hand man had dispatched a member of his team to recover a set of documents that, if released, would result in a total undoing of decades of success.

At the sound of footsteps, Cameron turned, his

pulse picking up at the sight of Warren Aceveda crossing the flagstone surface, impeccably dressed as always. His man walked behind him, dressed in camouflage gear, his long dreadlocks tied back with a bandanna. But the fact that he held a file in his hand was all that mattered.

Cameron stepped away from the railing and returned to the table set up with pitchers of ice and fresh lemonade. A bottle of rum and another of tequila sat nearby. "Warren, I hope you've come to make my day."

"I have indeed." Warren shook Cameron's hand before moving beneath the large umbrella out of the midday sun to pour himself a drink. "Though I suppose I should let Ezra do the honors."

Cameron hesitated briefly, then extended his hand toward the black man whose reputation for ruthlessness surpassed Cameron's own. "Mr. Moore. Good to see you again."

"As it is to see you, sir." Ezra Moore shook Cameron's hand, then handed him the file he carried. "Rest assured, I bring you what you need. You have no need to worry about the future of Spectra IT."

Don't miss Alison's newest book,
WITH EXTREME PLEASURE,
featuring more sexy men of SG-5 . . .

ONLY SOMETHING THIS DANGEROUS . . .

After three weeks in Manhattan, Kingdom Trahan is ready to get back to bayous, crawfish boils, and afternoons fishing on the Gulf. But before he can pull out of the parking garage, he meets a curvy detour. King noticed Cady Kowalski on the photo shoot he just endured—sexy and confident, with a waifish look that belies the way she corralled him into submission using only a can of hairspray. Yet Cady isn't confident now. She's bruised, edgy, and desperate to get out of town . . .

COULD FEEL THIS GOOD . . .

For years, Cady has been looking over her shoulder, wondering when the gang of drug-running criminals who killed her brother would make their move on her. She's grown used to having no one to turn to, no one to trust. But King isn't walking away—not even when their lives are threatened, again and again. Drawing Cady's pursuers out of hiding is the only way to end this, and it's also the most reckless thing they can do . . . short of diving into a red-hot affair from which there's no turning back . . .

To have Kingdom Trahan smart off to her about how she had handled things, when he hadn't been there to know what she'd been through, was the breaking point at the end of a day she could just as well have done without.

She left the laptop plugged into the socket on the table lamp and booting up on the extra bed as she headed for the bathroom. Telling him off through another shower curtain was not how she'd have chosen to say her piece, but she was in no mood to wait for the optimal time and place.

Unfortunately, her timing sucked. King wasn't yet in the shower. Oh, he was on his way, had the curtain pulled back, one foot lifted to step into the tub, but he was completely dry. And completely naked.

She quickly averted her eyes—just not quickly enough—from his muscled thighs and rump to his face, freshly shaved and still dotted with remnant blobs of shaving cream. "I'm sorry. I didn't mean—"

"Are you sure?" he taunted, laughing, before stepping beneath the spray and closing the curtain behind him.

Arrogant pig. Beast of a man.

And yet she stayed where she was, shutting the door, breathing in the stream as it began to smell of King.

"Was there something you wanted?" he asked her after sputtering out a mouthful of water. "Another look maybe? To share my hot water as part of your plan to fight global warming?"

The day she showered with him, they'd better pray for global warming because hell would be freezing over. "What I wanted was to tell you to mind your own business. You don't know anything about the last eight years of my life, or whether or not the choices I've made worked for me."

"You've been working dead-end jobs and bunking with dead-end roommates. That's all I need to know."

She felt her blood pressure rising, her anger coming alive. "Sounds to me like you're an expert at dead ends, recognizing them so easily the way you do."

"I spent a few years with nothing but a prison yard to run in, *chère*. Coming up against razor wire and walls lap after lap taught me a lot about dead ends."

"Maybe so," she said, pushing away her chagrin. "But that doesn't make you an expert on me."

"I never claimed to be. Hell, how could I be?" He sputtered more water, his feet squeaking against the floor of the tub. "You haven't told me enough to give me a chance. Most of what I do know I learned from McKie."

She closed her eyes, powering up to being really pissed off. "That's why you're acting like a shit? Because I didn't tell you everything?"

"No, I'm acting like a shit because I am one. I thought you might have figured that out by now."

"I'm guessing it takes longer than twenty-four hours for the shit factor to fully manifest."

He jerked back the curtain, fuming, his eyes red and fiery, and this time he didn't even bother with the rag. "If you're not going to get in here and scrub me down the way I like, then get the hell out of my bathroom so I can do it myself. This conversation is over."

Cady couldn't speak. King's chest was heaving, his cock rising, his stitched up head that he was supposed to keep dry soaking wet. This conversation was not over. He knew it as well as she did.

Discover the Romances of
Hannah Howell

More by Bestselling Author

Lori Foster

Bad Boys to Go	0-7582-0552-X	$6.99US/$9.99CAN
I Love Bad Boys	0-7582-0135-4	$6.99US/$9.99CAN
I'm Your Santa	0-7582-2860-0	$6.99US/$9.99CAN
Jamie	0-8217-7514-6	$6.99US/$9.99CAN
Jingle Bell Rock	0-7582-0570-8	$6.99US/$9.99CAN
Jude's Law	0-8217-7802-1	$6.99US/$9.99CAN
Murphy's Law	0-8217-7803-X	$6.99US/$9.99CAN
Never Too Much	1-4201-0656-2	$6.99US/$8.49CAN
The Night Before Christmas	0-7582-1215-1	$6.99US/$9.99CAN
Perfect for the Beach	0-7582-0773-5	$6.99US/$9.99CAN
Say No to Joe?	0-8217-7512-X	$6.99US/$9.99CAN
Star Quality	0-7582-1008-6	$4.99US/$5.99CAN
Too Much Temptation	1-4201-0431-4	$6.99US/$9.99CAN
Truth or Dare	0-8217-8054-9	$4.99US/$6.99CAN
Unexpected	0-7582-0549-X	$6.99US/$9.99CAN
A Very Merry Christmas	0-7582-1541-X	$6.99US/$9.99CAN
When Bruce Met Cyn	0-8217-7513-8	$6.99US/$9.99CAN

Available Wherever Books Are Sold!

Check out our website at **www.kensingtonbooks.com**